Pretty Lovely Lies

A Dark Romance

Heidi Stark

Contents

"A gilded cage is still a cage"

– Lady Hale

To everyone willing to swim through a sea of red flags
just to find the smut

Before

ALINA

The chill bites into my bones as I peel back the edge of a greasy pizza box, my heart thumping against my ribs. Yara's small hands, nearly lost inside the sleeves of her too-thin coat, rummage beside mine, disturbing the rotting waste that fills the dumpster. Me and my daughter, once again scavenging for scraps, because that's our life now. Our new normal.

"Mama, I'm hungry," she murmurs, her voice muffled by the layers of clothing that are barely enough to keep the cold at bay.

I swallow the lump in my throat, fighting back the sting of tears. "I know, sweetheart. Me too. We'll find something soon, I promise." The words come out more confidently than I feel, even though my stomach is hollow.

Yara nods, her bright eyes scanning the decaying trash with an intensity that shreds my heart. She shouldn't have to do this—no child should. No human should. And yet, here we are, our lives reduced to this moment, this heartbreaking necessity.

The stench of spoiled food and despair hangs heavy in the air, mingling with the fetid odor. We're shadows in the encroaching dusk. Ghosts that aim to blend into the background as we take only what we absolutely need. It's never wise to stand out here, for any reason, let alone when you're unprotected and vulnerable. Alone.

The guilt gnaws at me, sharp-toothed and relentless. My Yara, who once knew warmth and fullness, now digs through garbage because of me. Because I chose to run from a gilded cage, where danger was served right next to untold wealth and other things dreams are made of. Unfortunately, sometimes the more we learn about dreams, the more we realize they're actually nightmares.

"Did you find anything yet?" she asks, hopeful. Her eyes light up as she pulls out a half-squashed loaf of bread and turns it in her hand to admire it like it's treasure.

"Good job, baby." Pride wrestles with the pain in my chest. She's so strong, my little girl—too strong for her tender years. But it's my fault she has to be.

"Let's check if it's still okay to eat," I say, brushing off the worst of the dirt and other debris, inspecting it for signs of mold or spoilage.

Her stomach growls, a small sound of suffering that stabs at me. I tear a piece off, examining it in the fading light before handing it to her.

"Here, eat this while we look for more."

She bites into it, a muffled thanks escaping between chews, and my soul cracks a little deeper. Polite and well-behaved, even while she's starving. I'd imagined a different life for us, one filled with laughter and love, not lurking in the shadows, hungry and hiding.

I have to make this right—for Yara. I'll build us a new life, far from the clutches of men like Luchenko, whose opulent meals were laced with silent and not-so-silent threats, punishments and obligations. This is all on me, and I won't let her down.

"Thank you, Mama. That tasted really good," she says after she finishes her bite, her voice a beacon in the gloom. I don't deserve her politeness, her appreciation. This little girl, so pleased with a stale piece of bread out of the dumpster, for goodness' sake. It's just not right. I draw her close, wrapping an arm around her narrow shoulders, vowing to myself that this will be the last time I hear her stomach roar.

"Come on, my sweet girl," I whisper, kissing the top of her head. "Let's keep looking."

Together, we turn back to the task at hand, searching for sustenance in a world that seems determined to break us. But we won't shatter, not as long as we have each other.

The cold seeps through my threadbare coat as I rummage deeper into the refuse, and my fingers are numb.

Despite being bundled in every layer she owns, Yara shivers beside me, her small form huddled against the harsh cold. Streetlights flicker above, casting long shadows across the alley that seem to mock our desperation.

"Remember when we lived with Luchenko? We had nice food, Mama," Yara's voice trembles, not just from the cold but from a longing for a past that was never truly ours.

A lump forms in my throat as her words trigger a flood of memories, and because I know that her mention of his name must mean she's really starving.

I feel some relief that she calls him by his last name, not the more conventional title he prefers. Grateful that children are like mirrors, reflecting what they hear often enough that they eventually start saying it themselves and even come to believe it.

Grateful that Yara is a smart girl, fascinated by long words she can roll around in her mouth, rather than simpler sounds like 'dada'.

The grand dining room under Luchenko's roof, where silver platters overflowed with delicacies, is a stark contrast to the scraps we claw at now. But those meals came at a price, because under each nourishing, delicious bite lingered the taste of fear and control.

"I know, baby." My voice is steady, but inside, I'm reeling, struggling against the guilt that threatens to overwhelm me. "But that came with its own dangers..."

I push aside the memory of Luchenko's steely gray eyes watching us from the head of the table, a silent threat in his every glance. His presence, a suffocating force that turned every nutritious dinner into an act of survival. His cruelness, unrelenting.

The way he began to look at Yara as she grew older, unsettling. Revolting, even. I try not to think about those times, and I pray she never remembers the darkness we emerged from. Let her remember the good food, the warmth of the heaters, having her very own room. The abundance of clothing and toys and music that made her feel spirited and carefree.

Yara looks up at me, the innocence in her eyes tearing at my resolve. "Are we going to be okay, Mama?" I know she doesn't ask me these questions to make me feel worse. She feels a joint sense of ownership with me, an obligation far beyond her years to help get us both out of this situation and into something more stable and secure.

"Hey, look at me." I tilt her chin up, forcing a smile that feels like it might shatter. "You deserve a true childhood, away from all this. I'll make us a better life. Just give me a little more time."

Her eyes search mine, seeking the promise of security and warmth I've vowed to provide. "Okay, Mama."

"Good girl." I squeeze her close, her small body a fragile reminder of what's at stake. "Let's go home," I say, although I use the word loosely. "We'll figure something out. We always do, right?"

"Right," she echoes, a ghost of a smile on her lips, mirroring my own forced optimism.

We walk back through the desolate streets toward our rickety encampment, past buildings that wear their decay like badges of honor. I fear I'm beginning to have far too much in common with them, and I refuse to let Yara succumb to the same fate.

With each step, I reaffirm my vow to build a future where Yara can thrive—a world away from the shadows of men like Luchenko. One where she never again needs to worry about where her next meal is coming from, or about having shoes on her feet. Or about the dangerous men who lurk in the shadows, waiting to pounce when she's in direst need.

In the quiet that follows, I feel her hand slip into mine—a small lifeline amidst the uncertainty. I squeeze it gently, and in that simple touch lies the weight of all the love and determination I possess.

We'll get through this, together.

Even if it kills me, as it has nearly done so many times.

Chapter 1

ALINA

I rap softly on the intricate, mahogany front door of Dominika's house, my heart drumming with a mix of anticipation and anxiety. This place always feels like stepping into another world—one where the shadows of our past don't linger in the corners, waiting to leap out. An ode to our former life, but without the toxic dangers.

The door swings open, revealing Dominika in all her polished grace.

The sight of her is a comfort. Her sharp, high cheekbones and icy blue eyes would normally intimidate, especially with the way her meticulously microbladed eyebrows boldly frame her face and her full lips exude a perpetually knowing look. But to me, they spell friendship and understanding. The unspoken bond of our shared childhood experience has tethered us together through many storms, and always will.

There was a time when I wasn't sure if I'd be able to ever come here again or resume my friendship with Dominika, given how things were left off what feels like forever ago. But it's not her fault she's related to... *him.*

"Alina, darling! Come in, come in!" Dominika exclaims, her voice echoing off the marble floors. I step inside, the warmth from the grand foyer wrapping around me like a plush blanket.

She leads me through the hallways adorned with expensive art, to a sunlit parlor where a table is set with a platter of scones and a delicate porcelain teapot. It's surreal, this opulence, compared to our scrappy childhood homes. And compared to the homelessness Yara and I experienced until recently.

"Sit down, make yourself comfortable," Dominika gestures towards a velvet chair, her gold bracelets clinking softly. She pours tea into two intricately decorated porcelain cups, the steam curling up like little spirits dancing.

"So he knows I'm here? I was scared to come, but you insisted..."

"Listen, I don't delve into my brother-in-law's mind because that's a scary place for anyone. But I do know he's busy wrapping up a big business deal overseas. One of his key men is threatening a mutiny of sorts, and Marie is giving him a hell of a time. He won't have a spare moment to give you a second thought."

I smirk at the thought of such a powerful man facing such simple struggles as a nagging wife whom he can't seem to get rid of. Even the wealthy put their pants on one leg at a time.

"One thing is certain. I need to get us out of here. I can't keep putting her through this," I confess, staring into the golden liquid, my thoughts drifting to Yara's innocent face and the darkness that seems to follow us.

The irony, sitting here with the sister-in-law of the man who caused so much of our pain. But sometimes, we become the closest friends with the blood of our enemies. We're drawn to what repels us. It's a counterintuitive survival mechanism.

"You know, I've been thinking of you, Alina," Dominika says, her voice warm despite her clipped speaking manner. "Brainstorming ways to get you both out of this situation."

"Well, I'm all ears," I sigh. "I've done everything I can think of. Reached out to agencies, applied for every type of assistance I could find." I look down. "Even panhandled. It at least got us into some fairly stable housing and I was able to find a part-time job, but that could be taken away at any moment and it's hardly enough to make ends meet. I can't risk having the rug pulled out from under Yara again, or your brother-in-law changing his mind."

I shiver at the thought. Luchenko is cruel. He likes nothing more than putting me on a leash, letting me think that I'm free, and then yanking me back roughly just when I think I have the chance of truly getting away from him. And I worry that as Yara gets older, his sadistic streak is only going to get worse. There's no way I would put her through what I was forced to endure. No fucking way.

Dominika reaches across the table, her hand warm on mine. "I do have an idea for you, actually. You could try online dating. Find an American man who will take care of you. Eva did that, and now she's happily married with three American babies and a massive mansion in the United States. Just think... wouldn't that solve all your problems?" Her eyes shine with a mixture of hope and concern. "You'd be far away, and under someone else's protection. Not even my brother-in-law would be able to fuck with you with those kind of resources under your fingertips."

I sigh. "I suppose there's a chance I could find someone that way. It's just....".

"Just what, Alina? I have all the patience in the world for you—you know that—but you're running out of options. You're doing so much better than last time I saw you, but like you say, it feels impermanent. Luchenko is unpredictable. I regret every day that I can't do more, but as you know, things are... complicated."

Dominika is the queen of understatements. My childhood best friend, from the worst part of town just like me, but she took a very different path. Marrying her childhood sweetheart didn't sound like a runway to financial success, but he joined a powerful enterprise and quickly worked his way up the ranks. Alongside his stepbrother. His cruel stepbrother, Luchenko, who grew up with a silver spoon in his mouth. Dominika is one of the lucky ones, that's for sure.

"You're so lucky, meeting Aleksandr when you were both so young. High school sweethearts." I smile to emphasize I'm truly happy for my friend. I could never resent her for being with a good man, or having a life that seems like the polar opposite of everything bad about mine.

"I know," Dominika smiles, but it's small, as if her successes make her feel guilty. "Not many people get to say they met the love of their life when they were both so young. Or that they can live in a place like this with everything they need. I'm grateful every day. I just want you to find the same happiness. Especially after all you've been through."

My brain mulls over Dominika's suggestion of meeting an American man online, and immediately begins to fill in the blanks with lots of 'what if' scenarios. It's something I've considered before, but there have always been reasons I've pushed the idea out of my head. Just like, until now, I've pushed aside ideas like dancing in a club or setting up some kind of webcam business. Still, things are becoming increasingly desperate as Yara gets older. I need to open my mind, to consider options that were previously closed off.

"But what about my mother?" The worry for her wellbeing has etched permanent lines on my forehead. "If she's still here, Luchenko could use her as a pawn. You know how he can get when he doesn't know where I am for any period of time. I can't let her be treated like that. I'll be terrified the entire time I'm over there. Who knows how low he would sink if he felt like he could never reach us again?"

"You can bring her with you," my friend shrugs. "She might have to wait for a while, for immigration processes to go through. But you'll be able to fly her over to live with you eventually." Dominika's voice is reassuring, but it doesn't quite reach the tight knot of fear in my chest.

I think about my mother, aging in her cramped apartment. She's always taken care of me as best as she could, and I'm embarrassed I haven't been able to return the favor in her later years. There were many times she snuck Yara and I into her tiny residence in the government-run eldercare facility, even when it could have risked her being thrown out onto the streets herself. When she insisted on sharing her meager food rations when she risks running out herself. I find myself distancing myself from her occasionally so she doesn't put herself at risk for me and Yara. Compared to her, we're young and capable, resourceful, and I hate to lean on someone who also has nothing.

"But how do I know I can trust these men online?" The question tumbles from my lips before I can stop it, revealing the quiver of uncertainty beneath my brave mask. "I could be leaving one problem for another, just far away from everything and everyone I know."

"How do you know you can trust the men you meet in person? Is that really any better, or more of a guarantee they'll treat you well?" Dominika counters, her bold eyebrows knitting together in gentle reproach. "I think we both know that's not the case."

Her eyes scan toward a photo on the mantel, a family picture that I always try not to focus on. She's right, though. I met Luchenko in person, in what could be described as a more traditional way, and look where that got me. That said, if all of the horrible things hadn't happened, Yara wouldn't exist. So, despite the pain I had to endure, I wouldn't change anything for the world.

"I don't know..." I bite my lower lip. "It just seems too risky, especially with a child to think about." I wrap my hands tighter around the teacup, seeking comfort in its warmth.

"You can deal with a broken heart, Alina. You've done it before and you can do it again." She says it with such conviction, as if believing in me enough for both of us. "This isn't about falling in love. Think of it as a transaction of sorts. It's about keeping you and Yara safe."

"Maybe you're right," I sigh. "Besides, it feels like I've tried just about everything else. It's time for a change, and I'll do anything to give Yara the life that she deserves."

Dominika nods. "Just be careful, Alina. I know I'm the one suggesting this, but there are risks attached. Vet people thoroughly, and trust your gut." She pauses and scans the room, as if she's suddenly concerned our conversation is under surveillance. Which is a definite possibility. "The last thing any of us need is another Luchenko in our lives."

Chapter 2

ALINA

The computer screen glows in the dim room, casting shadows over Yara's sleeping face. The hard drive chugs and churns, struggling to navigate even the simplest web pages. Having access to a computer at all feels like a miracle, courtesy of a government program that attempted, yet largely failed, to provide technology access to the poor. My heart pounds as I slowly scroll through page after page of dating profiles, searching for something—anything—genuine. I almost give up several times as the internet intermittently cuts out, each disruption forcing me to start over.

Come on, Alina. You didn't come this far to back out now.

With a deep breath, I click the blinking 'Join Now' button and start filling out the profile. Name, age, location...the basics.

Then the open-ended questions. Hobbies. Interests. Dreams. Three things that feel like distant and frivolous luxuries. *Dumpster diving. Keeping my daughter safe from sex pests. Having at least one guaranteed meal a day without having to shack up with my lunatic baby daddy.* I smirk at my honest answer and delete it immediately.

My fingers hover above the keys. Dreams. I have so many, yet none at all. Safety. Security. A place to finally call home.

Home. The word aches inside my chest. When was the last time we truly had one?

I glance at Yara, her chest rising and falling steadily under the frayed blanket. She's the only home I need. Everything else is just details.

The cursor blinks impatiently. Come on, details. Spill your guts so some stranger can decide if you're worth his time. Or so he can figure out how to use the information against us later.

Worth his time. As if that's ever been the problem. More like whether we're troublesome enough to discard when the novelty wears off. Around here, men have a particular penchant for shiny new things—especially shiny, new, young things.

With a sigh, I start typing.

Dreams of safety, security, and stability. Of walls that don't whisper of what they've seen, and doors that lock to keep the darkness out. A place where my daughter can grow without fear of what's around each corner.

Where I can finally breathe again.

Is that too much to ask for? In this life we've been given, maybe. But I have to try. For Yara, I'll always try.

Of course, I don't word my profile in such a brutally honest way. Instead, I remain upbeat and vague in my responses, as if everything is fine. *Yoga and poetry. Travel and existentialism. A world filled with kindness, an unlimited supply of art supplies for my daughter, and excellent coffee for me.*

One of the biggest lessons I've learned is that nobody, except those very closest to you, actually wants to hear your problems—sometimes, not even them. Hearing the truth makes people feel bad, and nobody likes to feel bad.

I finish the profile, add a photo of us from happier days, and click to make it live.

And now, we wait.

The next day

I help Yara with her homework at the table, half an eye on my computer for any notifications. With each passing hour, my hope deflates like a sad, wrinkled balloon.

Of course no one is interested. Why did I think anything would be different this time? Sure, I'm what might be considered pretty. Beautiful, even. But I'm a single mother and I'm not as young as I used to be. And there's plenty of supply around here when it comes to beautiful, young women without children who would do just about anything for the promise of a better life.

Yara looks up from her math problems, her brow furrowed. "Still nothing, Mama?"

I force a smile and brush her hair from her eyes. "It'll happen, darling. These things take time."

Her expression says she knows I'm lying, but she nods and returns to her work. No twelve-year-old should have eyes that sad. That wise. And I feel guilty for even telling her that I'm trying this plan. Exposing her to the idea that we need a man to save us and that being on some flesh farm of a dating app is going to change that. But she's smart, and I feel like it's better to be honest than to keep things from her.

Secrecy is what led to our current situation, and it's not what is going to get us out. Plus, I need more than anything for her to know that I'm trying, and that I'm not settling for this life for either of us.

When my computer chimes at last, I startle. With shaking fingers, I reach for the mouse and click to read the message.

Man 1: Hey beautiful, you looking to come to America?

My stomach sinks. I've seen this before—these conversations generally turn into a thinly veiled offer for a green card marriage, cash in exchange for whatever they want. A sea of scammers, ironically preying on people more vulnerable and with much less than them.

Yara peers at me, hope flickering to life in her eyes. I rub at the tension gathering behind my forehead and type a reply.

Me: Thank you, but I'm really just looking for someone who understands me and what I'm trying to build for my daughter.
Man 1: Sounds like you need to loosen up a bit. Come have some fun I can show you a good time.

I sigh. That's what all of them want. Money or sex.

I end the conversation and block his profile. When several more messages come in, all with the same sleazy overtures, I close the app altogether.

Yara's gaze drops back to the table, her shoulders slumping.

"It's okay, kitten," I say, reaching out to squeeze her hand. "We knew it might take time to find someone good."

Someone who wants us, not just what he can take. But with each leering message, my faith in finding that person dwindles.

In this life we've been given, hope is a luxury I can't afford.

Hope, after all, can be even more dangerous than its absence.

The next day, I open the dating app with low expectations. But a new message catches my eye. The sender's name is Gerald.

Gerald: Hi Alina, nice to 'meet' you. Your profile got my attention. Not just your beauty, because you are absolutely stunning, but the strength I see in your words. I hope you're having a wonderful week. Tell me, what dreams do you have for you and your daughter in America?

A genuine question. No mention of sex or money or unrealistic promises. As if he actually read my profile and didn't just jerk off to the pictures and slide into my DMs. I read through it again, searching for the hidden agenda, but find only sincerity. Of course, he could just be a more complex scammer or creep than most, so I'm still on guard.

But this is much more promising than any of the prior conversations men have tried to start on the app.

Heart quickening, I type a reply.

Me: Hello Gerald. It's nice to meet you. I hope you're having a wonderful week as well. That's quite a question to start with. We have many dreams, but the most important would be for a safe and stable life, a fresh start.

I add *'Maybe that's too much to hope for'*, but then backspace until it's deleted. It sounds too cynical, too raw, and again, nobody truly wants to hear another's problems.

Gerald: A fresh start isn't too much to ask for. With your spirit, I believe anything's possible. And I must say, the idea of adding two beautiful ladies to my life is quite the incentive to help make those dreams come true.

I laugh in disbelief and delight, a knot of tension in my chest unraveling. When was the last time a man's words made me feel valued, rather than degraded? And the fact I have a daughter doesn't seem to have phased him in the slightest.

Me: You have quite a way with words, Gerald. And here I thought charm was a lost art.

His response is instant, despite the agonizingly slow internet connection.

Gerald: Around you, my dear, I'll endeavor to be nothing less than charming. Now, tell me more about yourself and the delightful little girl in your photos. I want to know everything.

Everything. No one has ever wanted to know me, all of me, the good and bad and in between. But in his request, delivered with playful gallantry, I sense only genuine interest.

Maybe Gerald will disappoint like the others. But for now, I have a chance at real connection—and the possibility of hope restored. With a smile, I begin to type.

The conversation with Gerald continues over the next few days, and I find myself eagerly anticipating the familiar ding to notify me of an incoming message.

Gerald: Imagine weekends exploring cities you've only read about, Yara attending the best schools, and you, Alina, finally having the peace you deserve. I want to give that to you.

My breath catches at the images he evokes, a life of safety and adventure and opportunity for Yara. And fun! But it's too fanciful. Men don't give such gifts without wanting something in return.

Me: It sounds like a fairy tale, Gerald. One I'd like to believe in, though life has taught me to be cautious of fairy tales. Besides, have you read them... like, really read some of them? Shiny on the surface but very dark when you come to learn the true, underlying meaning.

His cursor pauses, but I can't be sure if he's thinking of a response or if it's just the regular dragging of our internet connection.

Gerald: Let me be the one to show you that some fairy tales can be real and bright and positive. Just give me, give us, a chance.

He always seems to know what to say.

I hesitate, my fingers hovering above the keys. In my periphery, Yara stirs in her sleep, muttering something unintelligible. The sight of her, vulnerable and dreaming, hardens my resolve. For her, I would face any danger.

Me: We've learned to be wary of chances, Gerald. Promises too easily given have a way of disappearing like smoke. I want to believe everything you say, but if you want to prove your sincerity, we'll need more than pretty words. I hope you can understand that having a daughter in the pictures raises the stakes for me.

The moment I hit send I regret it. *Shit!* Was that too forward? Too brutally honest? I've probably burned this relationship before it had a chance to get off the ground.

But Gerald's reply comes quickly.

Gerald: Of course, I understand your skepticism completely. What can I do to put your mind at ease? A video call? Gifts to show my generosity? A visit in person? You need only ask, Alina. I will do whatever it takes to gain your trust.

My heart flutters with mingled anticipation and anxiety. Visits and gifts could be mere manipulations, but a video call would reveal more of the truth. It would show more about him, without the obligations some men associate with gifts, and without any expectations that might come with meeting in person. I drum my fingers on the table as I stare at the screen, deep in thought.

How far do I dare to push when hope is finally within reach? But if Gerald is different, he'll understand my need for caution. I take a deep breath. I'm hesitating only because I worry this might be pushing things too far. But if a video call is too much to ask, then this never had the potential to go anywhere anyway. Yara stirs again, her body twitching as if caught in a nightmare, and I make up my mind.

Me: A video call would be a start. Let's see if the man matches the charm—because you are very charming—before we get carried away. When are you available? Our internet connection is quite volatile so it won't be the best picture quality, but we should be able to get it to work if we wait until outside of peak hours.

Gerald: For you, I'm available anytime. How about tonight? Say, in an hour? I'll send you a link to connect, and we can talk for as long as you'd like.

Tonight. My nerves flare, but beneath them an ember of excitement simmers. Whether it quickly fizzles or fans out into a full-blown inferno remains to be seen, but the time has come to find out. I need to act quickly before someone younger, someone childless, captures his eye.

But I also know I can't seem too desperate. The right men find it off-putting, while the wrong men find it irresistibly alluring. Those men target the broken, the vulnerable. And after all I've been through, I rank near the top of that list.

Me: Tonight it is. We'll see what the evening brings.

Gerald: The evening will bring nothing but excellent conversation and friendship, I assure you. I'll send the link shortly. It's a date, Alina. Our first of many, I hope!

I sign off with a mix of anticipation and nerves churning in my stomach. After so much darkness, is it possible to find the light? In a little under an hour, I'll have the start of an answer.

With a deep breath, I brace myself for whatever is about to come.

Chapter 3

ALINA

I sit in the dim glow of my laptop screen, my heart pounding against my ribs. The cursor blinks expectantly as I smooth down flyaway hairs and straighten my sweater.

My wardrobe is sparse, but it still took me almost an hour to pick out an outfit and get ready. I need to look demure but attractive. Sane but interesting. Fun but not too much fun. Smart but not too smart. Witty but not silly. Feminine but not emotional. No pressure.

I take a deep breath as I click the call button, and within moments, Gerald's face fills the screen. My breath catches. Even pixelated, his classically handsome features and tailored suit exude effortless charm. He's definitely the same man from his profile pictures, yet somehow even more attractive.

"Alina," his smile seems to caress my name. "You're even more beautiful than your pictures."

Heat rushes to my cheeks. "You look nice, too." I resist the urge to fidget with my hair again.

His eyes crinkle at the corners, his voice dripping honey. "Just nice? I thought I'd dress to impress for our first real meeting."

I force a playful eye roll to hide my nerves. "Fine, you look very dashing and handsome. Like the classic American dream man with your dimple, and your chiseled jaw with straight, white teeth. Happy?"

"With you? Always." He winks and my stomach flutters traitorously.

Get it together, Alina. This is just flirting, doesn't mean anything real. But then he tilts his head just so, looking at me in a way no one else ever has, like I'm the only light in a dark room, and my doubts start to waver. His gaze doesn't bear the hunger of a predator the way so many men's do. Maybe he really does want to get to know me, and maybe there is hope.

What if this sophisticated, worldly man could be my second chance? The key to the life Yara and I have only dreamed of?

I shyly meet his gaze. "I'm really glad we're doing this, Gerald. I just...I hope I don't disappoint you. Things are different over text than by video, and video is different than in person."

His expression softens. "Oh Alina, you could never disappoint me. I meant it when I said you're special. I could tell from the moment I read through your profile, and I can't wait to get to know you better."

My lips curve into a smile, the first real one all day. Maybe, just maybe, this will turn out to be something real after all.

As we continue to chat, my gaze darts around the edges of the video frame, taking in glimpses of Gerald's home. I search for signs of deception, any tiny inconsistency between his words and what lies visible on my screen. But all I see behind him are the rich dark woods, artfully arranged bouquets of exotic flowers, crystal decanters glinting in the low light—everything about his surroundings exudes luxury and comfort. From what I can see, if anything he's underplayed what he would be able to offer.

I glance around at my humble surroundings and instantly feel embarrassed at our relative poverty. I'm perched on a rickety folding chair in our cramped living room, the peeling wallpaper and threadbare carpet a constant reminder of our hand-to-mouth existence. Gerald seems utterly at ease, like a king holding court, and, although he's not saying anything to make me feel judged, I feel small and shabby in comparison.

A thought flashes through my mind. Could a man like him, who oozes wealth and sophistication, ever feel at home in my modest little apartment? I imagine him recoiling at the thought of sitting on our lumpy couch, wrinkling his nose at the lingering scent of boiled cabbage.

Maybe this video date was a mistake. We live in different worlds, quite literally.

But then Gerald smiles, his eyes crinkling at the corners, and despite my doubts, I can't help but smile back.

"It really is so wonderful to finally see you, Alina. I'm so glad we had the chance to meet each other over video," he says.

His voice is like velvet, enveloping me in warmth. I knows flattery when I hear it, but something about his tone just feels genuine. For a moment, the vast differences between us fade away, and we're just two people seeing each other clearly for the first time.

"I meant what I've been saying, Alina. I want to give you and Yara the life you deserve," he says earnestly. "A big beautiful house, no money worries, everything your hearts desire."

He gestures to the open floor plan behind him, at the marble floors and designer furniture. "I have plenty of space here. My hope is that one day, as our relationship grows, we'll get Yara's room painted her favorite color, fill it with toys and anything else she likes. Only the best for my girls."

My eyes widen. It's like he's voicing my most secret hopes and dreams—a safe, comfortable home for my daughter where money and security aren't an endless source of stress and anxiety. I glance over at Yara, sleeping soundly in the fetal position. This sweet, resourceful girl who will spend hours happily sketching flowers on a scrap of butcher paper because that's all we can afford in terms of 'toys'. My heart clenches.

"You really mean that?" I ask hesitantly. "It's really important to me that we don't make her any empty promises. And we hardly know each other. I don't expect you to be promising me the world, let alone the two of us."

Gerald's expression softens. "I would never do that, Alina. If there's one thing I can promise, it's that I never make a promise I can't keep."

I blink back tears, overwhelmed by the rush of emotions. After so many disappointments and heartbreaks, Gerald's words feel like a lifeline, a dream I had stopped allowing myself to imagine. For the first time in forever, I feel a spark of hope for our future. I want to believe Gerald, to trust that he can give me and Yara the stable life we have always dreamed of.

However, old hurts have made me wary. I know that these things can come at an unbearable cost.

Gerald seems to sense my hesitation. He leans toward the camera, his gaze intent.

"I know it's hard to trust again after you've been let down before... and while you haven't gone into detail, I get the sense that it's happened to you and maybe more than once. But I promise you, Alina, I'm not like those other men. I would never hurt you or Yara."

His voice rings with sincerity. I feel my doubts start to slip away.

"Oh Gerald," I say softly. "I'm so glad I met you. I know we've only recently begun to speak, but I'm starting to think you might be one of the kindest, most wonderful human beings I've ever known."

Gerald's eyes crinkle at the corners as he smiles. "I feel the same way about you, my sweet Alina. I knew from the moment we met that you were special and that it would only be a matter of time before we are together."

As the conversation continues, any remaining awkwardness fades away. It feels like a mutual sharing of our hopes, fears, and dreams, and I find myself telling him things I've rarely confided to anyone. Yet, I keep my guard up when it comes to Yara. And there are certain things that will always remain locked away—things I can never share with anyone.

It feels like we're connecting on a level I've never experienced before, like fate is righting itself and illuminating a path forward. Deep down, I know that I've found someone truly special in Gerald.

Eventually, I end the video call, my heart unusually full. I sit in silence for a moment, letting the conversation replay in my mind.

Euphoria wars with caution inside me. Gerald seems too good to be true—a handsome, wealthy man willing to sweep me and Yara into a life of comfort and security. It's a dream I'd never dare dream before.

Yet at the same time, how can I not chase this glimmer of hope? After years of struggling alone, barely keeping a roof over our heads and sometimes failing to do so, Gerald represents everything I've longed for. Safety, stability, a good life for Yara. No matter what doubts linger, I have to take a chance on this.

I glance around my shabby apartment, at the peeling paint and thrift store furniture. Stacks of overdue bills threatening disconnections and late fees threaten to tip off countertops and rickety tables.

The contrast with the glimpses of opulence I saw in Gerald's home couldn't be starker.

Gerald can offer us so much more. But I worry it's a mirage that will disappear if I reach for it. That I'm hinging too much on one person I barely know, and that this momentary calm will give way to just another storm.

I take a deep breath, steadying myself. I have to be brave, to silence the doubts holding me back. This could be Yara's and my one chance at real happiness.

I can't let fear stop me from seizing it. If Gerald is true to his word, he could give Yara the remaining childhood and young adulthood I always wished I could provide for her.

"Have faith," I whisper to myself. "Maybe, just maybe, good things do happen sometimes."

I won't know unless I take the leap. With Gerald, I feel hope stirring again. I cling to it, willing myself to believe that our luck is finally about to change.

Chapter 4

ALINA

Gerald's handsome face hovers over mine. He tips my chin up to face him, assertively taking my jaw between his large thumb and forefinger. I meet his gaze, my stomach flip-flopping with excitement at what he has planned for the evening.

"My dear Alina," he says, his deep voice resonating through my core, "Prepare to be taken care of, just the way you deserve."

He shoves me down onto the plush leather couch, and my body tingles at the coldness and rich scent of the fabric. As I sink back, the couch envelops my body in a comforting cocoon. His eyes bore into mine with a hunger I've never seen before.

He takes hold of each of my knees and yanks them apart, exposing my bare pussy to his gaze. I shiver, both excited and terrified by the intensity in his eyes. In most cases, I'd feel vulnerable, and I do here too. But it's in a way that thrills me. I anticipate his every move, the way he takes control of the situation adding to the intensity of his every touch.

He's still himself, still Gerald, but there's something else lurking beneath the surface tonight, an animalistic need that makes my heart race and my core clench with anticipation.

"Look at you. Such a beautiful pussy," he growls, gazing down at me. He moves in to get a closer look, running his finger down my lips in a way that makes me shudder, longing for him to enter me. His finger reaches my clit and I moan. I arch my hips toward him as he begins to gently rub my clit, each stroke building the intensity within my core.

"Tonight, it's all about you," his voice is a low growl that sends shivers down my spine. "I want to worship every inch of this beautiful body of yours, to show you just how much I desire you." His words are at odds with the possessive way he grasps my hips, adding to the thrill.

He dips his head and I cry out as he gently takes my clit into his mouth and begins to suck.

He moves his head away, teasing. "Do you like that, little lamb?" he says, his nickname for me making me feel giddy, possessed.

"Yes," I gasp. "Please... please don't stop. I need you."

He smirks, and once again lowers his head, his tongue extending to tease my clit, lapping up and down.

I squirm with pleasure, my hips continuing to arch toward his face. Desperate for more of his expert touch. Craving more than just his tongue. I close my eyes, reveling in the sensation as he fans his tongue against my clit and breathes warm air gently over my pussy.

He hums, and the vibrations rock me from my pussy throughout my core.

I moan, "Gerald, yes. Fuck yes," as he continues to lap and suck, the sensation within my core continuing to intensify.

My thighs begin to shake, and a moment later the orgasm hits me. I cry out as I come hard, my heart pounding in my chest, and instead of pulling away he yanks me closer and continues going to town on my clit. My hips buck and strain, my pussy clenching over and over again as waves of pleasure radiate through me.

It's only once my orgasm subsides that he finally pulls his head away from my pussy, his hands still firmly grasping my upper thighs. God, he looks extra hot peering up at me from down there, my juices still coating his mouth and chin.

"Did you like that, little lamb?" he growls. "Are you ready for more?"

Still breathless, I pant, "More?"

"Yes, more," he rasps. "Surely you realize we aren't close to being done here? Not until I give you more pleasure than you've ever felt in your life. That's part of what comes with being with me," he adds.

I allow myself a lazy smile. I've done it now. Found a man who wants to take care of me in more ways than one. Someone who enjoys going down on me and is clearly very good at it. It's like winning the lottery of men and tongues. I take a deep breath, letting my body reset while I wonder what he has planned next.

He gently attaches restraints to my wrists and ankles and carries me to the bedroom, where he secures them to the four corners of the bed. I bite my lip to stifle a moan. I've been tied up before, but never like this. With the expert restraints and the juxtaposition of gentleness and care with the hardness of a man who knows exactly what he wants.

My breath catches as he trails feather-light kisses down my neck, his tongue flicking at my pulse points, sending shivers racing down my spine.

His lips brush my collarbone, leaving a trail of wet heat that makes my toes curl and my pussy clench, and I arch my back towards him, craving more.

He chuckles, low and delighted, as if he knows exactly what he's doing to me. "So impatient," he teases, swirling his tongue around my nipple before sinking his teeth into the hardened peak.

I moan, "Gerald," as sensations of pleasure shoot from my nipple straight to my core, my thighs squirming in pleasant protest. My back arches even more, my hips bucking against the bed in search of friction, my ankles and wrists tugging against the restraints.

I still can't quite believe this is happening. This handsome, wealthy man, focused one hundred percent on me and my pleasure.

He continues his sensual onslaught, his lips and tongue leaving a trail of fire in their wake as he makes his way down my stomach. My heart pounds in my chest, my breathing ragged as he once again nears my center.

"Please," I beg, not caring about any pretense of composure. "I need you now." Part of me wants him to go ahead and eat my pussy all day, but there's a larger part of me that craves having him inside me. I want him to fuck me, right now.

He looks up, his eyes dark with lust and something else I can't quite decipher. With one swift motion, he frees himself from his pants and positions himself at my entrance. He stares into my eyes, his handsome face etched with the same want and need I feel.

"I've wanted this since the moment I laid eyes on you," he growls, before plunging into me, filling me completely, his every thrust a testament to his need and desire.

And as our bodies become one, as the world around us dissolves into nothing but gasps and moans and the rhythm of our aching hearts, I know that this isn't just some one-time rendezvous.

This is the start of something... more.

As if reading my mind, he pants into my ear as he continues to thrust his rock-hard girth into my drenched pussy. "This is just the beginning, my love. I'm going to worship you every day for the rest of our lives, because you are my queen and you deserve nothing less."

His words add to the pleasureful sensations that race through my body. I cling to him like my life depends on it, my nails digging into his back as he pounds into me with a primal intensity that both thrills and terrifies me. This man has unlocked something inside me that I'd thought long dead.

He grips my hips, my body on fire as he moves above me, my wetness coating his hard length. "Tell me you like it rough," he growls, his voice a low rasp I barely recognize.

"Yes, I love it rough," I moan, my eyes clouded with lust and desire, and that's all the invitation he needs.

Untying my restraints with expert efficiency, he flips me onto my stomach, lifting my ass into the air.

I gasp as he plunges into me from behind in one swift motion, burying himself in my pussy. He's like a man consumed, as if every fiber of his being is on fire for me. With each thrust, he seems to lose himself more and more in my tight heat.

I respond by clenching myself around his cock like a vice grip.

As if the universe approves of our union, another orgasm rips through me. At the same time, I feel Gerald's body tense and he shudders as his own orgasm grips his body. His moans entwine with my cries as pleasure shudders through both of us, my pussy clenching tightly onto his cock as he pumps his seed deep inside me.

I know in this instant that my life will never be the same. He's everything I longed for, yearned for, and the chemistry between us is even more intense than I could ever have imagined.

He slides out of me and I turn over and reposition myself on the pillow next to him, tucked into his side. As we lay there, catching our breath, our limbs entangled in the aftermath, I know I'm in deep trouble. Of the best kind. I've never felt this way about anyone before, and it terrifies me.

But for now, I don't care. I'm just lost in the warmth and hardness of his body, the feel of his skin against mine, and the way our bodies fit together like missing puzzle pieces.

"I'd do anything to keep you close. This is something that can't be faked, can't be manufactured," he whispers. "We're the real deal. Meant to be together, just like this."

I nod and smile lazily, feeling deeply relaxed, all my stresses melted away if only for this moment.

"And don't you even begin to think we're done, little lamb," he smiles back at me. "We're just getting started. I'm far from finished with you yet."

"You're insatiable," I breathe, turning so my back presses against his chest as we lay tangled in the sheets. Our bodies are still slick with sweat, our hearts pounding in tandem.

I've had many men want to fuck me before, but never like this. Never so attentive to my needs, their smooth words never backed up by their actions when it came down to it.

But Gerald is clearly very different. A gentleman with just the right amount of rough edges.

We lay in silence for a moment, lost in our thoughts.

"I like you from this side too," he murmurs in my ear, his voice low and gravelly, sending shivers down my spine. He runs his hand over the contour of my waist and hips, my body electrified by his touch. "Also, I have something for you."

He props himself up on one elbow.

I turn to face him, curiosity etched on my features.

He reaches for an antique jewelry box on the nightstand and opens it, withdrawing a delicate gold necklace. Dangling from the chain is a glittering emerald, its color reminding me of the depths of my eyes.

"It's beautiful," I breathe, my fingers trembling as I take it from him.

"It's nothing compared to you," he says, his voice laced with sincerity.

My heart thuds in my chest as he fastens the clasp around my neck. I can't deny the thrill that courses through me.

"It suits you," he smiles, admiring his gift around my neck. Admiring me.

I blush, the weight of the stone suddenly making me feel self-conscious. What is this life? A man worshipping my body, fucking me really good, and now lavishing me with expensive gifts?

"How did you know I like emeralds? And delicate necklaces like this?" I quirk a brow.

"You said you wanted a hand necklace, but I thought this was more fitting."

It takes me a minute and then I burst out laughing. "Oh Gerald, your sense of humor is wild." I raise my hand to run it along the delicately linked chain around my neck. "But I'll take it."

"Now," he says, his voice dripping with desire, "let me show you just how much I like this necklace on you."

Before I can protest, he flips me onto my back, his body hovering over mine. His eyes burn with a hunger that sends a shiver down my spine.

"I really have been thinking about this for weeks," he growls, his hand trailing up my thigh, teasingly close to where I already ache for him again despite having had him only minutes before.

"Me too," I gasp, arching my hips towards him, unable to hide my need.

"Dirty girl," he growls, his eyes darkening with lust.

His hand wraps around the delicate chain of my new necklace, tugging me closer to him. Heat pools in my core as I realize his intentions.

"Gerald, I..."

"Shh," he soothes, capturing my lips in a searing kiss. "Just feel it."

With one swift motion, he enters me again, and I gasp into his mouth, the sensation of the necklace's cold metal against my heated flesh sending shockwaves through my body.

"That's it, baby," he groans, his voice a feral growl in my ear as he thrusts deeper, the emerald against my sensitive skin sending me into a whirlwind of pleasure and pain.

I moan, my nails digging into his broad shoulders, my body craving more of his possessive touch, despite the danger that I sense lurks just beneath the surface.

"You feel so good," he growls.

The power dynamic between us shifts with each thrust, our roles blurring like the lines between right and wrong. He's in charge, but he's also treating me as his goddess, taking me to heights of ecstasy I didn't know existed.

"Say it," he suddenly demands, his voice harsh as he buries himself to the hilt.

"I..." I pant, feeling myself teetering on the edge, the conflict within me mirroring the warring emotions in my heart.

"Say it!" he growls again, twisting the necklace and sinking his teeth into my neck.

"I..." Submission tastes like adrenaline on my tongue as I find myself whispering the words I never thought possible.

"I love you," I gasp. And as the words escape my tongue, I realize that I mean them. My body responds, reaching climax, my body trembling in his iron grip.

"Good girl," he growls, before joining me in the oblivion, his thrusts becoming erratic, marking me as his, body and soul.

As we lie panting, entwined in each other's arms, I know that nothing will ever be the same again.

"Shh," Gerald soothes me, stroking my hair as he slowly withdraws, his touch gentle but still possessive. "I've got you."

He reaches for a silk handkerchief and wipes us both down, his movements efficient and practiced. He has clearly been here before, in this aftermath of seduction.

But, right now, it's as if I'm the only thing he cares about. And I'm happy to be his obsession, his sole focus. He can worship me all he wants.

Gently, he helps me put my lingerie back on, his hands lingering on my skin, etching himself onto my very being.

"I'll be back for you, Alina," he whispers, his voice a dark promise, his eyes cold and calculating as he pulls away. His focus instantly shifts, his mind now back on the next business deal as he puts his clothes back on and quietly leaves the room.

Alone in the wreckage of our tryst, I take a deep breath and stretch as I exhale. I know there will be no escape from the web he's spun around me, like the silken threads of a spider entangling its prey.

But that's okay, because I don't want an escape. I just want Gerald.

I lie here like this for a while, and then, feeling the last remnants of our passionate encounter still coursing through my veins, I shiver as I finish getting dressed.

I tuck away the silk handkerchief that bears traces of both of our essences. This handkerchief, probably worth hundreds of dollars, used for aftercare.

A symbol of Gerald's wealth, and his taste in the finer things. Which now apparently includes me.

With Gerald now absent, my mind returns to a whirlwind of conflicting emotions. He just provided me with a level of intimacy I'd never thought possible. Yet, deep down I still have doubts.

As I finger the necklace that drapes prettily against my throat, the emerald glinting under the soft overhead light, I still fear our connection is tainted by ulterior motives. But at least the sex is out of this world.

I wake with a start, reorienting myself to my dark and cramped apartment, Yara snoring softly as she sleeps next to me.

My face flushes and my heart flips in my chest as I realize I was dreaming. And what a dream it was.

If Gerald turns out to be a fraction of the man that visited me in my slumber, we might really stand a chance.

Chapter 5

ALINA

Dominika and I sit closely together over a small table at our favorite little cafe, nestled in a corner that feels like a slice of peace in our otherwise chaotic city. The aroma of freshly ground coffee beans mingles with the scent of rain-washed streets outside. Fresh coffee, a luxury I could never justify, but something Dominika is able and happy to treat me to every now and then.

I lean in, ready to divulge my secret. "I've met someone. I bit the bullet and tried your idea of the online app, and I've been talking to this guy..."

Dominika's eyes light up with curiosity and excitement as she takes a sip of her latté, the pale golden crema swirling in her mug. "Oh really? How exciting! Who is he?"

"He's from America. A businessman. His name is Gerald." I can't help the blush that colors my cheeks, feeling a mixture of pride and nervousness. "And I think he might be the one," I blurt out.

She quirks a brow. "The one? As in *the one*? Wow! How long have you been speaking?" She probes, her voice tinged with both interest and caution.

"Only a couple of weeks. But he's swept me off my feet. He wants me to go and meet him somewhere." The words tumble out, laced with a hope I've not allowed myself to feel in years.

"Does he know about Yara?" Her concern shifts towards Yara now, always protective, always thinking about what's best for my daughter. Her unofficial godmother, she sneaks assistance our way whenever she can to supplement my meager earnings. If her husband knew, and worse yet if the organization he works for knew, she could get in a lot of trouble. For that and her friendship, I'll be forever grateful.

"Yes, of course. She's one of the first things I told him about. I won't even speak to someone unless they're theoretically prepared to include her in their world," I say quickly, feeling the need to assure both Dominika and myself that I'm making the right choices.

"Well.. that's good, I think," she says, studying me over her coffee mug. "What did he say when you told him about her? How did he react?" she presses, her gaze fixed on me, searching for any sign of doubt.

"He seemed excited. He asked lots of questions about her hobbies and what she looks like." I recall Gerald's reaction, and how I consciously tried to interpret his questions as interest rather than something more sinister.

It's difficult, being a single parent dipping their foot into the dating pond. You want the other person to show just the right amount of interest—not enough and you know it's not going to work, too much and it's creepy—and potentially very dangerous.

Dominika leans back, her expression turning serious, "Well, be careful what you wish for, dear. I know I suggested this to you, but a single man who takes too much interest in your daughter is never a good thing." Her words strike a chord of fear in me. As if I need reminding the world is full of creepy, misogynistic assholes that prey on women and girls.

"I know. I worry about that constantly, but I really haven't gotten that sense from speaking with him. It seems more like he's trying to show he understands that I'm a single parent and that having my daughter as a priority in my life isn't going to change just because of a relationship." I find myself defending Gerald again, wanting to believe in the good.

"Okay, well, make sure you know him first, before you introduce her to him. She's had so much instability already. And so have you," her voice softens, filled with empathy for our battered, yet resilient little duo.

"You think I don't know that?" I snap back, a hint of frustration leaking through. "Of course I'm not going to meet him for the first time while she's there."

"I know you know," Dominika says, squeezing my hand. "You really should wait a fair amount of time, though, until you're certain about his intentions," she advises, always the voice of reason in my sometimes too-hopeful world.

"Well, you don't need to worry. We've started talking about meeting in person, just the two of us. That should enable me to vet him properly," I try to reassure her, and maybe myself too.

"A few days together isn't the same as day-to-day life. Just be mindful of that," she says. "I mean, I have a friend, Anoushka, who met a man from America. He took her away on a dream vacation and she fell head over heels, but then he turned out to be really abusive. Trapped her in his house. She ended up in a woman's shelter after he beat her so badly she was almost unrecognizable."

Dominika's story sends shivers down my spine, the harsh reality of her words threatening to ground my fleeting dreams.

"You're scaring me now, Dominika. You're the one who encouraged me to do this in the first place," I retort, the fear and doubt starting to seep in.

"I know, I know. I just want you to go into this with both eyes open. I know how much you've been through. And I understand your desire for a new life that both you and Yara deserve. I just don't want you to get hurt in the process. Luchenko may be a very bad man, but as they say, better the devil you know sometimes." Her sincerity is palpable, her worry for us genuine.

"You're not suggesting—" I start, incredulous at the thought of ever going back to that life.

"No, never," she quickly clarifies, concern etching her features. "I don't think you should be near him. Speaking of which, has he tried to contact you recently?"

"Not directly," I shake my head. "But I know he's always near—him and his men. I feel like they're constantly watching, waiting. We're at the part of his cycle where he's so busy with other things that he can't obsess over us, but it's only a matter of time, and I worry if I don't leave soon, he'll try to take Yara again," I confess, the weight of our situation heavy on my heart.

"Understood. And yes, my husband has mentioned how busy the business is at the moment. Just don't jump into something worse because you're scared of a 'what if' situation," she warns, her gaze steady on mine.

"Dominika, I love you but you're sending me very mixed messages." I sigh, feeling torn between the promise of a dream and the reality of our past. My best friend's tendency to speak out loud can be great for generating ideas and analyzing options, but it can be very confusing once you've already made a life-changing decision.

"I know, I know. I'm sorry. Look," she sighs, squeezing my shoulder with affection, a gesture that feels like a lifeline. "I hope that you can appreciate I'm coming from a good place. There are so many things to consider here. And I just worry about you. I want the best for you. You're my best friend." She smiles at me, her eyes kind. "Plus, I'll miss you if you move all the way to the United States, even though it seems like that might be the best option for both of you."

Her words bring a small smile to my face. "You can always visit, Dominika. If Gerald has half the financial means he says he does, and from what I've seen on camera during our video calls, you could practically have your own guest wing whenever you wanted to see me!"

Her laughter, light and genuine, fills the space between us. "Well, wouldn't that be amazing. Let's go into this with a positive attitude. Just be wary, and take notice of any red flags."

As I nod, taking in her advice, the café around us buzzes with life, a stark contrast to the seriousness of our conversation. It's a poignant reminder of the world moving around us, oblivious to the impending decisions that could alter the course of my and Yara's lives forever—a fragile bubble that might burst at any moment.

Chapter 6

ALINA

I sit on my bed, staring at my phone screen as Gerald's voice fills my ears. He tells me all about his latest trip to Dubai, describing the towering skyscrapers and shimmering desert sands. I'm transfixed by his words, imagining myself standing beside him, taking in the exotic sights and sounds.

"Alina, are you still there?" Gerald asks, breaking me from my thoughts.

"Sorry, I'm here," I reply, feeling a flush rise to my cheeks. "It just all sounds so fascinating, and I guess I was daydreaming about what it might be like to visit a place like that someday. Can you imagine it? Riding on camels alongside each other in the desert? Fabulous."

"Good. So you're open to traveling and you clearly have a sense of adventure... because, well, I've been thinking about something," he says, a hint of excitement in his voice.

"What is it?"

"Video and phone calls are great, but of course I want to meet you in person. Like, really meet you. I know we've talked about it in theory, meeting up somewhere down the line. But I think we should do it sooner rather than later. And I have the perfect idea."

My heart races as Gerald describes the tropical island getaway he has in mind. I can almost feel the warm sand between my toes and the gentle breeze on my skin.

But then fear creeps in, as it tends to do. What if this is all too good to be true? What if Gerald isn't who he seems to be? After all, it wouldn't be the first time I've been tricked and trapped by a powerful man.

"Alina, are you still there?" Gerald's voice breaks through my thoughts again.

"Yes, sorry. It just sounds...amazing," I say, trying to sound upbeat.

"Ah, I knew you'd love it. We could have our own little paradise, just the two of us. Even if it's only for a couple of days."

My stomach tightens at the thought. I want to trust Gerald, but my past experiences have taught me to be cautious.

"Can I think about it?" I ask, hoping to buy time. After all, I don't even have a passport. I also don't want to seem too keen, like I'd just up and fly away to vacation with any old stranger I met off the internet.

Even a devastatingly handsome stranger who's promising me and my daughter the world.

"Of course, take all the time you need." His voice is kind. "But I promise, Alina, this will be worth it. I want to show you how much I care about you. And," he adds, as if reading my mind, "I don't want you worrying about anything when it comes to expenses or paperwork or anything like that. You mentioned you haven't left the country before, and I would be happy to get a passport for you."

My heart leaps at this offer, at what is probably a small kindness to a man like Gerald, but one that means so much to me.

The call ends, leaving me alone with my thoughts. Can I really take a chance on this man? Or will it just lead to more pain and disappointment?

I lay back on the bed, closing my eyes and imagining myself on that island with Gerald by my side. It's tempting, so tempting. An absence of responsibilities, even if only for a couple of days. Exhilarating yet terrifying, like standing at the edge of a cliff and peering down.

Part of me longs to throw caution to the wind and dive into this new adventure with Gerald. To let him sweep me off my feet.

It's as if he's awakened something in me—a thirst for more out of life than just scraping by day-to-day.

The photos he shared of pristine beaches and elaborate hotel suites are so different from anything I've ever known. Sure, Luchenko provided a degree of opulence, but never an international vacation. That wasn't part of the deal, and certainly not something his wife would tolerate.

But then I hear Yara's voice in my head, reminding me of my responsibilities as a mother. I know I can't just leave my daughter behind, no matter how much I long for adventure and connection. It's selfish. Wrong. Dangerous. I barely know this man. What if he isn't who he seems? I've been hurt before by men who made big promises they didn't keep.

"Maybe I shouldn't go," I whisper to myself, feeling the weight of the decision ahead.

But then again, if I never go, I never stand a chance of creating this new life for us.

For Yara.

Needing advice, I once again meet with Dominika, this time at our favorite park. Sitting on a weathered bench surrounded by lush trees, I tell Dominika about Gerald's offer.

Her face reflects both protectiveness and excitement as the breeze gently rustles her shag haircut. "A tropical vacation with a handsome stranger? It sounds like a fairy tale," she says. "But Alina...remember what we talked about. Promise me you'll be careful. Make sure it's not a fairy tale with a dark twist. I don't want you getting hurt again."

I nod, knowing Dominika speaks from a place of love. "I don't plan to do anything reckless. But maybe...maybe I should take a chance. I've spent my whole life playing it safe and look where it's gotten me. Don't I deserve a little adventure?"

Dominika squeezes my hand supportively. "Yes, you absolutely do. And I am excited for you. I just want you going into this cautiously. Guard your heart, but if it feels right...go for it. You have to kiss a few frogs sometimes to find your prince... just make sure they're not frogs that leave you with permanent scars."

I smile, emboldened by my friend's encouragement. I'll move slowly with Gerald, but for the first time in years, I feel a spark of hope that something extraordinary awaits.

I return home feeling lighter than I have in a long time. I call Gerald, butterflies swirling in my stomach. When he answers, his deep voice sends a thrill through me as I imagine hearing it in person.

"I've been thinking about it, and I've come to a decision," I say, my heart beating fast. "I'd love to join you on the trip."

Gerald lets out an exclamation of delight. "Wonderful! You won't regret this, Alina. We'll have such an adventure together!"

He begins eagerly detailing his plans—the exclusive resort with private villas, the secluded white sand beaches, the candlelit dinners and couples' massages. I picture it all in my mind, allowing myself to get caught up in his enthusiasm.

Then Gerald's tone softens. "But most importantly, I want you to feel safe with me. Cherished. This trip is about exploring what we might have together, not the extravagance."

His words melt my lingering doubts. Perhaps Dominika was right and my fairy tale awaits after all. I've protected my heart for so long, but now maybe it's the time to open it to new possibilities.

"I trust you, and I'm excited to go on an adventure with you," I say sincerely. "I can't wait to discover where this journey leads us."

Gerald's relieved exhale comes through the phone. "You won't regret placing your faith in me, Alina. Our adventure begins soon, my little lamb."

Little lamb. His choice of words floors me, mirroring his nickname for me in my steamy dream about him. What are the chances? It's like the universe is sticking a blinking neon arrow over his head and screaming 'Go for it'!

"Why did you just call me that?"

"Little lamb? You just have this pureness, innocence... cuteness about you."

Wow. Even his nicknames are perfect. Although I know a few people who wouldn't describe me as pure *or* innocent.

But my excitement is tempered by a nagging concern—leaving Yara, even for a short time. Though capable, she is only twelve, and we've scarcely spent a night apart. I'd leave her with my mother, but it's strictly against the rules of her home, and there's no way Yara could realistically hide out for several days without someone noticing her.

Sensing my hesitation, Gerald says gently, "I know being away from Yara worries you. Tell me what would make you comfortable leaving her."

I consider his question. "I'd need to know she's being cared for by someone truly trustworthy. And that I can still be close, even from afar."

"Of course," Gerald immediately replies. "I'll arrange for a nanny—someone vetted and capable of tending to Yara's unique needs. You can video chat daily, and Yara can call anytime she wants. Does that work?"

I exhale in relief, touched by how sincerely Gerald tries to accommodate my misgivings. How he anticipated my concerns without me having to explain. "Yes, I believe so, that sounds good. Thank you."

"Yara's wellbeing matters to me because you matter," says Gerald. "I'll always respect your priorities and make them mine, too."

Bolstered by Gerald's reassurance, I gather my courage to speak with Yara.

I sit her down, taking her small hands in mine.

"You know I met someone special, Yara. Mr. Gerald. He wants to take us both on a trip soon, but I have to go and meet him first, to make sure it's safe. You'd stay here with a nanny."

Yara's lip quivers. "You're leaving?"

"Just for a short while, sweetheart. And we can talk whenever you want."

"Will he be mean like Mr. Luchenko?" Yara asks worriedly.

I squeeze her hands. "No, my love. I don't believe so. But remember, if anyone makes you uncomfortable, you tell me right away. Even if they say to keep it secret. Okay? And your grandmother will be close by as well. We'll make sure you're both safe."

"Who is the nanny? Are they nice? Will they do dance routines with me?"

Her questions make me chuckle. I stroke her hair gently. "We'll find someone kind who will keep you company, I promise."

Yara nods bravely. "I'll miss you Mama. But I'm glad you're going on an adventure."

I hug her tight, my hopes and fears intermingling.

I just pray that my trust in Gerald is warranted, and that our journey together will lead someplace beautiful.

Chapter 7

ALINA

The moment I clear customs and step into the arrivals area at the small island airport, I'm greeted by a tall, thin stranger in a suit. "Miss Petrov?" he inquires politely.

I nod at the man, wondering how he's able to wear an immaculate white shirt and long slacks in the humidity and heat that have enveloped me since the moment I stepped off the plane.

"Mr. Cranshaw sent me to collect you, ma'am."

Interesting. I guess I'd expected Gerald to greet me himself. The man must notice my confusion as he follows up with, "He had an important business meeting and wanted to make sure he wasn't late in picking you up."

I nod. "I see.. well, thank you for coming to get me."

"Of course," he beams. "Anything for Mr. Gerald. Did you have a good flight?" He chitchats as I identify my luggage on the carousel and he helps me to grab it and place it on a large cart. "I'm Kenneth, by the way."

"Yes, it was really nice, thank you!" Everything went as scheduled from the time I woke up and headed to the airport, Yara and the nanny waving as I walked out the door and hopped into my waiting taxi. As if the universe was giving me yet another sign that I'm absolutely on the right path.

I felt like a movie star the whole way here, drinking mimosas and chatting with the flight attendants throughout our flight. It's been years since I last flew—not since the early days with Luchenko when he'd take me on short local flights to fancy boutique hotels—and I was worried I might be afraid. But the only part that frazzled me a bit was when I arrived on the tiny tropical island and had to make my way through customs and immigration clearance.

There's something about authority—particularly men in uniform—that always puts me on edge. It's a tickle of discomfort, a fear that I'm suddenly going to be hauled away, even though I've done absolutely nothing to warrant that, to my knowledge. I'm not sure if it's the uniforms, the firearms, the serious expressions on the men's faces, or something else, but it had me tense even here. Where I'm from, we're taught not to trust law enforcement for a reason, after all.

Kenneth loads my luggage into a sleek black SUV and opens the back door for me. I hop in, inhaling the rich scent of leather upholstery. A driver and a fancy car to pick me up... so far, Gerald seems to be the wealthy man he claims to be. Not that his money is the only reason I'm here. But you never know—with so many catfish stories and horror tales of bait-and-switch schemes, I'm relieved to see that Gerald appears to be who he says he is

"How long have you known Gerald?" I ask Kenneth as we make our way down the palm tree-lined road on the way to the hotel. I figure I may as well take this opportunity to gather any insights. I am here partially to vet him after all, so I may as well see what Kenneth knows. Or rather, what he's prepared to share.

"I've worked with Mr. Gerald for about three years now, ma'am," Kenneth beams, the pride evident in his voice. "He took me under his wing when I was assigned as his driver, and I've been working for him ever since. I accompany him all over, really. Including on his vacations." With his free hand, he gestures at the palm trees that line the highway.

"And does Gerald invite lots of ladies to these islands for romantic vacations?"

A concerned look passes over Kenneth's face, but just as rapidly he seems to recover. "I, uh—I'm not meant to discuss Mr. Gerald's private life, ma'am. I hope you can understand."

I quickly wink and smile in an attempt to put him at ease. "I'm only teasing, Kenneth. If that was a test of loyalty, you just passed with flying colors."

Kenneth laughs awkwardly. Shit. I hope it doesn't get back to Gerald that I'm inquiring about other women. I don't even really know why I asked. It just kind of came out.

I change the subject, asking Kenneth more benign questions about where he's from and what he likes to do for fun.

He seems relieved by the change in conversation and I decide not to press things further.

It's important that I start this vacation out on the right foot, and—who knows—Kenneth could end up being an ally down the road if I need one.

We enter a winding driveway through a large, ornate gate emblazoned with the luxury resort's prestigious logo. Immaculately curated vegetation and vibrant flowers line the roadway, and I wind my window down to inhale the strong, pleasant scent of hibiscus and jacaranda.

We pull up at the valet stand and I go on ahead while Kenneth figures out the luggage and vehicle situation.

"Alina!" Gerald's voice echoes through the grand lobby of the luxurious hotel, his eyes gleaming with excitement. I recognize him immediately, just as handsome as he was in his photos and during our many video calls, but the 3D version with muscles and angles that the sunlight hits in all the right places.

After a warm embrace that gives me pleasant tingles, he places his hands on both of my upper arms and steps back to take in the full length of my appearance. He beams. "Wow, Alina, just look at you. You are so very beautiful. I knew you were stunning, but video calls don't do you justice."

I find myself blushing. He's just as smooth in person as he was on our calls and via text.

His energy is also contagious. He's as comfortable here as I imagine him to be in a boardroom, securing one of his mysterious business deals. He takes my hand with confidence and leads me towards the reception desk, his tailored suit swishing with each step.

"Sorry for the uptight outfit," he gestures at his clothing. "I'll change into something more appropriate later. I just had a business meeting on Zoom and needed to look the part. Didn't want them to think I was running around playing golf instead of making wise investment decisions on their behalf."

Again, interesting. So he brought suits. I thought this was a trip where we could get to know each other, not for me to sit in the room or by the pool or whatever while he talked commerce.

He must notice the look of slight confusion on my face. "Don't worry," he says. "I've scheduled plenty of time for us. I just have a few things I need to take care of that couldn't be moved." He smiles at me and places a hand on the small of my back. "I hope you understand... and I can assure you that getting to know you is my top priority."

His eyes roam down my body, and it's hard to explain how it makes me feel. Admired, I guess. But also in a slightly predatory way. I don't entirely hate it, but I don't love it either. Maybe I'm just slightly irritated after the flight and news of his work obligations.

"I have a surprise for you as well. Several, actually," he grins.

I eye him warily, my past experiences with surprises leaving a sour taste in my mouth. "What surprise?" I ask, half-joking, half-serious. "You're not about to tell me we're jumping out of a plane or something, are you?"

"Ah, you'll see," he says, winking at me. "But first, let me check us in." He turns to the receptionist and flashes a charming smile, his fingers tapping on the marble counter impatiently.

As we wait for the keys to our room, I take in the opulent surroundings: sprawling gardens dotted with palm trees, a glistening pool that stretches as far as the eye can see, and a pristine private beach that shimmers under the tropical sun. It's all so overwhelming, so out of my league.

I've been to a couple of nice hotels before, but those were all back in the home country, and it was with Luchenko. Thankfully, those memories are now well in the past and fleeting at best. Thank goodness for the power to forget.

"Here we go," Gerald says, handing me a key card. "Our suite is this way." He gestures towards a grand staircase, his hand brushing against mine.

I swallow nervously, the walk to our shared hotel suite suddenly making things very real. I hadn't really thought about the fact we'd have one room to share right off the bat. But we have been talking for a while, and he is a handsome man.

I need to stop being so uptight. Yara and my mother are both safe and sound back at home, and I deserve to let my hair down a little. Gerald is a successful, powerful man, and he wants to spend his time with me. I should be grateful.

We ascend the stairs, my heart racing with anticipation. The door to our suite looms before us, and Gerald pauses for effect. "Ready?" he asks.

I nod, my palms sweating.

He swings open the door and leads me inside, his hand on the small of my back. My eyes widen as I take in the plush furnishings, the panoramic views of the ocean, and the king-sized bed that beckons seductively.

"Wow," I breathe, feeling a lump form in my throat. "This is... amazing. I think this might be the most breathtaking sight I've ever seen."

"Only the best for you," Gerald murmurs, his lips grazing my ear. I shiver, my senses on high alert. "And, forget this view, I think *you* might be the most breathtaking sight I've ever seen."

My stomach flip-flops at his words, making me realize I'm not used to this type of attention. He threw a lot of compliments my way via video and text, but these kinds of things just hit differently in person.

As the day wears on, we explore the hotel grounds, lounging by the pool and sipping cocktails under the shade of a parasol. Gerald is the perfect host, attentive to my every need and desire. Our conversation flows easily, and I admire the way the sun hits his well-defined body. He's an attractive man, and I'm here on a free vacation with him. I should be relaxed, carefree.

But as the sun begins to set, I can't help but feel a twinge of unease.

"Do you really have to work tonight?" I ask him as we watch the sky turn pink and gold.

"Unfortunately, yes," he says with a sigh. "I'm sorry, I know it's not ideal. Especially this being our first day together and all. But the time zones make it difficult to schedule things, and—don't worry—I'll be back soon enough."

I nod, trying to hide my disappointment. "Okay, I'll just... hang out here for a bit."

"Good girl," he says, planting a kiss on my cheek before disappearing into the hotel. Although I'm still disappointed by his work obligations, his use of those words get me thinking about what might happen when he's done with work for the evening, and I feel a pleasant twinge deep in my core.

Left alone, I wander towards the beach, my toes sinking into the soft sand. The waves crash against the shore, their rhythm lulling me into a sense of peace.

But as the darkness creeps in, so does my fear. What if this is just what it's like to be with Gerald? A lifetime of mysterious business meetings and time spent alone?

I shake my head, trying to dispel the negative thoughts. This is supposed to be a romantic getaway, a chance for us to connect and explore our feelings for each other. I'm such an overthinker, I'm extrapolating one unfortunately timed business meeting into a lifetime of clandestine meetups and a neglectful partner. And yet, I can't shake the feeling that something isn't quite right.

As I make my way back to the suite, I hear a commotion coming from one of the nearby restaurants. Shouts and crashes ring out, sending a chill down my spine. I quicken my pace, my heart racing with fear.

As I pass the restaurant, I see Gerald at the center of the chaos, his eyes blazing with anger. He's shouting at a group of men, their faces twisted in fury.

I freeze, unsure of what to do.

"Alina!" he calls out as he notices me, his voice piercing through the noise. "Get over here!"

I hesitate for a moment before hurrying toward him, my heart in my throat. As I reach his side, he grabs my hand and pulls me close.

"Stay with me," he says, his eyes blazing. "No matter what happens, don't let go."

I nod, my fingers trembling in his grasp. The tension in the air is palpable, the danger real. And yet, I can't help but feel a thrill of excitement at being by Gerald's side in this moment of crisis.

But who are these men, and why are they here? How does Gerald even know anyone on this small tropical island? I'm so confused.

As the men close in, I brace myself for whatever comes next. For better or for worse, I'm in this with him now.

I inhale sharply to steady my nerves as the men approach, their hostility rolling off them in waves. Gerald's grip on my hand tightens, but his face remains an impassive mask.

"Let's talk this through," Gerald says calmly, though I can detect an undercurrent of danger in his tone. "There's no need for violence."

The apparent leader of the group, a burly man with a scar down his cheek, spits on the ground. "You think you can hustle us and just walk away, Cranshaw?" He cracks his knuckles menacingly. "I don't care how rich you are, you're gonna pay."

My heart pounds in my chest. Gerald's expression is cold and calculating, even in the face of a threat. A thrill of fear and excitement runs through me.

Gerald smiles, but it doesn't reach his eyes. "I won fair and square. Just accept you lost."

In a flash, the scarred man throws a punch, but Gerald dodges it smoothly. Chaos erupts as the men all rush at Gerald at once.

I'm shoved to the side as Gerald meets them blow for blow, his tailored suit soon spattered with blood.

I watch in awe at his vicious grace, mesmerized despite the violence. With an efficient combo, he drops the last man groaning to the ground.

Gerald turns to me, his chest heaving, his eyes alight. He pulls me close again, the thrill of the fight still surging through him.

"Do you see?" he murmurs in my ear. "I want you to remember this night for the rest of your life. And that I'm not one to be crossed."

I feel his heart pounding against mine, and realize my own is racing to match it. Being with him suddenly seems dangerous, but not for the reasons I thought it might be. And it's kind of exciting.

Gerald takes my hand and leads me away from the groaning men. Adrenaline still courses through me as we walk back toward the main lobby.

"Let's get out of here," Gerald says, his voice low and controlled once more.

We head outside into the warm tropical night.

The sounds of steel drums float on the breeze as we stroll along the beach, hand in hand. Torches flicker, casting a golden glow over Gerald's handsome face. He gazes at me intensely and I feel weak in the knees.

"Dance with me," he murmurs, drawing me close. We sway together under the stars to the island rhythms. Gerald runs his hands along my body and I melt into him.

"Any requests?" he asks.

"Your choice," I smile.

"As you wish," he grins. "Don't say I didn't give you a warning," he says over his shoulder as he approaches the band between songs.

As he walks back, the sounds of a steel drum version of a popular song strike up behind him.

I laugh with joy as he takes both of my hands in his and we dance together, my head on his chest.

Gazing up at him, under the star- and moonlight, a surge of emotion hits me. His eyes meet mine and I sense he feels the same.

"I—" I begin to speak, but Gerald silences me, dipping his head until his mouth meets mine in a passionate kiss.

His lips are soft, his kiss commanding, causing my pussy to clench as a dozen butterflies are released in my stomach.

"Are you hungry?" Gerald asks as the song ends.

His question makes me realize I'm famished, and my stomach grumbles in response. He hears it and laughs. "I take that as a yes. Come with me, beautiful," he says, taking my hand once again and leading us back to our suite.

Chapter 8

ALINA

Gerald orders us an intimate candlelit dinner delivered to our balcony.

He feeds me bites of lobster, brushing his fingers against my lips. "You're exquisite," he whispers. "You're like a dream."

"So is this food," I reply, blown away by the buttery, delicate flavors of the lobster and the rest of the sumptuous spread laid out before us. A girl could get used to this.

Afterward, he leads me to the bedroom.

I flush as I remember my dream, way back from when I first met him online. Will the real Gerald be as kind, as attentive, and as focused on worshipping me?

My expectations are sky-high, unrealistic, and yet having experienced him in dream form I know that anything less would be a disappointment.

My heart pounds as Gerald's hands gently hikes up my skirt, slipping off the black lace panties I bought especially for the trip. His massive hands part my thighs, his gaze cold and calculating as he kneels before me. I shiver, the room's cool air adding to the anticipation of what's to come. He leans in, his charming smile fades into a more serious expression as he surveys my nakedness.

"Spread your pussy for me, baby," he growls, his voice low and guttural. I quiver at the dominance in his voice, and it instantly makes me wetter. Slowly and obediently, I part my lips, exposing the dripping wetness that pools between my thighs. God, I need him.

He dips his head and his tongue flicks out, lapping at my clit like a predator tasting its prey. My hips buck upward, helpless to the sensations coursing through my body.

"Oh, fuck, Gerald," I moan. His name, once so foreign, now a sweet release on my lips.

Gerald chuckles, the vibrations of his laughter sending shockwaves through my core. "That's right, baby, but call me daddy," he growls, slipping two fingers inside me while his tongue continues to worship my clit.

"Gerald... daddy, I'm going to come," I pant, gripping the sheets tightly. Calling him daddy only makes my pussy clench further, makes me grow even wetter. It always felt like a weird thing to say during sex, forced almost, but with Gerald it's incredibly hot.

He doesn't relent, only redoubling his efforts. "That's right, sweetheart. Good girl. I want to taste every drop of your cum," he growls, his voice thick with lust.

The way he says cum, like it's the filthiest word ever spoken, sends me hurtling over the edge.

My back arches, my orgasm tearing through me like a freight train.

"Oh, fuck! Oh, fuck, daddy!" I cry out, my head thrown back as wave after wave of pleasure washes over me.

Gerald stands, wiping his face with the back of his hand. "Delicious," he growls, his expression pleased as he gazes down on me as I recapture my breath.

And then he lifts me up from the bed and carries me over to the window, pressing himself against me from behind as we both gaze out at the city lights. his cock hardening against my heat. "You feel so fucking good, Alina," he groans, his voice rough with need. "I need to be inside you."

"Oh, God, so do you," I gasp, my hands pressing into the cool glass pane, my hips arching backward, tempting him to drive himself into me.

My enthusiasm only fuels his need, and he slams into my pussy hard from behind, my body taking every inch of him.

It's like I was made for this, made for him, and I don't want it to end.

I can tell by his movements that he can feel the pressure building in his loins, and that he won't be able to hold back.

My breasts smash into the window each time he plows his hard cock into my pussy, and I moan at the cold sensation of the glass against my hard peaks.

With one final, powerful thrust, he comes inside me, his climax tearing through him like a storm, yanking me over the edge with him.

With a lingering glance at the twinkling tropical scene before us, he takes my hand and leads me back to the bed where we both lie down. I nestle into the crook of his arm, draping my thigh over his torso. We remain entwined, panting and struggling to catch our breath, neither of us willing to let go or let this moment end.

"You're dangerous, Alina," he says, finally finding the words.

I laugh, a breathless sound. "I know."

My words seem to send a shiver down his spine, and he trembles slightly. "With you, I feel like I'm in deep, deep trouble, you know?"

"Oh, I very much feel the same way about you," I reply. "It feels like our worlds were destined to collide, and there's no going back now."

"You're right about that," he says, his tone with a slight edge to it. "There's no going back."

We lie there in silence for a moment, enjoying the feeling of each other's sated bodies pressed against each other.

"I can't get enough of you," he growls. And then he makes it clear that he really does feel this way.

He flips onto me on the plush king-sized bed, his body hovering over mine as he drives into me relentlessly.

I moan his name, my nails digging into his back, my body arching up to meet every thrust. My body blazes with desire, lust clouding my vision as he continues to plow my pussy.

"You like it rough, don't you, little lamb?" he growls, his voice low and guttural.

"Yes," I whimper, my hips bucking against his, my wetness soaking the expensive sheets below them. "God, yes. Don't stop."

He obliges, his pace becoming even more frenzied, his grip on my hips bruising as he brings me closer and closer to the edge.

I can feel another climax building, and from the way his body begins to tense, I know he's not far off either.

"You're mine," he growls, his teeth clenched in unadulterated pleasure. "Say it."

"Yours," I gasp out, my walls squeezing around him in delicious spasms. "Oh, God, I'm yours!"

That's all it takes. With a primal roar, he comes, spilling himself deep inside me, marking me as his.

As he collapses on top of me, panting for air, I can't help but think how addicting this feels, him making me his, owning me in the most primal way possible.

My chest heaves against his, my body still trembling from my orgasm. God, how did this happen? Can life really be this good? Is Gerald really the one?

But it's hard to think about that now, not when my body still hums with pleasure and his warmth envelops me like a second skin.

Gerald props himself up on one elbow, gazing down at me with a satisfied smirk. "You know, Alina, I wasn't sure if you really had it in you."

My heart stops. Is this where the other shoe drops, and he says something cruel?

"To come so hard," he finishes, winking at me.

Relief floods me, but only slightly. I know I'm in deep, and the more time I spend with him, the harder it would be to walk away if things didn't stay as perfect as this.

But I don't have a choice.

My life, and my daughter's, depend on it.

As I drift off to sleep in his arms, I try to push any worrying thoughts out of my head and just focus on what this is. A magical connection between two people.

A connection that I've worked so hard for.

After years of heartache, abuse and running, I'm finally getting what I deserve.

I awake feeling more rested than I have since I can remember. The morning sun streams through the windows, bathing the room in a bright, cheerful glow.

Slowly, I get out of the insanely comfortable bed, my muscles aching in ways I haven't felt in a long time.

As I shower, the warm water cascading over me from the rainforest shower head like a comforting massage, I reflect on the past evening.

I find Gerald in the kitchen, pouring himself a steaming cup of coffee.

"Morning, sunshine," he greets me, and I join him, wrapping my arms around his strong frame. "I trust you slept well," he says, his dark eyes dancing with mischief.

"Like a baby, thanks," I reply, trying to keep my voice even, hoping he won't hear the lust in my voice.

He smiles, dangerous and deadly. "I'm worried though."

I quirk a brow. "Worried? About what?"

My own anxiety suddenly clenches in my stomach. Comments like that always make me feel instantly guilty, even when I haven't done anything. Like I'm about to be found out for something.

"You're too good, Alina," he explains, his smile growing wider as his gaze trails over my body as if remembering every inch of it from the previous night. "Too perfect. No one's that flawless, not in my world."

I blush. "You flatter me. And are clearly going through your delulu era. But last night was..." I begin, at a loss for words.

"Just the beginning," Gerald completes my sentence. He turns and tilts my chin up, and kisses me deeply. I know being with him won't be easy, but I'm ready to take the leap based on how the last night has gone, and now this morning.

I lean into him, resting my head on his chest.

The fresh morning air and the sound of the rolling waves relax me. I feel content, almost giddy.

"Seriously, Gerald... I've never experienced anything like last night," I say softly. "Being with you makes me feel like...like Cinderella at the ball. Like all my dreams are coming true." It's true. I haven't experienced anything like his tenderness, combined with a place like this.

Yes, I had a few luxury vacations with Luchenko, but it was different. He was rough. Worried only about his own satisfaction. Gerald seems so much more... attentive.

Based on the violent display last night, I can see he has a ruthless side, but towards me he just seems tender, caring. Rough in all the right ways, and only the right ways.

Gerald strokes my hair. "You deserve to be treated like a princess, Alina." His voice rumbles pleasantly in his chest. "No, scratch that. Like a queen. I want to give you the whole world. And Yara, too."

I smile, comforted by his words and at the sound of my daughter's name, but a small voice of doubt still lingers in my mind. Gerald seems too good to be true.

Will this magical feeling last?

Or will it shatter like a glass slipper when the clock strikes midnight?

Gerald tilts my chin up, his gray eyes boring intensely into mine. "I know you've been hurt before," he says, as if reading my thoughts. "But I promise, what we have is real. I won't let anyone hurt you again. You're here with me now, and I'm going to prove to you that I can give you and your daughter the world that you both so very much deserve."

He kisses me deeply, possessively, stealing my breath. I cling to him, pushing aside my doubts for now and losing myself in his passion. The rest of the world fades away.

Right here, right now, I feel like the luckiest girl in the world. And that I'm unequivocally doing the right thing by my family.

"You're right, though. That was pretty amazing. You told me you liked it rough, but that was... just, wow," he says. "I was hammering you really good."

This man really does seem too good to be true. Charming, wealthy, *and* with a cock many woman will only ever dream of.

Every move he makes is deliberate, controlled, confident. He wants to be in charge of the situation, that much is clear.

But he's so attentive, and part of his wish to control in the bedroom seems to be focused on making me come.

He's like the whole package. Maybe I did do something right to deserve this.

"I've never had so many orgasms at once in my life."

"Ah, my dear Alina. That's because you hadn't met the right man until now."

I laugh. "Well, you're right about that. I'm just grateful that now we have each other."

"Me too, my love. Me too. I can't wait for all the wonderful things we'll do together. I truly believe we're going to set the world on fire. You, me, Yara. A whole family unit taking things over."

Chapter 9

ALINA

The rest of the vacation seems to pass by in a whirlwind—lounging by the pool, sipping cocktails, indulging in great food, engaging in deep conversation, enjoying mindblowing sex, and repeating the cycle. It's hard to believe it's already our final evening together.

The amber glow of the setting sun reflects off the gentle waves, bathing us in its soft light. My bare feet sink into the warm sand as he takes my hands in his, his emerald eyes glinting with excitement.

"Alina, my darling. From the moment I met you, I knew you were the missing piece of me. I know this is fast, but sometimes when you meet someone you just know." Gerald grins as he lowers to one knee and presents a dazzling diamond ring. I gasp as he asks, "Will you make me the happiest man in the world and be my wife?"

My heart flutters wildly in my chest. After so many years of hardship, his proposal fills me with a sense of hope and joy I'd long forgotten. I want nothing more than to begin our new life together. Gerald and Yara and me. A family.

"Yes, yes of course I'll marry you!" I exclaim.

Gerald sweeps me into his arms, twirling me around before capturing my lips in a passionate kiss. As we embrace on the beach, the future feels bright.

In the afterglow, we walk hand-in-hand along the shoreline as Gerald describes our lavish life to come. "I'll take you to the finest restaurants in New York, and we'll redecorate my penthouse just for you. Anything your heart desires, it's yours," he purrs, squeezing my hand. "And Yara too, of course," he adds. "You're a package deal. My queen and my princess."

His promises soothe my lingering doubts. With him by my side, perhaps Yara and Mother and I can finally live in true safety and comfort.

I rest my head on his shoulder, daring to believe our troubles are behind us. As the sun dips below the horizon, we seal our future with another deep kiss.

Despite the joy of the moment, however, I can't shake a lingering unease.

Being engaged to Gerald, even uprooting and moving all the way to the United States, doesn't fix everything.

Luchenko will no doubt be furious at his loss of proximity to me, and determined to drag Yara and me back into his web. He has an army of lawyers, and his name is on her birth certificate.

I need to tread carefully here.

The warm tropical breeze suddenly feels chilling. This paradise is only an illusion, with the dark dangers of my past lurking just out of sight as usual, waiting to shatter this potential for my and Yara's happiness.

Gerald notices the shift in my mood. Pulling me close, he rubs my arms soothingly. "What's wrong, my darling? You're trembling."

I hesitate, and for a moment I consider telling him. But it's too soon to trust him with my fears.

I can hardly tell him that, even in this gorgeous location, and even after a beautiful proposal, I can't stop worrying about Luchenko finding us once he discovers this plan for a new life.

That the contrast between this bliss and the misery I escaped makes me feel like I'm living on borrowed time.

Gerald tilts my chin up, gazing into my eyes. "You're safe, Alina. I know that's of most concern to you and that there are things in your past you're not ready to tell me. But all that matters is that you and your family—our family now—are safe. I applied for your fiancée visa today, by the way—the immigration office will expedite it. We'll be in America before anyone back in your old home will be able to get to you."

My eyes widen in surprise and excitement. "You did? That's wonderful!" I throw my arms around his neck.

Gerald chuckles, holding me tight. "I'll take care of everything, my dear. So you can focus on our future, not the past."

His reassurance lifts my spirits. With Gerald's aid, perhaps we can finally outrun our demons after all.

I pull back slightly, looking up at Gerald with a furrowed brow. "How soon do you think we'll be able to bring Mother over? I can't bear the thought of leaving her behind."

Gerald brushes a strand of hair from my face, his expression softening. "I know, I know. It won't be long, just be patient. Immigration is a process, and we have to take it one step at a time. But bringing her to the US is my top priority, and I'll pull all the strings I have available to me to get her here as soon as we can."

His voice is gentle yet firm. I search his eyes, and am comforted by the certainty I find there. I've spent so long adrift, forced to rely only on myself—and now here is someone offering to share the burden. Someone with untold resources and the ability to actually stand by his word.

"You're right, you have everything under control," I concede with a small sigh. "I'm just so used to handling everything alone. It'll take time to adjust to having help."

Gerald smiles, pulling me against his chest once more. "You've been so strong for so long, Miss Independent. Let me be your rock now."

I nod, the tension easing from my body as I lean into his muscular frame. I listen to the steady beat of his heart, letting it drown out my worries. With him by my side, the future seems bright with hope.

I close my eyes as the sounds of the island wash over us. The hypnotic rhythm of the waves is a stark contrast to the chaotic symphony that dominated my days until now—sirens, shouted threats, pounding footsteps giving chase through darkened alleys.

Here, there is only calm and the enveloping hug of the gentle ocean breeze.

I bask in the sensation, allowing myself to get lost in this moment of peace.

Is this really how things are going to be for us from now on? No more looking over my shoulder, no more nights spent huddled and listening for the strike of heavy boots against the floor. Is that life really behind us now?

Still, as Gerald's words of reassurance echo in my mind, I can't ignore the flicker of doubt that clings like a shadow. The promises of a future together, a new life—it seems almost too good to be true after so many years of fear and struggle.

Can I dare to hope that our troubles are truly behind us? That this time, escape would lead to freedom rather than yet another period of borrowed peace?

I cling to Gerald tighter, praying that his certainty and comfort will be enough to dispel my lingering reservations. I want so badly to believe his pretty, lovely promises, to embrace this new chance with an open heart capable of feeling true joy.

No matter Luchenko's reach, or the dangers that might lurk in wait along our path, I refuse to let them steal this happiness.

Not when I've finally glimpsed the light after so many years spent wandering in the dark.

Chapter 10

ALINA

The scent of cinnamon and yeast envelops me as I enter the kitchen. Mama stands at the table, her forearms dusted with flour as she kneads dough with practiced hands.

I slide onto the bench across from her, my heart hammering. Now's the moment to break the news. Bittersweet, given the ramifications.

"Mama, I have news."

She glances up, her tiny but strong hands still working the dough. "What is it, child?"

I take a deep breath. Just say it quick, like ripping off a bandage. "I'm moving to America with Gerald."

Mama's hands still. Concern clouds her eyes. "Alina, are you certain? You've only known this man a short time. Just because he sweeps you off your feet by taking you to some fancy tropical island doesn't mean he's who he says he is."

"I know, but—"

She holds up a floury hand. "Listen to me. Men make big promises they rarely keep. If something seems too good to be true, it is."

Doubt creeps in. She has a point—I only met Gerald a few short months ago, and we've only spent a few days together in person.

But no, I've thought about this a lot and decided I can't let fear rule me.

"He's not like that, Mama. I trust him." I lean forward, willing her to understand. "If you'd met him in person, you'd feel the same way."

She searches my face. "I hope you're right, child. But please, promise me you'll be cautious."

"I promise." I reach across the table and squeeze her floury hand.

No matter what the future holds, nothing can break our bond.

Mama looks thoughtful as she resumes kneading, working the dough with practiced motions.

"You know I only want what's best for you, right Alina?" Her voice is gentle. "My concerns come from experience, that's all."

I nod, knowing she speaks the truth. Mama's keen eye and wisdom has guided me well over the years.

Yet something in me resists her doubts now.

"Gerald has proven trustworthy so far," I say firmly. "I've watched for red flags, and haven't seen any."

Mama raises an eyebrow. "It's easy to put on an act at first. To show you who they want you to see. For some, they can keep up the pretense for months, even years." Her expression turns solemn. "But eventually, the cracks appear and the real person emerges." She pauses. "And if you haven't seen any red flags at all, then it sounds like you have blinders on. Because every man has some kind of a flag."

I lean forward, unwilling to back down. "What if this is who he truly is, though? A good man who cares for me, and who would do anything for me and Yara? And seriously... the only thing I've found not to like about him so far is that he doesn't like pickles."

Mama's face softens a bit at my stubborn hope, and she smirks at the pickle reference. She reaches across the table and pats my hand.

"Then I'm wrong, and you have my full blessing, Alina." A hint of a smile touches her lips. "I'll look forward to visiting you both in America someday soon."

Her words lift my spirits. I knew convincing Mama wouldn't be easy, but her tentative acceptance means everything.

"I promise we'll bring you over to live with us as soon as we can. Gerald's already talking about starting your immigration paperwork the moment we're married."

"Let's hope for the best," she says, nodding. "But don't let worrying about me cloud your judgement. And just promise me you'll be careful."

I meet her gaze directly. "I promise, Mama."

No matter what the future holds, I'll enter it with open eyes. Mama gave me the gift of wisdom, and now I have to find the courage to follow my heart.

Mama squeezes my hand gently before returning to kneading the dough. I watch her strong, nimble fingers work the pale mound. Baking has been her passion since girlhood. Even in our darkest days after Papa died, Mama always managed to conjure up sweet breads to fill our bellies and spirits.

Looking at her now, I feel a pang of guilt. I want her blessings for this new chapter of my life, but I would forge ahead regardless if she put up a fuss.

I have to, for Yara.

Still, having her support makes things much easier.

"You've given me so much, Mama," I say softly. "I don't want to seem ungrateful, or like I'm running away and abandoning you."

She pauses, dusting flour off her hands before facing me again. "Oh Alina, you have nothing to feel guilty for. A mother's greatest joy is seeing her child spread her wings and fly. I always knew you'd do amazing things."

I blink back sudden tears. "I'll send for you, as soon as I'm settled. Yara will need her grandmother's guidance."

Mama chuckles. "And her cooking! American food is so bland, or so I've heard."

We both laugh, the sound lifting the mood.

No matter what comes next, our bond will remain as strong as ever.

I smile through my tears as Mama comes out from behind the counter and wraps her arms around me the way she has since I was a little girl. Her arms are frailer now, but the meaning behind this simple act is as powerful as ever.

Inhaling the scent of yeast and cinnamon that always clings to her, I'm instantly transported back to childhood. To long days spent watching her bake in her cramped kitchen, learning at her side.

She's taught me so much over the years—how to roll out dough, shape intricate braided loaves, and test when cakes were done with a toothpick.

But more than recipes or techniques, she's imparted wisdom. Patience while waiting for dough to rise. Care in choosing ingredients even when you have hardly any food in your pantry. The value of putting love into everything you create.

I cling to her tightly, knowing I'll carry those lessons with me wherever I go. They're woven into the fabric of who I am.

She pulls back, cradling my face in her flour-dusted hands. "You'll write?"

I nod, not trusting my voice. "Of course, and we can do video calls as well. I'll help you get it all set up before we leave."

"And I know you'll take wonderful care of my granddaughter. Gosh, I'm going to miss her."

"Of course, Mama." I managed a watery smile, instantly feeling guilty for taking Yara away. "And I know she'll miss you too. I'll make sure you can video chat all the time."

She kisses my forehead. "Good. Then I have nothing to worry about. I'm so proud of you, Alina, for never settling or accepting what life gave you."

I hope she's right. That the roots she's given me will be enough to flourish in new soil.

Drawing a shaky breath, I stand, my heart brimming with equal parts excitement and fear.

But bravery isn't the absence of fear, it's moving forward despite it.

And for Yara, I will find that courage.

Chapter 11

ALINA

"**Y**ara," I say, gesturing for her to come over. "I need to talk to you."

I'm equal parts excited and apprehensive about having this conversation with her. Revealing that we're about to make a life-changing move is no small deal.

The opportunities available to her in America, compared to here, make my heart swell with anticipation and pride.

But at the same time, I know I'll be ripping her away from the life she knows—her friends, the school she's settled into, and her beloved grandmother. This brings immense guilt.

Nonetheless, I'm convinced that we'll be a million times better off than if we stayed. The comforting blanket of familiarity isn't enough to outweigh the risks and dangers that come with staying.

Yara looks up from where she's sorting through her clothing. Her big blue eyes are filled with curiosity and a hint of apprehension.

"Okay, Mama," she says, coming over to sit next to me on the couch.

"Listen, sweetie," I begin, taking her hand in mine. "Now, you know I've met Gerald and gone on vacation with him."

"Yes," she nods. "Mr. Gerald seems like a nice man."

"Well, we're going to be leaving to go and live in America with him. He's promised to take care of us."

"Really?" Yara's face lights up with excitement, but then a shadow flickers across her features. "What's he like, Mama? Is he mean like Mr. Luchenko?"

Her question pierces my heart. The innocence of her query belies the depth of her understanding, shaped by shadows of our tormented past.

She's always been so perceptive. Even as a very young child, Yara possessed an uncanny ability to see through façades—a trait that both comforts and worries me as we face this new chapter.

"Really," I confirm, relieved by her initially positive response, but then I hesitate. "I need you to understand something, Yara. This man is different from Mr. Luchenko, but we still have to be careful."

Choosing my words with care, I attempt to educate Yara on the importance of vigilance. "He seems very nice, but humans can be tricky. You'll discover this as you grow older."

My advice is layered, an attempt to prepare Yara without instilling undue fear. "If he ever does anything to make you feel uncomfortable—no matter how big or small—you must let me know straight away," I instruct, laying the foundation for a trust that must never be broken.

Yara looks thoughtful. "Even if it's just a small secret?"

I nod. "Especially if it's a small secret. Because one thing is certain in this life: little secrets are bad news. They lead to big secrets."

"Okay," Yara nods, looking serious now. "What should I do if he's not nice?"

"Tell me right away," I instruct. "No matter how small it seems. We have to trust each other, okay?"

"Okay," Yara repeats, nodding again.

"I'd rather that you tell me something that you think might be happening, rather than worrying that you got it wrong, okay?"

I squeeze her shoulder and smile. I can feel Yara's trust and love like a warm blanket around my heart.

She nods and squeezes me back.

"Good girl," I say, standing up. "Now let's get packing. We have a long journey ahead of us."

As Yara nods, I can't help but feel a sense of hopefulness mingled with fear.

This new life will be full of unknowns and challenges, but at least we'll face them together.

And without Luchenko and his men lurking around every corner.

I zip up the last suitcase and heave it onto the pile, and take a deep breath to steady my nerves.

This is it. The moment we've been waiting for.

My thoughts drift to Gerald.

Our relationship has developed quickly, though we have been talking for months.

He seems perfect—kind, successful, and attentive.

When I met him on vacation, he appeared to be everything he claimed to be over video and chat.

Still, I can't shake off the feeling that something might go wrong. I've been hurt before, and I don't want to expose Yara to any further danger.

All men start out nice enough, until they're not any more.

The purpose of our leaving is to escape Luchenko's clutches and provide the best life possible for Yara, not to place her in harm's way of a different kind.

"Mom?" Yara's voice interrupts my thoughts.

I blink and refocus on my daughter. "Sorry, what is it?"

"I know it's kind of babyish, but can we bring my stuffed bear with us?"

Yara holds up her raggedy teddy bear, the one she's had since she was a baby, its fur matted and worn.

"Of course," I smile, understanding the need to cling to a shred of comfort and familiarity. "He can come with us."

"Yay!" Yara beams, hugging the bear tightly.

It's moments like this that make me feel grateful for what we have.

Despite our past traumas and hardships, we still have each other. And that's all that matters.

The fact we're going to escape to a much better life is just icing on the cake.

"Okay, let's finish packing," I say, picking up a shirt from the floor. "We don't want to miss our flight."

Yara nods, and together we continue packing our things. The suitcases are almost full, and I take one last look around the apartment. It's almost empty now, devoid of any memories of the special times we shared here.

"Well, this is it. Are you ready to say goodbye to this life and enter our new phase?" I ask Yara, the question just as much for me as for her.

"Yes," Yara replies, holding her bear close.

"Then let's go."

I pick up the suitcases, tipping them onto their wheels, and lead the way out of the apartment.

It feels funny, leaving with just the clothing on our backs and a couple of pieces of luggage. But it's all we have and, until now, it's really been all that we've needed.

Plus, Gerald has promised that he'll get us anything else we need when we get there.

As we walk down the stairs, carefully navigating the wheels of the rickety suitcases so they don't snap off, I feel a pang of sadness. We're leaving behind the only home we've known for years.

It was an accomplishment getting off the streets and into this place. I hold back tears as I remember the pride I allowed myself to feel as the keys were handed over to me, and I knew Yara would never need to set foot in a dumpster again to forage for scraps. This place has poignant memories.

But I also feel a sense of almost overwhelming excitement. We're starting a new chapter, one filled with hope and possibilities.

"Are you scared, Mama?" Yara asks, looking up at me, sensing my emotions.

"A little," I admit. "Change can be scary. But we'll be okay. We have each other."

"Forever?" Yara asks, her eyes wide.

"Forever," I promise, giving her a reassuring smile.

We step out into the early morning, and I take a deep breath. The air is crisp and fresh, and the sky is tinged with pink and orange. It's a new day, a new beginning.

"Let's go," she says, and together we head toward our future.

I glance down at Yara as we walk, taking in the trusting innocence in her eyes. I know moving to another country won't be easy, but I'm determined to shield her from further pain.

As we near the bus stop, I squeeze her hand. "Remember what we talked about earlier? About secrets?"

Yara nods, her expression serious.

"I meant every word," I continue. "No matter what happens, no matter where we go, you can always tell me anything. Even if it's scary or you think it will make me angry or sad. I will always listen."

Yara throws her arms around my neck. "Okay, okay, I get the point, Mama. I promise I'll tell you all my secrets," she says earnestly.

I smile and hug her back tightly. "And I promise to keep you safe, always."

We stay embraced for a long moment, drawing strength from each other.

Then the bus pulls up, and we climb aboard, ready to face the future side by side.

As we settle into our seats, I gaze out the window at the streets passing by. I feel like I know every crack in the pavement, every corner store with their rickety awnings and handwritten signs. This neighborhood had been our whole world for so long.

I glance over at Yara, who is curled up under my arm, already drifting off to sleep. I gently stroke her hair, feeling a swell of emotion.

That tiny apartment had been our refuge, our sanctuary from the storms of life.

That neighborhood, where I watched Yara grow from a baby into a bright-eyed twelve-year-old.

Now we're leaving it all behind, venturing into the unknown.

The promise of a better life tugs me forward, but uncertainty haunts our steps.

I tighten my arm around Yara.

No matter what comes, I vow to myself, I will protect this child with everything I have.

She will never suffer again.

The bus accelerates as we leave the city limits, mile by mile putting distance between them and the past.

I take one last look at the receding skyline, bidding it a silent farewell as my heart lurches in my chest.

Emotion threatens to overtake me, and I blink back tears.

Then I turn to watch the road ahead, towards the new horizon before us.

Wherever we end up, whatever happens, we will face it together.

Me and Yara against the world.

I hold on to this thought like a lifeline. As long as we have each other, we can survive anything.

The sun begins to rise, casting a warm glow over the bus.

I watch as the light spills over Yara's face, illuminating her features. A sense of hope fills my heart.

We're leaving behind the darkness of our past and stepping into a new day, a new life.

"Mama?" Yara stirs, rubbing her eyes. "Are we almost there?"

I smile down at my daughter. "Not yet, my love. But soon."

Yara nods, settling back into her seat.

I turn my attention to the passing scenery as we near the airport. I find myself dreaming of our new future—the potential of having hobbies and interests that until now have seemed frivolous and reckless, maybe even some new friends.

The bus pulls into the station, jolting me out of my thoughts.

I gather our bags and stand up, motioning for Yara to follow.

We step off the bus, taking in the bustling airport. It feels chaotic, exciting, the cacophony of other departing travelers serenading us into the next chapter.

"Come on, let's go find our new home," I say, taking Yara's hand.

Together, we head toward the check-in desk, ready to start our new life.

Chapter 12

ALINA

The terminal bursts into view as we step off the jetway, a kaleidoscope of light and sound.

Yara's hand clenches mine, her eyes round with wonder.

"Mama, is this really America?" she whispers.

I sweep my gaze over the crowds, the glowing signs, the sheer vibrancy of it all. There are American flags everywhere, the patriotic red, white and blue emblazoned on signs and decor.

I half expect to see a group of frat bros playing beer pong with red solo cups off in the distance. Or maybe an eagle or two flying past while Bruce Springsteen belts from the speakers.

"It's even brighter than I imagined, little bird."

We weave through the river of travelers, Yara sticking close to my side.

She cranes her neck, trying to take it all in. "It's just like the movies!"

My pulse quickens, my skin tingling. A new chapter for us. A chance at a life free of fear.

I squeeze Yara's hand, meeting her shining eyes with a smile. "We're really here."

She beams, skipping beside me. "Everything is so big and colorful. When can we ride in one of those yellow taxi cabs?"

A laugh bubbles up as I imagine us cruising the streets of New York. "Soon, little bird."

For a moment, I have the urge to run. To skip the part where we meet Gerald. To take Yara and just escape into this giant country and find a life just for us, maybe in a big city or just a simple, tiny town. It doesn't really matter.

But I know that's not how it works.

And Gerald is a nice man who wants to take care of us. We need him.

I try to shake off this reckless urge. It's just nerves, fear of the unknown.

Fear of past choices dictating my future.

I don't know what awaits us in this new chapter, but seeing the hope in Yara's eyes, I feel the knot in my chest loosen. We're far from the darkness now. This glittering world is ours to explore.

And I'll do anything to make it her wonderland.

Gerald is waiting for us at the arrival gate, leaning casually against a pillar. He's impeccably dressed as always, not a hair out of place.

When he sees us, his face splits into a dazzling smile.

"There are my two favorite ladies," he croons, sweeping me into a tight embrace. His cologne envelops me, subtle and expensive.

Releasing me, he reaches out a hand to shake Yara's, and she nervously reciprocates.

"Don't be shy, little one. I don't bite." He winks, and Yara allows herself a small smile, glancing up at him with shy curiosity.

"Shall we?" Gerald gestures grandly towards the exit.

As we step outside, a sleek black car awaits us.

The driver opens the door with a small bow.

I gape at the luxurious interior as I climb in, Yara right on my heels.

She runs her hand excitedly over the plush leather. "Mama, this is like the cars on those TV shows you like to watch."

I laugh, suddenly self-conscious about my penchant for American reality TV.

"Only the best for you," Gerald says indulgently, sliding in beside me.

He snakes an arm around my shoulders, his thumb brushing my collarbone. A shiver races down my spine as I think back to the last time he touched me this way.

We drive away from the crowded city into gentle hills dotted with mansions. Yara presses her face to the window, oohing and ahhing.

Finally, we pass through an ornate gate and pull up to the grandest house yet.

My jaw drops.

Gerald chuckles. "Welcome home."

The inside is even more breathtaking. Vaulted ceilings, chandeliers, paintings in gilded frames.

Yara darts from room to room, her laughter echoing.

"I can't believe this," I murmur.

Gerald's eyes crinkle. "You deserve it, darling. I told you I'll give you the world. So you'd best start believing."

His hand on my back is warm, his words intoxicating. For the first time, I let myself believe that we've found our haven.

Yara's room is the pièce de résistance.

She gasps, dashing inside. The walls are her favorite pink and teal, the shelves overflowing with toys and books. A four-poster bed is draped in lace and tulle, and next to it is a vanity festooned with all manner of makeup and hair decorations.

"For me?" Yara breathes.

Gerald places a hand on her shoulder. "All for you, princess."

Yara throws her arms around his neck.

He laughs, patting her back. "Why don't you explore while I show your mother her room?"

Taking my hand, he leads me down the hall.

Our room is just as lavish, with plush carpet and gauzy curtains around the king-sized bed.

Gerald comes up behind me, hands circling my waist. "Only the best for my queen," he murmurs in my ear.

I shiver as his lips graze my neck. When I turn in his arms, his eyes blaze with hunger.

"Tonight, after Yara's asleep..." His fingers trail down my spine.

I flush but don't pull away.

For all he's given us, don't I owe him this?

Besides, our vacations proved the bedroom is just another place we're extremely compatible.

Gerald tips my chin up, kissing me deeply.

I cling to him, dizzy.

Maybe this is exactly where we're meant to be.

After tucking a sleepy Yara into her massive new bed, I find myself drawn back to the window overlooking the moonlit grounds.

The day's events whirl through my mind—the opulent mansion, Yara's unbridled joy, Gerald's heated kisses.

My heart swells with hope, but trepidation lingers.

Can this be real? Have we truly escaped our past struggles?

I want to trust Gerald, to believe his promises.

But experience has taught me that nothing gold can stay that way. Because nothing is pure and everything is just painted with a fake coating.

Eventually, it starts to peel, leaving nothing but decay, disappointment and shattered dreams.

I wrap my arms around myself, shivering even though the night is warm.

In the distance, a dog barks, jolting me from my reverie.

No, I can't let old fears poison this new beginning. Yara deserves this chance at happiness.

I turn from the window, resolve steeling my spine.

The past is done.

Our future begins now.

Morning dawns bright and clear.

Yara bursts into my room, still in her new pink pajamas. "Mama, come see!" she cries, tugging my hand eagerly.

I let her pull me along, her enthusiasm infectious.

She draws me to the French doors and flings them open. Beyond lies a garden, flowers nodding in the breeze.

"Isn't it pretty?" Yara dances outside, her face upturned to the sun.

Watching her spin joyfully amidst the blossoms, I feel lightness in my chest.

No more dim, cramped rooms and rationed meals. Yara can be a child again.

I kneel and she runs into my arms. "We made it, little bird," I whisper, hugging her close. "We're safe now."

Yara looks up at me, eyes shining. "I love it here, Mama."

"Me too," I say, meaning it with my whole heart.

This is our haven, our fresh start. And I'll do anything to make it last.

Over breakfast in the grand dining room, I marvel at the spread—fruits, pastries, eggs and sausages. More food than Yara and I have seen in weeks, each item more flavorful than the last.

Gerald sits at the head of the long table. He wears a fitted white polo shirt that sets off his tan and highlights his muscular physique.

He flicks through the business pages of a newspaper, preferring the old-school feel of an actual paper rather than scrolling through news on his smartphone.

"Eat up," he urges with an easy smile. His presence is both reassuring and unsettling. But I can't fully trust this lavish lifestyle he's granted us. Despite his hospitality, it just seems too good to be true.

Yara digs in happily while I pick at my plate. I know I'm hungry, but I can't force myself to eat.

Gerald notices my hesitation. "It's a lot, I know," he says gently. "But I promise, you'll get used to it."

I meet his gaze. Under the charm, I sense something darker in his eyes.

But I swallow my misgivings and force a smile. "We appreciate everything you've done for us."

Gerald leans forward, voice low and earnest. "This is your home now. I'll take care of you, like family."

His words kindle a fragile hope inside me. I want to believe them with every fiber of my being.

That Yara and I have finally found a safe harbor after years adrift.

"Thank you," I say softly.

I reach over to clasp Yara's hand, allowing myself to feel hope just for a moment.

After breakfast, Yara excuses herself to go and peruse more of the grounds while I retreat to my room. At the window overlooking the sprawling estate, I take a deep breath. For the first time in so long, I feel like I can breathe freely, without fear nipping at my heels.

This is our chance, I tell myself. Our new beginning.

I squeeze my eyes shut and make a silent vow—I will fight to the death to protect the life we're building here.

Eyes open, I gaze out at the lush grounds and smile as I see Yara skipping by and then talking to something that looks a bit like a duck.

"Here's to our new life, little bird," I whisper.

I must be strong, for Yara's sake. Her happiness means everything to me.

I straighten my spine and lift my chin. The past is behind us. Ahead lies the promise of joy.

And I will do whatever it takes to fulfill that promise for my daughter.

For her, for us, I will make this work.

Chapter 13

ALINA

Gerald approaches me as I stare out the window, taking in the expansive grounds and mentally comparing it to the tiny apartment Yara and I just left behind.

"You don't seem like yourself," says Gerald, his brow furrowed. "The you that I've got to know up until now, I mean."

I frown. He's right. I'm not myself.

"I'm sorry, I don't mean to appear ungrateful." I pause, trying to find the right words. "We just got here, and you've already done so much for us. It's just a lot of change at once, I guess. As a mother, you always feel this overwhelming sense of responsibility for your child. You question every decision you make, wondering whether it's in their best interest, or if you're being selfish."

"Alina," he places his hand on my shoulder and gives it a gentle squeeze, "I may not have known you for that long, but what I do know is you don't have a selfish bone in your entire body."

"Well, I appreciate you saying that," I sigh. "But am I really worth risking everything for? What if you change your mind and then we're out on the streets? Or worse, we get deported back to the life we left behind?"

"You have nothing to worry about. Without you my life is nothing, Alina."

"And what of Yara?"

"That's a silly question, my love. You've always been a package deal. Like I've said since the day we met, I'll take care of your daughter as if she were my own, and I'll protect her as fiercely—or maybe even more so—as I'll look after you."

He gestures around the palatial room where Yara continues to squeal with excitement every time she makes a new discovery. "See? Doesn't this go a long way to proving my intentions are real?"

"It does..." It's hard to argue with a man who has just spoiled your daughter rotten after she's gone without for so long.

I flash back to her joy at rummaging through the dumpster and finding a tiny stale piece of bread, and my stomach flip-flops at the contrast with her current situation.

"Let me show you more," he says.

"But—"

Gerald puts up a hand to silence me. "Alina, little lamb... please, just let me show you."

He takes me by my hand and leads me to our bedroom where his lips brush against mine, feather-light and teasing.

His hands slide around my waist, his body pressing mine firmly against the wall.

He growls low in my ear, "I've been dying to taste you again."

His tongue darts out, tracing a hot line from my earlobe down my neck, sending chills down my spine.

God, why does he have this effect on me?

My hands tremble as I reach up to grip his shirt, as if I need something to hold onto to keep from melting into his arms.

His lips find mine once more, this time with more hunger. His tongue invades my mouth, tasting every crevice, possessing me in a way no man ever has.

I can't help but surrender to him, my legs weakening with each sensation he ignites within me.

His hand moves up my thigh, the fabric of my dress offering scant resistance against the warmth spreading through me.

I moan into his mouth, my body aching for more.

Gerald's hand continues its ascent, pushing the fabric of my dress up until he reaches the lace of my panties.

He growls, "I knew you'd be wet for me."

His fingers slip beneath the lace, finding me slick and ready for him.

I arch my hips into his touch, moaning as he expertly finds and rubs my swollen clit.

"Gerald... I can't," I pant, not quite sure if I'm protesting or begging him for more.

He only chuckles, his fingers delving deeper, curling into my wetness, and oh, God, it feels so good.

"You can," he rasps in my ear, his hot breath sending shivers down my spine. "Tell me how bad you want me, Alina."

"I... I..." I stammer, my cheeks flushing red with the knowledge that I'm a goner with just a few well-placed touches. "Fine, I want you, okay? Just... please don't stop."

Gerald chuckles in response, his fingers picking up the pace, rubbing me in time with the music.

My nipples peek through my bra, aching for his touch, my core throbbing for him.

"That's better, baby," he growls. "I knew you'd come around."

The continued friction of his fingers against my clit pushes me over the edge.

My world shatters around me, my core contracting in the most mind-blowing orgasm of my life.

I cling to Gerald, my nails digging into his broad shoulders as waves of pleasure wash over me.

As I come down from my high, I rest my head on his shoulder, my heart pounding wildly in my chest.

"Thank you, Gerald. That was—"

Before I can finish my sentence, his lips are on mine again, silencing me.

His tongue invades my mouth, flavored with lust and desire, and I moan, collapsing into his embrace.

Gerald's hands roam my body, leaving a trail of fire in their wake, until he reaches between my legs once more.

This time, he rips away my drenched panties.

My head spins with need as he buries two fingers inside me, working them with expert precision.

"Gerald," I whimper, arching my hips into his touch. Screw everything—my doubts, my hesitations—this feels too good.

His lips trail down my neck, my nipples hardening in their wake.

He reaches my core, lapping at me like a starving man.

My knees buckle, but Gerald holds me up with ease.

His tongue flicks my clit, making my toes curl.

"God, Gerald, don't stop," I cry out, my eyes squeezing shut.

He chuckles darkly, only spurring me on more.

I grab handfuls of his silk sheets as he continues to feast on me, and I spasm around his fingers and tongue.

He knows my body too well, better than any man other than him has a right to.

"Come for me, Alina," he growls, his voice dripping with dominance.

And come I do, my orgasm exploding through my body like fireworks on the Fourth of July.

My nails dig into the sheets, my entire body shaking as a surge of pleasure sweeps over me.

"Gerald," I pant, collapsing onto the bed.

"I'm not done with you yet, my dear," he purrs, flipping me over onto all fours.

I hear a cap being popped open, and then feel the cool sensation as Gerald applies lube to my back entrance.

Before I can protest, he begins to work his thick cock into my ass.

I cry out as he slides all the way into me, stretching me in a way I've never been before.

"Gerald!" I scream, caught off-guard by the unexpected intrusion.

"Relax, baby," he soothes, thrusting in and out, his grip on my hips tightening. "You've always been made for this."

Despite my shock, I find myself giving in to the sensations. The fullness, combined with his fingers still teasing my clit, is overwhelming. My second orgasm is building now, larger than the first, a tsunami of pleasure ready to wipe me away.

"Gerald, I can't take any more!"

"You can, and you will," he growls, slamming into me harder, sending me over the edge.

Our mingled cries of ecstasy fill the room as we come together, my world shattering into a million pieces.

As our breathing slows, I turn over in Gerald's arms, our hearts beating in tandem.

That was like nothing I've ever experienced.

Every one of my nerve endings feels individually raw, and my head hums in the afterglow.

Finally, it seems like I've done something right.

But then why is there a niggling feeling in the back of my head?

Chapter 14

ALINA

A *couple of weeks later*

I walk into Yara's room, expecting to see her curled up with a book or staring at her brand new smartphone that now seems permanently attached to her hand.

It hasn't taken long for her to acclimate to more of an American life, and the comforts afforded by a life with Gerald.

Instead, she's sitting by the window, staring out at the darkening sky.

The light from the sunset casts an orange glow on her face, highlighting the sadness in her eyes.

"Hey," I say softly, sitting down next to her.

"Hey," she responds, her voice barely above a whisper.

I wait for her to speak, sensing that something is bothering her.

"How was school today?" I ask.

I can't imagine it would be easy, settling into not just a new country and home, but also to a new school and classmates and all that comes with that.

Especially at the age of twelve, when hormones are running rampant and classmates hone their words like weapons.

"School's fine," she finally mutters, but her lack of enthusiasm speaks volumes. Yara loves to learn, and this is not like her.

"Is something wrong?" I ask, placing a hand on her shoulder.

Yara hesitates before speaking. "Everything's so different here, Mama. The way they talk, the games they play...I don't fit in."

I feel a pang of guilt, wondering if it was a mistake to uproot our lives and move to the US. But I push those thoughts aside, focusing on Yara's words.

"Have you talked to anyone at school? Made any friends?" I ask gently.

Yara shakes her head. "It's hard. They all seem so...different. I'm the odd one out, and they think it's funny."

I take a deep breath, trying to think of a way to help her adjust. "Maybe we can find some cultural events or groups to join, meet other people who understand what it's like to be new here."

I've done a bit of research online, but I must admit, that kind of investigation gave way to more exciting pursuits like exploring the new house and making vacation plans with Gerald.

Yara nods slowly, but I can tell she's still hesitant. "Can I tell you something?" she asks, her voice small.

"Of course," I say, sensing her need to confide in me.

"Today, some girls were making fun of my accent. Saying I think I'm better than everyone because we live in Gerald's fancy mansion," Yara whispers, her eyes brimming with tears. "They said I'm a silly bitch and that I think I'm pretty but I'm not."

My heart breaks for her, anger boiling inside me at the thought of anyone saying such cruel things to hurt my child.

"Those girls are just being mean," I say firmly. "You're not better than anyone, but you're also not less than anyone. You're unique and special, and they don't have the right to make you feel otherwise." I pause, and take her hand in mine and meeting her eyes. "And they're right, you *are* pretty. They're probably very jealous of this stunning young girl who has just joined their school. They're probably worried you're going to steal all their boyfriends."

I wink at her.

Yara nods, a small smile crossing her face. "One of their boyfriends did say hello to me at lunch, and the meanest girl of all, Denise, seemed to get really mad."

"See? There you go. You just keep being your wonderful self and eventually they'll get tired and move on to the next target."

"Thanks, Mama," she says, leaning into me for a hug.

As I hold her close, I can't help but think of the stories I've heard about high school life in America.

A sliver of doubt creeps in.

Did we escape one life of isolation and uncertainty, only to land in a new place where we feel like outsiders?

Despite trying for so long to escape it, part of me suddenly yearns for the simplicity of our old life back home.

But I push it aside, focusing on my daughter and our new life together.

There's no going back now.

This is just a speed bump, something to be expected when you change countries and enroll your child in a new school.

We'll make it work, no matter what challenges come our way.

I hold Yara a little longer, wishing I could protect her from the cruelty of the world. But I know I can't shield her from everything.

"It'll get better, Yara," I say, as much to reassure myself as her. "We just need to give it more time."

Yara nods, but I can see the apprehension lingering in her eyes. The same apprehension I'm trying hard to fight back.

This mansion, a symbol of our new life, suddenly feels like another gilded cage. Isolating us from the normalcy we so desperately want.

But, I remind myself, this cage comes with Gerald's kindness and attentiveness, not Luchenko's cruelty.

I need to get over my past so I can embrace my future, or I risk losing everything.

I pull Yara in for one more hug, holding her tight.

No matter what doubts creep in, I won't let them take root.

I made the choice to bring us here.

Now I must find a way to make it feel like home.

The next few days go by without incident.

Yara seems to be more settled, and even brings home a couple of assignments where she received an A grade. I'm so proud of her adaptability and tenacity.

As I sit in the sunny nook of the kitchen, I glance at a romance novel without really letting the words sink in, my mind drifting to other things. Suddenly, Yara's voice startles me from my thoughts.

"Mama, can I talk to you about something?"

She perches on the edge of the seat cushion, fiddling with the hem of her skirt.

I imagine she's been given a hard time again at school.

I swear, if these petty girls don't lay off I'm going to march down there and give them a piece of my mind.

"Of course, sweetheart. What is it?" I keep my voice as calm as possible, trying not to add to whatever's bothering her.

Yara takes a shaky breath before speaking. "I heard some girls at school talking about Gerald. They were saying bad things."

I stiffen slightly but try to keep my voice steady. "Oh? What kind of things?"

"That he's...he's not a good man. That he's hurt people before." Yara's eyes are downcast. "And that you're not the first, you know, wife he's brought over from another country. That it's all just a show and you're..."

She trails off, but I can fill in the rest.

My fists clench at the thought of such poison being spread about my fiancé, and how that makes my daughter feel. And me, if I'm honest.

"Yara, look at me." I tip her chin up gently. "It's just idle gossip. You know how people love to talk about those more fortunate than themselves. They see this mansion and the lovely clothes Gerald got you for school, and they just can't help themselves."

I smooth back her hair, offering a reassuring smile.

But inside, I feel that familiar flicker of doubt. What do I really know about the man I've entrusted our future to?

No. I can't go down that road.

Not when Yara needs me to be strong.

I'm not going to let some pre-teens and their immature fairy tales ruin this for us.

"This is just part of adjusting to our new home. Try not to let it get to you."

Yara nods uncertainly. I pull her in for a fierce hug, as much to comfort myself as her.

We sit in silence for a while, doubts swirling.

But I can't let them take hold.

I made my choice. Now I must find a way to quiet the storm brewing inside us both.

Chapter 15

ALINA

"I don't know what to do." My tone is hushed, but the room is large and I feel like my every word is echoing, magnified for everyone in the neighborhood to hear.

"Is everything okay?" Dominika asks, her voice rife with concern even through the phone.

"Yes.. yes," I say quickly. "I don't mean to worry you... I just..."

"Spit it out. You *are* worrying me," she says.

"Okay well, this is going to sound silly, but... everything is going really well for the most part. He's lavished more gifts on Yara than any girl could ever use, the mansion is gorgeous, he seems nice...."

"Have you slept with him yet?" She interrupts me, clearly wanting to cut straight to the chase.

I laugh. "Yes, Dominika. And that was great, too. Best of my life, even."

"So what's the problem?" Confusion is palpable in her tone. "You're calling me to complain because you've found a wealthy American who can rescue you from all your problems over here, who lavishes you with attention, has an amazing cock, a gorgeous mansion, who accepts and spoils your daughter with gifts... I'm really concerned that you're going to overdose on *good things*, Alina! Should I call the police?"

I smirk as I take in her words. She's right. How am I being such a stress cadet over all of these positives?

"Haha okay, I know I sound silly." I pause and bite my lower lip. "I'm guess I'm just... not used to this."

"Well, that's understandable," she replies. "Luchenko may have money, but thoughtfulness is not his strong suit."

Again, Dominika is the queen of understatements.

She continues. "He uses his finances as a weapon rather than something that can make people's lives better. That's what you grew to expect. And then after all the housing and food uncertainty... give yourself a break, Alina. For God's sake, you're hard on yourself. Let yourself feel comfortable with the idea that things can be good."

I sigh. "You're right. I'm always waiting for the other shoe to drop. The entire way over here I worried that I was forgetting something, as if I couldn't drive down to the store to get a toothbrush or something. And then I had a minor panic attack coming through immigration. And then meeting Gerald... the blood was rushing so hard in my ears I thought I was going to pass out."

"But you're safe now, Alina. Yara's safe. You're further from my diabolical brother-in-law than you've ever been. This is your chance to make a life for yourself, and for your daughter. A life that you've worked so hard for and that you've always dreamed of."

I frown. "But I feel so selfish, Nika. Maybe I should have kept us back there and just tried to do more of what I was doing. Picked up another job so we could stay somewhere nicer in a few months when I saved up enough money."

I feel myself spiraling as I consider all the what-if's.

"Alina? Listen to me," Dominika's voice is firm, as if she can see my mental state unraveling through the phone.

She knows me too well.

"I know this acceptance of people showing you kindness and generosity doesn't come easily to you. But I want you to remember, you're a great mother. And an equally wonderful friend and general human being. This is your time."

She pauses, as if trying to find the right words.

"Now, it's your turn to relax and enjoy the ride. Things can only go up from here."

I thank her and we hang up, agreeing to talk again soon. Pondering her words, I wonder if she's right.

Or if she just wants me to be happy so badly that she has blinders on, too.

That's the problem with being let down over and over again. At the first sense of opportunity for real happiness, you either jump into it while ignoring every possible red flag.

Or, perhaps worse, you start to conjure up red flags where there are none, robbing yourself of the potential for any actual joy.

Fuck, I hate being a human sometimes.

One thing is clear. Right now, good things are happening.

And I'm determined, for Yara's sake, to keep this string of good luck going for as long as it possibly can.

At the first sign of trouble, I'm out.

But for now, we get to enjoy everything positive that being with Gerald, and that being in America, can possibly bring.

Chapter 16

ALINA

It's less than a week later that everything changes, and I begin to realize that Gerald really isn't what he has claimed.

That's as long as he's able to keep up the façade before it finally breaks down in an epic explosion.

It all starts when Yara refuses to eat the cereal that he picked out for her.

She's polite about it, but he takes it as insolence and slams his fist on the table, scaring her.

I immediately send her to her room, furious.

"She's not your child, Gerald. You can't discipline her like that," I try to explain.

"Well, she shouldn't act like such a spoiled brat in my house," he growls, his eyes narrowing at the uneaten cereal growing soggier by the minute. "The way I see it, if someone does you the kindness of giving you a nice meal, you eat it. I asked around and all the local kids are obsessed with it. It's all over their Snap Tock or whatever it is they're using these days."

I try to placate him. "Look, I'm sure she'll regret not eating it. But you must understand... everything here is new for her. The packaging, the labels. Things look different, they sound different, they taste different. What seems like a small thing to you is massive for her right now. Surely you can see that. Please give her some grace."

He sniffs and looks down his nose at me from across the table. "My house, my rules. And politeness and gratitude are baseline requirements."

My heart races a little faster. "But she's my daughter, Gerald. She barely knows you. Please leave the discipline to me. And she was polite... you just didn't like that she didn't want what you were offering."

He glares at me, his expression so cruel it sends a shiver through me. It's as if his whole face changed, the kind, attentive man now long gone.

"You belong to me. When will you finally understand that I own both you and your insolent little... Yara?" His words are a chilling declaration of ownership, even as he just about spits out my daughter's name in apparent disgust. "I had a feeling she was going to be an issue, but I need her to be here with you."

The air in the mansion is thick with tension as I take in the reality of our situation.

The grandeur and generosity I once admired now feels like a trap, closing in around me and Yara.

It's all an illusion, a façade that obscures something much darker.

My veins turn to ice at the mention of her in this way. "Don't say her name like that. And she most certainly does not belong to you. Neither do I."

"Yet you've accepted my kindnesses so far," he sneers.

"As if I had a choice."

My eyes narrow, suddenly clicking that he's not the man he's been making out to be. Visions of Luchenko's cruelty flash into my mind.

"Sometimes we do what we need to survive, Gerald. You, of all people, should know that."

He circles around me, his polished Oxfords clicking on the shiny marble floor.

"But there has to be part of you that wanted it. Otherwise, you could have refused. Everybody has a choice, Alina."

His eyes glimmer cruelly.

"You made yours, and now it's like you're changing the narrative to make things fit the way you want them to."

I want to cry that sometimes, when you're a mother, you have to switch your mind off to your own wants and needs. To put this creature you brought into the world above anything at all, including yourself.

That it was never about me and never will be for the rest of my time on this earth.

But I know that will just further highlight my weak spot. My reason to be.

Yara.

Not that he isn't cruelly fixated on her anyway.

"What changed, Gerald? You've been so kind, so caring."

He sneers at me. "Nothing's changed as far as I'm concerned. I'm just peeling back the curtain so you can see how things are going to be from now on."

Everything hits me all at once.

The secretive calls.

The dangerous-looking men always lurking in the background.

Never feeling like I can be alone with my thoughts.

The extra attention on Yara.

I feel like an idiot.

He's displaying the classic narcissistic tendencies that I've unfortunately come to know too well. The tropical vacation, our first weeks here—all classic love bombing techniques designed to sweep me, and Yara, off our feet.

Behind it? A cold, calculating man with unknown intentions for both of us.

God, I really do feel stupid.

But I so wanted to believe his promises.

I know that knights in shining armor don't exist, but he just seemed so... genuine.

Looking back, maybe I just heard what I wanted to hear, what I needed to in order to allow myself hope for a better future. For Yara, and even for myself.

His attempt to distort reality only strengthens my resolve. I meet his cold gaze unflinchingly.

This isn't my first rodeo with a dangerous and powerful man who lied about his true intentions.

"The only choice I had was to protect my daughter, no matter the cost to myself."

Gerald scoffs. "How very noble of you. But we both know you're not that selfless."

He brushes a strand of hair from my face and I fight the urge to recoil.

"From the moment I became a mother, my own desires ceased to matter," I say sharply. "Everything I've done has been for Yara. Every sacrifice, every compromise—it's all been all for her."

I think of the countless sleepless nights, the soul-crushing work, the pieces of myself that I've given up along the way.

The tears I've swallowed when Yara has asked about her father.

The birthdays and holidays spent working while Yara was home alone, or with her grandmother who is becoming less and less capable of taking care of her granddaughter or herself.

Gerald leans in, his breath hot on my cheek. "That's quite a martyr complex you've built for yourself," he murmurs. "But we both know you're only human."

I meet his gaze unflinchingly, defiance burning in my eyes.

I would burn this whole mansion down if it meant protecting Yara.

"You know nothing about me," I say coldly. "You never will."

I turn on my heel and leave the study, Gerald's amused laughter echoing behind me.

"I'll be sharing more information soon on how you can both live up to my expectations," he calls out.

I stalk down the hallway, my fists clenched at my sides.

I can feel Gerald's eyes on my back, but I refuse to turn around.

Not now, not ever.

My mind races.

I don't know what he has planned for us, but it's suddenly become clear that every day here is a risk to Yara's safety just as if we were back home.

Every day is a gamble with our lives.

But, no matter what he has in mind, I refuse to let Gerald win. I will protect my daughter, no matter the cost.

I walk briskly through the mansion's opulent halls, my heels clicking sharply against the polished marble floors. But the extravagant decor that once dazzled me now feels garish and oppressive.

This is not the fairytale palace Gerald promised—it is the gilded cage I feared. But without even the meager resources I had at home. Friends, my mother, a better understanding of the system and resources. Our own space, away from Gerald.

Even with Luchenko nipping at our heels over there, it seemed more palatable.

They say better the devil you know, and now I'm beginning to think that's true.

I reach the heavy oak door of Yara's bedroom and slip inside, immediately comforted by the sight of my daughter sleeping soundly, her chest rising and falling in a steady rhythm.

I perch on the edge of the four-poster bed and gently brush a strand of hair from her face.

A fierce protectiveness wells up inside me.

"I won't let him hurt you," I whisper into the quiet room. "I'll find a way out of this, I swear it."

She stirs slightly in her sleep but doesn't wake.

I watch her for a moment longer, then head back out into the hallway, newly invigorated.

I won't accept defeat.

My love for my daughter outweighs any fear or doubt.

As I descend the grand staircase, the mansion almost seems to mock me with its extravagance—the crystal chandeliers, the antique vases, the original oil paintings.

I was tricked, and worst of all I fell for it hook, line and sinker because I wanted to believe that something, anything, good could happen to us.

But it's all a façade. This place is a prison and Gerald holds the keys.

However dire it seems, though, I'm determined to pick the lock and get us out of here. I won't be intimidated or manipulated any longer.

A fire has been lit within me, fueled by my fierce desire to protect my child. I refuse to let another powerful man try to destroy us.

I will find a way out.

For Yara's sake, I have to.

Chapter 17

ALINA

The golden light filtering through the massive windows does nothing to warm the ice in Gerald's eyes.

The kindness and warmth that once seemed to pour from them is gone, leaving me wondering if I ever imagined them in the first place.

My heart slams against my ribs as he prowls towards me, backing me into the corner of the room.

The antique chaise longue digs into the backs of my knees, trapping me.

"The way the system works, Alina," he rasps, "is that I have complete control."

His hand curls around my throat, just firm enough to remind me of his strength.

Of my helplessness.

"I have the option to rescind your immigration paperwork at any time."

No. This can't be happening.

We were happy, weren't we?

I search his face for any trace of the man I thought I knew, but there's nothing familiar in those arctic eyes.

Only hunger.

The thrill of the hunt.

I scrabble at his wrist.

"But that's not true!"

My nails leave red crescents on his skin. He doesn't even flinch.

"I really did believe we were meant to be! I trusted your promises. My intentions were good!"

A Cheshire cat grin splits his face. "But they don't know that."

His fingers tighten, cutting off my breath.

Spots dance before my eyes.

"And when it comes to immigration, the American citizen has all the power. And you know what I've heard happens in immigration prisons, Alina. Especially to young children nearing their teenage years."

Yara. The thought of my daughter in a place like that—no. I won't let him take her. I'd kill us both first.

I sag against him, playing the obedient fiancée.

As his grip loosens, I stomp on his instep and elbow him in the solar plexus.

He grunts, stumbling back.

I bolt for the door, my heart in my throat.

If I could just make it outside, get help—but then, he's right. Where would I go? Immigration will take his side and deport me. Us. Maybe even send us to prison.

I can't put Yara through that. After everything she's been through already...

A bruising grip closes around my upper arm, yanking me off my feet.

I crash to the marble floor, pain exploding through my knee and hip.

Gerald looms over me, his eyes glacial, his mouth twisted in a snarl.

"You stupid bitch. I always keep my promises, and if you don't do exactly as I say, immigration will be here so fast to haul your ass off to prison you won't know which way is up."

His boot connects with my ribs, stealing my breath.

"They might even leave your precious daughter with me. For safe-keeping."

Icy terror floods my veins.

There is no escape.

I'm well and truly trapped, just like he planned.

Gerald has won a game that I didn't even know we were playing.

I struggle to my feet, clutching my bruised side. Every breath sends a stab of pain through my chest.

Gerald watches me with those dead, predatory eyes.

Waiting.

Knowing I have no choice.

I swallow hard against the bile rising in my throat.

For Yara, I would do anything.

"What do you want from me?" The words taste of ash and defeat.

A slow, sinister smile creeps across his face.

"That's better. I knew you'd come around."

He straightens his cuffs, the picture of nonchalance.

"You'll be working for me now. Doing as I say, when I say it. And the first order of business..."

His gaze turns hungry, raking over me in a way that makes my skin crawl.

"You're going to help me acquire some new...merchandise. Pretty little things, just like yourself... just like Yara."

Revulsion and horror twist my gut.

He wants me to lure other women into his web, like a spider feasting on flies. Girls, too.

I shake my head in mute denial.

"Don't shake your head at me. It makes perfect sense. Yara will also be assisting us. Having someone around her age will help us to more effectively lure new meat."

My stomach seizes and I feel bile rising in my throat.

My sweet Yara, being used to help capture other girls, luring them into a life of sex slavery.

"No, you wouldn't—"

Gerald tsks. "Come now, Alina. Did you really think you were that special and I really just wanted you to come here to be my wife?"

His mouth contorts into a cruel sneer.

"You know what's at stake here. Or shall I call immigration to come collect you and your daughter right now? Those cages I've seen on the news look less than comfortable... and the violence and rapes... I wouldn't wish that on my children. Not when they could be staying in a place like this in exchange for a few small favors."

He gestures at our sumptuous surroundings.

A different kind of cage.

Bile rises higher in my throat, acid and unstoppable. I turn just in time, retching onto the polished marble floor.

Gerald makes a noise of disgust. "Clean that up, you messy creature. And then we'll talk about your new job responsibilities."

He leaves me here, crumpled on the floor in a pool of my own sick. Broken. Beaten. With no way out and nowhere left to run.

I stay here for a long time, unable to move. Unable to think past the horror of what's being asked of me.

Finally I drag myself upright, my limbs as heavy as lead.

There are cleaning supplies under the sink in the adjacent bathroom, and I scrub at the floor until no trace of vomit remains.

As if I could erase the memory so easily.

When I'm done, Gerald is waiting in his study.

I hover in the doorway, not wanting to cross the threshold. Not wanting to enter the lair of the evil man who's managed to trap me because I wanted so badly to believe in something good.

God, I feel stupid now.

He looks up from some papers on his desk, his eyes cold.

"Come in. Sit." His tone brooks no argument. I perch on the edge of a chair, tense as a bowstring.

"Here is what will happen."

Gerald leans back, steepling his fingers.

"You will go to clubs, bars, anywhere you can find lonely young women. Chat them up, get friendly. Then invite them back here under some pretext."

His lips curl.

"You can be quite charming when you put your mind to it."

I frown as pain sears through my head. It's like the gravity of what he's asking me to do is hitting me full force. He doesn't even have to touch me to have a physical impact on me.

I don't want to ask questions, but I also have an almost perverse need to know where I would be leading these women if I do what he's asking me.

"And what happens then... to them, I mean—"

He waves his hand at me as if impatient at my question. "Once they're here, we dose them with a sedative we've acquired. When they wake, they'll find themselves...indisposed. Ready to be sold to the highest bidder."

He shrugs.

"Simple as that. If you do your job well, your daughter stays safe and untouched. If not..."

He leaves the threat hanging.

I stare at him, unable to form words around the horror choking me. He wants me to lure unsuspecting women to their doom. To a fate worse than death.

And if I don't, Yara...

Bile rises in my throat again, but this time I swallow hard and manage to keep it down. For now.

Outwardly I remain motionless, frozen.

Inwardly my mind races, searching for an escape from this nightmare.

There has to be a way out.

There has to be. I must find it, or die trying.

Gerald stands, smoothing his jacket. "You have your orders. Now get to work. And be warned, I have no patience for subpar results."

He exits the room, leaving me alone with the devil's bargain he's forced upon me.

I remain motionless for a long time after he leaves, trying to process the depravity of his demands.

Lure innocent women to their doom or watch my daughter suffer and possibly die.

There is no choice at all, and we both know it.

When I can finally move again, I go to Yara's room and gather her in my arms, clinging to her as she babbles about her day. The thought of anything happening to her makes me feel physically ill, a cold knot of terror taking up residence in my stomach.

I would do anything to keep her safe. Even if it means becoming a monster myself.

Later that night

I dress up in a slinky red dress and too-high heels, hating myself more with every step as I venture out to prowl the clubs for Gerald's next victims.

My stomach churns the entire time, but I force on a flirty smile and strike up conversations, trying to seem casual and as if I'm out for a night of uninhibited fun and revelry just like everyone else.

But it's no use. I feel awkward and nauseous, and anyone paying attention probably notices I seem a bit off. Nobody bites. But I know I can't keep putting this off.

If I fail at this, if I can't bring myself to lure these women to their doom, Yara will die. I need to find another way to protect her, even if it means sacrificing myself.

As closing time approaches with no success, relief and worry both flood me.

I've failed my first test, but for now I haven't lured any other innocent people into Gerald's evil trap, and Yara and I are both still alive.

He can't expect results on my first day. I need a little more time to figure a way out of this nightmare.

There has to be someone who can help us. Someone I can tell the truth without them thinking I'm insane. The key is finding them before Gerald realizes his new toy is broken beyond repair.

I pray for the chance to keep searching as I make my way home, dreading facing Gerald and the punishment my failure might bring. But Yara's life is worth any cost. I would endure anything to ensure her safety.

Absolutely anything.

I walk through the front door of the mansion with leaden steps, my heart pounding. Gerald will be waiting to hear about my success, eager to start the 'training' he has planned for his new recruits.

How will he react when I tell him I failed? I'm really taking a punt that he won't come down too hard given this is my first time trying.

The foyer is empty, but I hear voices coming from the study down the hall. Gerald's smooth, cultured tones, and a woman's laughter in response.

My stomach drops as I realized he's succeeded where I failed, and already brought a victim into our home.

Summoning my courage, I walk to the study and find Gerald casually draped across the leather sofa, a glass of brandy in one hand. A stunning brunette sits beside him, gazing at him with smitten eyes.

My entrance catches her attention, and she frowns at my presence, her territorial instincts flaring to life.

Gerald glances up with a shark's smile, noting my pale face and trembling hands. "Alina, darling, you're just in time. Our guest was wondering where you were. I was about to send a car for you."

His meaning is clear: he knows I failed, and is punishing me by making me witness his conquest.

The nameless woman's frown deepens at the obvious intimacy in his tone. She shifts away from him, regarding me with unveiled suspicion.

Gerald chuckles and wrapped an arm around her shoulders, pulling her close once more. "No need to be jealous, sweetheart. Alina is part of the package."

Revulsion rises in my throat like bile at his words. I force it down and summon an answering smile. "Of course. My apologies for keeping you waiting."

Gerald's eyes gleam, seeing my capitulation. "There, you see? All is well. Now, we were just discussing how we might entertain our guest this evening."

His fingers trail down the woman's arm in a possessive caress.

"Any suggestions, darling?"

I swallow hard, wrestling with the urge to scream. To attack him and try to destroy the monster he's just revealed himself to be.

But one wrong move would mean Yara's death. I have to play his game, at least for now.

There has to be a way out of this, if I'm patient, if I can endure his cruelty. I will find it, no matter the cost.

"I'm sure we can think of something," I say softly. "After all, we aim to please."

Gerald's laughter echoes through the room, a dark promise of what's to come.

Chapter 18

ALINA

The Past – approximately 11 years ago

The chandelier's crystals refract the light, scattering it across the ball-room in a dizzying display. I pause to steady myself, smoothing my hands over the beaded bodice of my gown. The dress cinches too tight, and the heels are too high. Even the air feels perfumed and cloying, threatening to choke me. But this is how he likes me to look, how he insists I present myself. He'd have it no other way, and he always gets what he wants.

Luchenko appears at my side, his smile not reaching his cold eyes. "You look stunning, meelaya."

I stiffen, bile rising in my throat at the familiar endearment. This man had once made me feel safe, protected. Now his presence evokes nothing but dread.

"Don't call me that," I say sharply. "You lost the right long ago."

His expression remains impassive, but his fingers dig into my elbow. "I'll call you what I wish. I've always admired that defiant streak of yours, meelaya. Makes things more... exciting."

A shiver goes through me at the thinly veiled threat in his words. I survey the room, taking in the guests' sidelong glances and hushed whispers. They all know I'm nothing but Luchenko's plaything, a carnal distraction while his precious wife is out of town.

At first, it was embarrassing knowing that they knew. But, after so many parties spent embarrassed, shrinking like an expired flower in the corner of the room, shying away from the rumors, I decided to embrace it. To play the part of Luchenko's love interest, holding his hand and hanging off his arm and every word at these types of events.

Because it was much easier that way, I quickly learned. Luchenko has a massive ego, and having a young and attractive woman constantly by his side is part of the persona that he's so carefully curated. While his wife is out of town, at least.

At first, I was pampered. The finest clothing, jewels, food. Even a couple of vacations that were well-timed with his wife being off on extended family trips. He paid for everything I needed, no questions asked.

And I accepted the gifts, because I'd always had nothing and finally I had something.

And that felt really, really good.

But after only a month or so, everything changed. The world shifted on its axis.

My period didn't come.

I'd lost quite a lot of weight very quickly, because I know Luchenko prefers his women on the thinner side, so initially I put it down to that. But after a couple of weeks, there was still no sign and I started to notice subtle changes in my body. My breasts ached, my skin seemed different.

And deep down, I just knew.

Of course, it was hard to keep the pregnancy a secret. As my body continued to change, Luchenko noticed my growing belly and breasts. It's hard to hide the nausea caused by morning sickness. And, of course, he noticed I didn't have my period. Finally, he had his doctor visit and he confirmed my state.

The birth of our daughter only tightened Luchenko's hold. We called her Yara, which I told him means 'small butterfly', which is true. But what I didn't share is that it also means 'strong'.

Because I knew she would need to be strong, just like I would.

Luchenko immediately saw her as a possession, a means of controlling me. The thought of him molding her young mind, twisting it as he had my own...it made me ill.

Before, it was just me. He could hurt me, threaten me. Even threaten to hurt my mother, withholding her access to medications and restricting her food rations.

But with Yara here now, it's changed his sick game. He now has this thing to hold over me—this vulnerable being—and I've found myself completely at his mercy.

Trapped. The word echoes in my mind. But not for much longer. I will find a way out of this gilded cage, even if I have to claw my way free.

I force myself to smile, though it feels more like a grimace. "If you admire me so much, why do you insist on parading me around like one of your possessions?"

Luchenko's grip on my arm tightens painfully. When he speaks, his voice is a low rumble meant only for me.

"Never forget who you belong to. All of this—" he gestures around the opulent ballroom "—exists because I allow it. And I can take it away just as easily."

I meet his cold gaze unflinchingly, anger simmering in my veins. "I belong to no one. Least of all you."

His eyes narrow. For a moment, the sounds of laughter and clinking glasses faded away. There is only Luchenko's hulking presence before me, his scarred face inches from mine.

When he smiles, it's the expression of a predator spotting vulnerable prey. "Such spirit. I enjoy taming you. In fact, I find it one of my most satisfying pastimes."

Revulsion roils in my stomach, and I force myself not to recoil.

I will not let him see my fear.

With effort, I extract myself from his bruising grip. "If you'll excuse me, I need some air."

I don't wait for his response before turning on my heel. The sound of my footsteps clicking across the marble floor matches the rapid pounding of my heart.

These exquisite surroundings have become a death trap. And I will free myself from it, no matter the cost.

I stride out onto the balcony, the night air raising goosebumps on my bare arms.

Behind me, the muted sounds of the gala continue, a constant reminder of the prison I've found myself trapped in.

Out here, away from Luchenko's smothering presence, I can finally breathe.

But each inhale is tinged with fear.

Fear for myself, and the future that lies ahead for me and my daughter. Luchenko's daughter.

Luchenko's thinly veiled threats echo in my mind.

"Your aesthetic appearance has little to do with my plans for you and our daughter's futures. Beauty fades with time, and that's what initially attracted me to you, I'll admit, but it's not why I want you now. I have other uses planned for you."

His words chill my veins, goosebumps breaking out all over my arms and chest.

The thought of Yara at Luchenko's mercy makes my blood run cold. I have to find a way out of this, for both of us. But how?

I stare out at the city lights twinkling below me. We're so high up, untouchable in Luchenko's ivory tower. Just one of the many ways he keeps me under his control.

The sound of approaching footsteps makes me stiffen.

I don't need to turn around to know it's him. Luchenko moves with the self-assured gait of a man accustomed to dominating any space he enters.

When he speaks, his voice is deceptively gentle. "The night air hasn't chilled you, I hope?"

His solicitude is a lie. I know the monster that lurks beneath his charming façade.

"I'm fine," I say tightly. "I'd like to be alone."

Ignoring my words, he comes closer, crowding me against the balcony railing.

I force myself not to shrink away.

"So spirited," he murmurs. "I admire that in you, meelaya. But you forget your place."

His hand settles on my lower back in a mockery of intimacy, the gesture that young women are taught mean a man is taking care of us, guiding us as if we need a man to help us safely navigate the precarious balance of life. To steer us from room to room.

To keep us out of trouble and away from the threat of hysteria and other 'womanly issues'.

Disgust rises in my throat, but I swallow it down.

"And what place is that?" I challenge.

Luchenko's answering smile is slow, possessive. "At my side, as my devoted wife. In my home. In my bed." His hand slides lower in emphasis. "Precisely where you belong."

Rage burns through me, overpowering my fear. I shove him back with all my strength.

"I will never be your wife. You already have one of those, you've made that clear. And you will never have me, or my daughter, again."

For a moment Luchenko looks amused by my defiance. Then his expression hardens.

"Take care, Alina," he says softly. "You try my patience."

I turn away but he reaches out and grips my chin, forcing me to meet his cold gray eyes.

"You belong to me. Never forget that."

With that, he releases me and strides back inside, the echo of his footsteps ringing with grim finality.

I let out a shaky breath, wrapping my arms around myself.

I have to escape. Tonight has made one thing clear—Luchenko will never let me go willingly, and when he finds out about my condition the stakes are only going to get higher.

I look out once more at the city lights, steeling my resolve. Whatever it takes, I will find a way out.

I take a deep breath to steady my nerves before slipping back into the opulent ballroom. The laughter and chatter wash over me, a discordant backdrop to my churning thoughts.

Luchenko is nowhere to be seen. I'm not sure if that's a relief or even more unsettling.

His presence always looms, whether he's at my side or not.

I navigate through the sea of glittering gowns and tailored suits, keenly aware of the covert glances and hushed whispers following my passage. To them, I'm an object of fascination, the infamous mistress of the powerful crime lord. An outsider.

A server passes with a tray of champagne flutes and I snag one, taking a bracing sip. The bubbles do little to calm my nerves, and I feel guilty for imbibing alcohol that could compromise my judgement. But emotions threaten to overwhelm me, and so I decide to sip instead of cry.

After all, Luchenko doesn't like his mistresses to make a scene.

As I wander, fragments of conversations reach my ears.

"...shipments coming in from the docks tomorrow night..."

"...new territory in the south side..."

I pause as a familiar laugh rings out.

Craning my neck, I spot Luchenko's lieutenant, Viktor, holding court with a group of men. His cruel eyes glint with malice as he regales them with some tale.

"...and the little girl screamed for her mother as I squeezed..."

My blood turns to ice.

Viktor's grin only widens at their raucous laughter, the monsters.

Bile rises in my throat. I have to get away from here. Away from them. It's not just about me anymore.

I quicken my pace toward the exit, no longer caring who notices my hasty departure.

All I can think about is getting out of here.

I have to escape Luchenko's web, no matter what it takes. For both our sakes.

With a deep breath, I step back out onto the balcony, the cool night air raising goosebumps on my bare arms. Below me, the city sprawls out in a glittering expanse, deceptively peaceful from this distance.

If I stare long enough, I can almost pretend I don't know the ugliness lurking in its shadows.

Almost.

I shiver, rubbing my hands over my arms. How have I let things spiral so far out of control?

Memories of those early days with Luchenko come unbidden, when his charm and lavish gifts had blinded me to the darkness simmering underneath. He was there for me when nobody else was, provided me with things I never dreamed of.

And I was sucked in, thirsty for a life outside of the oppressive darkness. Believing that I could have more, that I somehow deserved more.

But that came with a catch that I was initially too blind to see.

By the time his true nature emerged, it was too late.

I was caught in his web, bound by threats both spoken and unspoken. The mother of his youngest child.

As I gazed out at the city lights, an idea begins to form.

Luchenko's empire may be vast, but it's not absolute. There have to be cracks, weaknesses I can exploit.

I just need help, allies outside his sphere of influence. Someone who can shelter Yara and I, and hide us beyond his reach.

The first step will be discreetly reaching out, making contact without raising suspicion. It won't be easy or without risk.

But I have to try, for my daughter's sake. For her future.

With this silent vow made under the night sky, I gather my resolve. I will find a way to cut free of Luchenko's web. No matter what it takes.

The allyship comes from the most unexpected of places. Luchenko's wife, Marie.

When she first approaches me, I'm dubious. For a moment, I think she might even try to take my baby.

But I soon learn that Marie is fierce and doesn't appreciate being humiliated repeatedly by Luchenko. We have more in common than I think either of us realized.

I no longer want to be in Luchenko's grasp, and she doesn't want me there either. She wants me out of their lives.

And my pregnancy and Yara's birth have only expedited her need for me to be well out of the picture. As it turns out, Marie is infertile. Seeing me with her husband's baby is like salt in a deep wound.

After prolonged negotiations, they come to a stalemate.

Luchenko lets me live my life away from his grasp, raising Yara.

This solves Marie the embarrassment of having his illegitimate love child paraded around in front of the world.

She's not stupid enough to think many people won't see right through it, based on timing alone, but it seems more palatable than having this baby thrown in her face.

So we're thrown out on the streets, discarded.

I sneak us in and stay with my mother whenever I can, but the rules are strict in her assisted living accommodation, and there's a high risk that by allowing us in she could be thrown out herself, with no place to go.

Her situation is more tenuous than mine. I'm relatively young, strong and resourceful. Mother, however, is elderly, somewhat frail despite her strength of spirit, and she needs medicine that's almost impossible to access while living on the streets.

Yet, despite being tossed aside like a piece of trash, I know that Luchenko still thinks about me. Obsesses about me.

He keeps track of my whereabouts, and from time to time I notice his men trailing me. No doubt reporting back.

I know beyond a doubt that Luchenko sees Yara as his possession. And that it's only a matter of time before he decides to take back what he believes is his.

Chapter 19

ALINA

Gerald's cruelty only continues to ratchet up over the next couple of weeks. I'm constantly on guard, hovering over Yara at all times, hesitant to let her out of my sight even for a moment.

He moves me from our master bedroom into another area, some kind of makeshift dungeon-looking room with a rickety bed and thin blankets, although occasionally he allows me to sleep in Yara's room.

As the sun rises one morning, a pale sliver of light creeps along the floor of the dingy basement, casting ugly shadows on the filthy walls.

It's a far departure from the palatial, immaculate parts of the mansion that Gerald lured me to.

I force myself to open my swollen eyes, every muscle in my body screaming in protest.

Sheer willpower is the only thing that keeps me from curling back into the fetal position and succumbing to the darkness threatening to consume me.

Despite the pain, despite the humiliation, I have to survive this.

For Yara.

Using the wall for support, I stumble to my feet, blinking away the bleariness in my eyes.

Slowly, I begin to search the room, careful not to make any noise that would alert Gerald's men to my escape attempt.

The door is locked, but the single window high up on the wall, covered in grime and cobwebs, offers a glimmer of hope.

Rushing over, I drag a rickety chair over to the window, and after several failed attempts, manage to wedge it against the wall.

The sunlight streaming through the cloudy glass is the most beautiful sight I've ever seen, even as it illuminates the grime coating the pane.

My aching muscles scream in protest, but I ignore them, knowing that every second counts.

With a deep breath, I wrench at the latch, wincing as it squeaks in protest.

Heart pounding, I glance over my shoulder, half-expecting to see Gerald's men barging through the door. But for now, I am alone.

Wedging my slender frame through the narrow opening, I breathe a sigh of relief as my feet touch the ground outside.

My exhilaration is short-lived as I realize I'm on the second floor, surrounded by tall fences topped with barbed wire.

A familiar dread begins to creep up my spine.

What am I even thinking? I would jump off the roof and then what?

Even if I did manage to escape, where would I run to? Even if I did manage to contact the authorities, what would I say?

Gerald could simply claim that Yara was his biological child, and in the time it took to verify that this wasn't true, goodness knows what fate may befall her at his hands.

I shudder at the thought of leaving Yara alone with him. With his men.

I've seen the way they look at her, and it's not so different from the way they look at me.

To escape now would be selfish. Too risky.

But it also might be the only way I can get help for us before it's too late.

In the distance, I hear the unmistakable sound of footsteps and voices.

Panicking, I scan my surroundings for any means of escape. My gaze falls on a rickety drainpipe, my only chance.

Ignoring my protesting body, I begin to climb.

Halfway up, I hear the shattering of glass, my captors hot on my trail.

Fueled by terror, I scramble upwards, the jagged edges of the rusty pipe tearing at my skin.

"No matter what it takes, I'll find you!" I whisper to myself, hoping Yara will somehow hear my promise.

With a defiant scream, I swing my leg over the fence and leap into the unknown.

But the feeling of freedom doesn't last long. I grunt as a heavy object smashes into my back and everything fades to black.

My heart races as I watch in horror as two of Gerald's men drag Yara away, her terrified cries tearing through my soul. "Yara! Be brave, my love! I will come for you as soon as I can." But the look in Gerald's cold eyes tell me my words might not be enough.

"She won't, Yara. She's lying," he taunts, "You're about to start a new life. Not the one you dreamed of with your mother, but a new life nonetheless. I can't wait to introduce you to my highest-paying clients. I think they'll be quite satisfied with you."

"G-Gerald," I gasp.

A chill runs down my spine as I turn to face him, his perfect features twisted in anger. His eyes flash with rage. "Oh, Alina, did you really think you could escape me?"

My stomach clenches as his words sank in.

I want to scream, but I know it would only scare Yara more. "Don't listen to him, Yara!" I plead, my voice shaking, "I will come for you. This will all be over soon."

I can't bear to think of what they might do to my innocent child. And this is all my fault. How could I have put Yara in this position?

"Please," I beg Gerald, desperately, "Just... anything. But don't touch Yara, I'm begging you."

Gerald's smile sends shivers down my spine. "Oh yes, you'll do anything if Yara isn't touched? Is that right? Anything at all? I just want to make sure I heard that correctly... in which case it's a bit of a shock, seeing how you just tried to escape."

"Yes, absolutely," I say quickly, without a second thought. My voice drops to a whisper. "Anything. And I'm so sorry I climbed outside. I don't know what came over me."

Gerald appears thoughtful, and he lifts his gaze to mine. "Alright then. In that case, she's safe... for now. But only if you do one thing without complaining."

I nod, not sure how to respond.

"You're in my world, now, Alina," his cold voice purrs as he approaches me. I freeze, my heart pounding in my chest as his muscular arm wraps around my waist. My head swims with panic, my earlier defiance evaporating like mist in the sun.

He yanks me against him, his cold nose brushing against my ear. "And now that I have you, I'm never letting you go. Not without a fight."

My vision blurs with unshed tears. "You're insane. Haven't you done enough?"

"Insane or brilliant?" his lips curve into a sardonic smile. "I'll let you decide that after you've met my latest acquisition."

The door opens, and a man with steely gray eyes and a scarred face appears. A shudder ran down my spine as I immediately recognize him. Maxwell. The stories I've heard about him... people speak about him in whispers.

"Take her," Gerald orders, gesturing towards me. "Make sure she's... prepared for tonight's event."

"No!" I struggle against Maxwell's iron grip, but it's no use. He half-drags, half-carries me into the adjoining bedroom, my stomach seesawing violently.

Tonight's event?

Maxwell locks the door behind us, his expression impassive. "Strip," he commands, his voice a low growl.

My hands tremble as I fumble with my clothes, desperate to stall for time. "W-Why?" I manage.

He doesn't even spare me a glance as he lights a cigarette. "You're the entertainment," he drawls, smoke curling around his head like a macabre halo. "And your little Yara? She'll be joining us later."

The breath leaves my lungs in a rush.

"Now!" Maxwell barks, and the coldness in his eyes sends a shiver down my spine. He's just like Gerald.

As the first tear trails down my cheek, I begin to undress. With shaking fingers, I unbutton my blouse, my breath coming out in ragged gasps.

I can't let him see me crack.

As I lower my jeans, I glance around the room frantically for anything I could use as a weapon. There has to be something.

With my heart pounding in my chest, I slide off my underwear and ball them up, praying for a miracle.

Gerald knocks on the door in mock concern about my privacy, and he enters the room. "Is she ready?" he asks as his lascivious gaze rakes over my naked body, sending a wave of revulsion through me.

I will not break in front of him.

"Now, get on the bed." His voice is like ice, sending a shiver down my spine.

This is not the man who promised to take care of me, who promised me the world.

It's not the same man who was attentive in bed, making me feel like a queen.

That was a all a lie.

Steeling myself, I climb onto the bed, naked and exposed, leaving my crumpled clothes on the floor.

My stomach lurches as he makes a call on his radio and four men enter the room, and I realize what he means by 'entertainment'. He wants me to submit to whatever his men do to me, and I have no choice but to comply if I ever want to see Yara again.

If I want to keep her safe and avoid the same thing happening to her.

He really is trying to break me.

The men all undo their belt buckles and unzip their pants, and my stomach roils as I realize what's about to happen.

The next few hours are a blur of pain and humiliation.

I try my best to dissociate, thinking of Yara's face and the promise I made to come for her.

I will find a way out of this. We will both get through this nightmare, together.

They might be able to ravage my body, but they will never take away the love that burns so brightly in my soul for my precious girl.

When it's finally over, I lie on the ground, shaking uncontrollably. My body aches physically and emotionally, and I've never felt more alone in my life.

Gerald's men drag me to a filthy corner of the room, where I curl up into a ball, trying to disappear from the world.

I know that Gerald is trying to dismantle me entirely by doing this, trying to shatter my spirit so he can fully claim me as his.

And, as I look down at the blood trickling down my legs and feel the stinging, bruised sensation caused by what took place today, I realize this may well be the closest I've ever been to letting that happen.

I lie there for a while, stained with the evidence of my violation. I feel filthier than I've ever felt in my life, inside and out.

I want to scrub myself for hours, but I also realize that's not going to take away the damage that's been done inside me. To my mind, to my soul.

In any case, I need to find a way out of this deceptively pretty hellhole and fast.

A while later, I hear the familiar clip of Gerald's Oxfords approaching the room.

"You've done well," Gerald said coldly, as he enters. "Your girl will be untouched for now. But remember, little lamb, you're both mine now. Even if you are a filthy whore."

I force myself to meet Gerald's cold eyes, my own blazing with defiance. "You can't break me, Gerald. No matter what you do."

"Oh, we'll see about that," he smirks, his eyes cold as ice.

With that, he exits with his entourage, leaving me in the company of my demons from past and present.

I try to push myself up, but the dizziness overwhelms me and everything once again fades to black.

Chapter 20

ALINA

Yara's small frame seems to shrink even further as she stands defiant in the grand foyer. The soaring ceiling and cold marble loom oppressively, dwarfing her twelve-year-old form.

Across from her, Gerald's imposing height and broad shoulders block out the light. His initially charming smile is a distant memory, replaced by a perpetual expression of terrifying iciness.

"I won't do it," Yara states, her voice quivering slightly.

Gerald's jaw clenches, his patience clearly waning. "You'll do as I say, girl."

Yara shakes her head, resolute. "No. I don't want to."

In an instant, Gerald's large hand is raised threateningly.

Yara flinches but stands her ground.

Watching unseen from the doorway, my heart leaps into my throat.

Every instinct screams at me to run, to beg Gerald's forgiveness before his temper snaps.

But I force myself to remain still and quiet, my pulse racing.

The hovering hand.

The small defiant frame.

In a chilling moment of clarity, I know with certainty that no amount of compliance will keep Yara safe here.

I've let Gerald have his way, done everything he's asked of me. I've suffered, endured more than many could. But clearly, it's not enough.

The tiniest thing could set him off, send him unraveling. And he's clearly willing to take out his anger on me. It's only a matter of time before Yara becomes his target.

Gerald's voice slices the tense air. "You will do as I say, Yara. No questions asked."

I have to get her out of here. The thought pulses urgently through my mind.

I watch Yara's brave stance, see the shadow of fear in her eyes.

My resolve solidifies.

I gently close the door to Yara's bedroom, sealing us into the lavish space. To me, the plush bed and ornate furnishings feel less like luxury and more like traps cruelly disguised as comfort.

Kneeling before Yara, I take her hands in my own.

My voice is hushed but steady with determination. "Yara, listen to me. We can't stay here any longer. We have to leave."

Yara's eyes widen, uncertainty and hope swirling within them. "But how, Mama? His men are everywhere."

"We'll find a way," I assure her, my mind racing through the possibilities. "It won't be easy. We'll need to be smart, and brave."

Yara nods, my outward display of courage seeming to kindle her own. "I can be brave, Mama. For us."

In low voices, we begin outlining an escape plan.

Yara describes patrol times she's observed, while I plot decoys and distractions. Her exceptional observation skills come in exceptionally handy. Pieces come together—secret signals, memorized schedules, hiding spots.

It's dangerous, but together we can do this.

As our plans solidify, our already strong bond continues to augment—partners united against a shared threat. Fear still lurks in Yara's eyes, but her stance grows more confident by my side.

I pull her close, my heart swelling with love and determination. Yara's arms wrap tightly around me.

"It's you and me against the world now, my butterfly," I whisper.

Yara nods into my shoulder. She pulls back to look up at me, her eyes glistening with a mix of fear and resolve. "It's you and me against the world, Mama," she echoes softly, both a promise and a plea.

I cup her face gently and press a soft kiss to her forehead, sealing my vow. In that moment, our embrace becomes more than just comfort—it's a shared determination to face whatever comes next. I feel Yara's body relax as I take her hands in mine, trusting in my strength. My own shoulders straighten with renewed purpose.

After a quiet moment, we step back, hands still clasped. There's much to do before we can attempt escape into the uncertain future. But united as mother and protector, I know I can conquer anything for my daughter's sake.

"Come, let's go over the plan again," I say gently. "We'll need to be ready."

Yara nods, squaring her slim shoulders. Her eyes shine with courage. Together, we turn back to our makeshift map, two hearts beating as one. No matter what trials await, we will face them hand in hand.

After we're done, I tuck the blankets snugly around Yara, who clutches her stuffed bear close. Though the lavish bedroom hardly feels like home, tonight it offers a brief respite.

"Try to sleep, butterfly," I murmur. "You'll need your strength for what's ahead."

Yara nods, her eyes already drifting closed after the emotional evening. I smooth back my daughter's hair, my heart swelling with tenderness and fear. So much weighs on this child's resilience.

After a last gentle caress, I step away, clicking off the lamp. Moonlight from the windows casts everything in silver and shadow. I pause at the door, casting one more lingering look at my slumbering child.

Yara looks small and vulnerable amidst the imposing opulence. But I know my daughter has a core of iron—she will not break under our captor's grip. As long as I get her out of here soon, before he can try to break her too.

As I step into the hallway, my silhouette transforms as I bring myself to my full height. The mansion sleeps, unaware of the tempest gathering within. But I am wide awake—a sentinel standing vigil, a warrior ready to battle for my child.

Let our captor underestimate me at his own peril.

I will tear the world apart for Yara's sake.

Starting with him.

Chapter 21

ALINA

The humming fluorescent lights do nothing to brighten the drab beige walls of the immigration office. I fidget in the hard plastic chair, my heels tapping an anxious beat against the scuffed linoleum floor.

Gerald's man shuffles his feet beside me now and then, his expression stony as he monitors me to make sure I don't do or say anything to cause Gerald concern.

The immigration lawyer Gerald appointed me flanks my other side, but I'm not under any illusion that he's there for me at all.

My fingers twist the strap of my purse as I glance around. The other immigrants waiting looked just as on edge as I feel. A baby wails while her mother bounces her gently, murmuring in a language I don't recognize. An elderly man clutches his cane, his rheumy eyes staring blankly ahead.

We're all here for the same reason—the hope of a better future. My future with Yara depends on this interview going well.

"Alina Petrov?"

I startle at the sound of my name, pulse racing. This is it.

I stand on shaky legs, smooth my skirt, and follow the officer to his desk.

He rifles through my file, his face impassive. I clasp my clammy hands in my lap, trying not to fidget.

After an agonizing silence, he looks up at me over his glasses. "Your petition seems to be in order. Provided your relationship with Mr. Gerald Cranshaw remains...intact, of course."

My stomach drops. Gerald.

This isn't about my merits at all—it's all about him, and he holds all the cards.

"I understand," I say softly, my fate crystal clear.

As long as I belong to Gerald, I can stay in America.

I belong to him.

The realization makes my skin crawl.

But if that's what it takes to keep Yara safe, so be it.

I will find another way, in time.

I stand on shaky legs, thanking the officer politely before I leave.

My steps grow more determined as I walk away, my jaw set.

Gerald won't control me forever. I just need to be patient.

I push open the bathroom door, grateful for a moment alone to collect myself. The interview has shaken me more than I want to admit.

I lock myself in the farthest stall, leaning back against the door. My breath comes in shaky gasps as the reality of my situation crashes over me.

I'm trapped, bound to Gerald by forces beyond my control. The life I've fought so hard to build here could be ripped away in an instant if I step out of line.

Hot, angry tears prick my eyes. After everything I've endured, to have my fate resting in that monster's hands...it isn't fair.

As I struggle to rein in my emotions, a flyer taped to the back of the stall door catches my eye. "Need help? Call this number for assistance with domestic violence or human trafficking."

A bitter laugh escapes my lips. If only it were that simple. Gerald's tendrils likely run too deep for me to outmaneuver him so easily.

Still...perhaps I owe it to myself and Yara to try. To at least make one desperate grasp for freedom before resigning myself to captivity.

My hand shakes as I pull out my phone, thumb hovering over the keypad. Do I dare?

I hesitate, my finger still poised over the number. If I go through with this, there will be no going back. Gerald's wrath will be swift and merciless if he discovers I'd tried to break free of his control.

Not just for me, but for my sweet Yara too. She would bear the brunt of his fury because he knows she's the one way he can truly get at me. The thought makes my heart seize with terror.

As much as I yearn for escape, I know rash action now might only make things worse. Gerald's influence likely runs deep, even into the very organizations claiming to help people like me.

Calling the number could be walking right into his trap, handing ourselves over and removing the sliver of autonomy we still cling to. The risk is too great.

I lower my phone with a shuddering sigh, tears streaking down my cheeks. The choice to stay is agony, but it's ironically the only way to keep Yara safe.

For now, at least.

Gerald's smug confidence in owning me is not unfounded. His tendrils wrap around every aspect of my life, backed by a network of complicity and corruption.

I'm not paranoid enough to think he had the flyer placed their himself as some type of warped test. Or that the first person who answered the line would be complicit.

But the one after that, or the one after that—no, it would only be a matter of time until word got back to him.

But that doesn't mean I'm giving up. If anything, this only strengthens my resolve to break free, somehow. I'll bide my time, plan meticulously, and when the moment is right, Yara and I will disappear like ghosts.

Gerald's days of controlling me are numbered. I just have to be patient and smart.

Wiping my eyes, I emerge from the bathroom, my head held high.

Now the real fight begins.

I steady my breathing as I walk back to the waiting area, each step deliberate. This isn't the time for panic or despair. I need to be focused, alert.

The fluorescent lights of the immigration office seem harsher now, almost blinding. The hushed conversations around me blur into white noise. All I can hear is the pounding of my heart, keeping time with each click of my heels on the linoleum floor.

I nod politely at the lawyer and Gerald's goon.

Outwardly, I'm the picture of calm.

Inwardly, my mind races.

They nod back at me and gather their belongings, ready to transport me back to the mansion.

The interview today had been meant to secure our future here. Instead, it has only cemented how precarious our situation really is.

We're trapped in Gerald's web, and even the authorities are tangled up in it.

But I refuse to lose hope. Gerald holds all the cards now, but I still have my wits. And I'll use them to slowly, methodically pick apart the foundations of his control. It will take time. Patience. Sacrifice.

I steel myself for what lies ahead.

For now, I have to play the role Gerald expected. Be obedient. Compliant.

All the while watching, waiting, gathering what I need to make our escape.

Although it may feel like it, this is not the end. It's only the beginning. The battle lines are drawn, and I won't stop until I win our freedom.

No matter what it takes.

Chapter 22

MORELLO

I push open the heavy metal door, the hinges creaking loudly in the stark silence of the empty hallway. My shoes echo against the cold concrete floor as I make my way toward the briefing room, my heart pounding. This is it. The break we've been waiting for.

I step into the fluorescent lights of the briefing room. Lynfield is already waiting, a manila folder in hand. His steel blue eyes meet mine, crinkling at the corners.

"Morning, Morello. Take a seat."

I sink into the chair across from him, clasping my hands on the metal tabletop.

Lynfield slides the folder to me.

I flip it open.

A headshot of a handsome man with a charming smile stares up at me.

"Gerald Cranshaw," Lynfield says. "We got a solid lead on him connected to the trafficking ring."

My pulse quickens. This guy's been untouchable for years. A real wolf in sheep's clothing.

"How'd we get this break?" I ask.

Lynfield grins. "Let's just say Gerald got uncharacteristically sloppy. Left a trail. Could be the opening we've been waiting for."

I nod slowly, my gears turning. This has to be played just right. One misstep and he'll slither away again.

But if I can get the evidence we need...

"I want you leading point on this," Lynfield says. "You're my best agent for a job like this, Morello. If anyone can nail this bastard, it's you."

"I won't let you down," I say, meeting his gaze.

Lynfield claps my shoulder. "I know you won't, kid."

I close the file and tuck it under my arm, resolve steeling within me. This time, Gerald won't get away.

For his victims, and for all the lives he's destroyed, I'll bring him to justice.

No matter what it takes.

I take a deep breath as I step out of Lynfield's office, file in hand. Time to get to work.

I settle in at my desk, spreading out the contents of the file. Crime scene photos, witness statements, financial records. Piece by piece, the web around Gerald grows clearer.

I stare at his headshot again. Those cold eyes hiding behind an easy smile. Acting charming while he profits off innocence sold.

It makes my blood boil.

I think of the victims, mostly nameless faces in the reports.

The girls lured by false promises. The boys kidnapped from their homes. All just pawns to him.

My thoughts fly to my nieces and nephews, and what it might mean for them to be put in the same situation. It makes my blood run cold.

There are some sick fucks in this world with a penchant for vulnerable women and children, and as long as there's demand there will always be people like Gerald to ensure a continuous supply.

My jaw tightens as I pin his photo to the board. I'll find the thread that unravels this whole operation.

And I won't stop digging until every lead is exhausted, every stone overturned.

For now, Gerald still thinks he's untouchable. But that's about to change. I'll be the one to finally wipe that smug grin off his face. And when I bring him in, it'll be the end of the line. No more vanishing acts.

I crack my knuckles and get back to work, fueled by purpose. The long nights are coming, but it'll be worth it to show the world who Gerald Cranshaw really is. I won't stop until justice is served.

I sift through the files, searching for any thread I can pull. Bank statements, phone records, travel documents. I pore over them, piecing together a timeline.

Names and potential shell companies start to emerge, alleged fronts for Gerald's network. Suggesting money trails winding through jurisdictions, with many assets hidden under layers of obfuscation. It's hard to find definitive links or any actual proof.

But I'm patient, methodical. The picture slowly starts to come into focus.

As I study a cargo manifest, something catches my eye. A shipment to one of Gerald's warehouses from a port in Odessa. And listed in the contents—'agricultural equipment'. Gerald Cranshaw is no farmer. And my instincts tell me to dig deeper.

I pull up a case file on Anastasia and Bodahna Kerov. Two sisters, kidnapped from a village near Odessa before being smuggled abroad. My heart sinks as I put it together.

They were that 'equipment'.

Reading their statements, I'm struck by their courage. They survived hell but hadn't given up. That is, until their charred bodies were found a few miles out of the city in an abandoned warehouse.

They are no longer of any use to me, rest their souls, but if I can find others like them, they could blow this whole case open.

I feel a surge of determination. This isn't just about the job anymore. It's personal. I have to get the remaining women and children safely out of Gerald's reach. And prove to them there's still good left in this world.

I add pictures of Anastasia and Bodahna to the board. "I'm coming for you," I whisper to them. "Just hold on a little longer."

Outside my window, the skyline fades to black. But I barely notice as I delve back in, following this new lead. The night stretches long ahead, but I'm more motivated than ever.

For his victims, I won't stop.

Not until I take Gerald down.

Hours later, I'm still poring over the files, looking for any thread I can pull to unravel Gerald's network. My eyes burn from staring at pages until the words blur together. But I can't stop. Not when lives hang in the balance.

Rubbing my temples, I glance up at the board. At Anastasia and Bodahna's faces gazing back at me. They look so young, so full of hope. Hope shattered. We won't fail the others like we did them.

"We're closing in," I tell them, as if they're proxies for any of the other victims who might stand a chance. "Just stay strong," I add, more to myself than anyone.

A soft knock at my door makes me turn. My partner, Nina, steps in bearing two steaming mugs.

"Thought you could use a recharge," she says, offering me coffee.

I manage a weary smile as I take it. "You're a mind reader."

She surveys the organized chaos of my office. "Late night?"

"Yeah. I think I've found a real shot here, Nina. It's looking like Gerald Cranshaw recently brought over a woman who he's treating differently than the others. Word on the street is he's taking her as his wife and wants to get her hooked up in his trafficking operations given her connections to... certain countries with ample supply."

Nina nods, understanding my determination is personal. "You'll get him, Morello. But you have to take care of yourself, too. Otherwise, you'll burn out."

Her words resonate through the fog of fatigue and frustration enveloping me. She's right. I'm no good to anyone if I work myself to death over this.

I take a long sip of coffee, feeling its warmth flow through me.

"Thanks for looking out for me," I tell her. "And for the coffee. I'll try to get some rest soon."

Nina squeezes my shoulder, then heads out to begin her shift.

I stare after her, grateful. With people like her on my side, I can keep fighting.

For justice. For people like Anastasia and Bodahna.

Turning back to the board, I steel myself. The nights ahead will be long and hard. But I'll gather the evidence to take Gerald down while keeping whoever I can safe. I'll find a way. I just have to believe that hope can defeat fear.

Chapter 23

Morello

My eyes burn as I stare at the screen, the glow casting dark shadows across my furrowed brow. I click through file after file, searching for the one thread that could unravel Gerald's web. The office is silent except for the soft shuffle of papers and the rhythmic tapping of keys.

"Every piece of evidence gets me closer," I murmur, rubbing my temple. This case consumes my thoughts, even my dreams. I have to be meticulous, strategic—one misstep could destroy lives. No pressure. And today I just happen to have one very compelling lead.

The bell on the diner door announces my arrival. I slide into the cracked vinyl booth where the witness sits hunched over, his shoulders tense.

The man's eyes dart around the diner's dingy interior.

"Talk to me," I say, my voice low.

The witness leans in. "Gerald's like smoke, man. Just when you think you've cornered him, he slips away. Got eyes and ears everywhere."

I nod, my brow furrowed in thought. This snake of a man has eluded justice for too long, putting profits over people. Destroying lives. But I'm patient—I will trap Gerald in his web of lies.

For Anastasia. For Bodahna. For the voiceless victims who deserve protection.

Failure isn't an option.

The witness slides a flash drive across the table. "It's all here—the shell companies, money trails. His whole damn operation."

He glances around again before meeting my eyes.

"This could nail the bastard. But watch your back. Gerald doesn't like to lose."

I pocket the drive, my pulse quickening. This could be the break we need.

"I'll be careful. Gerald's not the only one with connections."

Driving back to the office, the weight of the case presses down on my shoulders. I know the stakes—this is more than a career-defining case. If I stumble, lives will be shattered, lost in Gerald's web.

All the girls under his thumb, counting on me for justice.

I can't fail them. Won't let them down.

I tighten my grip on the wheel. The city lights streaked by as I focus on the road ahead.

Gerald thinks he holds all the cards, that he can intimidate and manipulate his way out. But he underestimates my determination, and the power of the agency that sits firmly behind me, providing access to untold resources and manpower.

For the voiceless victims, I will bring Gerald's empire crashing down. Whatever it takes. I just need one thread to unravel it all.

And now, perhaps, I hold it in my hand, the flash drive heavy with promise.

"Your move, Gerald," I murmur into the darkness. "Let's see you slither out of this one."

I stride into the office, energized by the potential evidence in my pocket. I gather my team of analysts, their tired eyes lighting up when I reveal the drive.

"This could be it," I say, plugging it into my computer. "Let's see what Gerald's been hiding."

We dive into the data, sifting through files and financial records. My pulse quickens as more concrete information about the shell companies emerge, including transactions tying Gerald to trafficking rings in Eastern Europe. It's all there—money trails, communications, shipments.

"This ties him directly to the operations," an analyst said. "We have near solid proof."

I nod, a fierce joy rising within me. "We've almost got the bastard."

Tempering my excitement, I know the job isn't done. "We need to verify every piece of data. Gerald's lawyers will pounce on any loophole. Our case needs to be ironclad. And there are still humans involved... humans whose lives are still very much at risk."

We work through the night, fueled by coffee and determination. Building an airtight case against the most dangerous and connected man we've ever pursued.

As dawn breaks, I step outside for some air. Stretching my weary limbs, I notice a black car idling down the block. Before I can react, it speeds away into the early morning traffic.

A feeling of unease washes over me. Has Gerald already gotten wind of our investigation? Sent someone to monitor me?

Back at my desk, I find a plain manila envelope waiting for me. No return address. Just my name typed across it.

A chill runs through me and I'm suddenly extra grateful each incoming mail item is meticulously scanned for explosives and other dangerous materials.

Regardless, I still open it carefully.

Inside is a single photo—me and the informant from earlier, meeting at the diner. A clear threat.

My jaw tightens. So Gerald wants to play games. Intimidate me into backing off. I stare into the mirror on the wall.

"You think you can scare me away?" I say to my reflection, as if Gerald himself watches from the glass. "Too bad I don't spook that easy."

I tuck the photo back into the envelope. Gerald is getting desperate if he's resorting to such tactics.

And desperation makes him vulnerable.

"Keep watching from the shadows all you like," I whisper. "We're coming for you."

I return to work, my resolve now hardened into steel. Gerald has no idea who he's up against. I will see this through, no matter the cost.

For the voiceless victims, I will bring Gerald down or die trying.

I head to Lynfield's office, the envelope in hand. I know I have to inform my boss about Gerald's thinly-veiled threat.

Lynfield's face is grave as I explain the photo's significance.

"This changes things," he says. "Gerald's making it personal now. And it sounds like we should be on extra high alert for a leak."

I nod. "He's rattled. Which means we're getting close."

Lynfield sighs, leaning back in his chair. "Be careful, Morello. Cornered men get reckless." His concern is evident in the crease of his brow. "I don't want you taking unnecessary risks."

"I know how high the stakes are," I assure him. "But we can't let Gerald intimidate us into backing down. Too much is riding on this."

Lynfield regards me for a moment before nodding. "You're right. We proceed, but watch your back. Gerald won't go quietly."

I leave the office, Lynfield's warning echoing in my mind.

I stop by my desk, picking up another photo of Anastasia and Bodahna. Despite attempts to get them off my mind, they've taken up permanent residence. I know they won't leave my thoughts until justice is done. Their innocent smiles fortify my resolve.

I will see this through, for them and all of Gerald's other victims. The man is slippery, but not untouchable.

Justice will find him, no matter how long it takes.

"I'm coming for you," I whisper to the photo. A promise to Gerald, wherever he lurks. A promise to the families of those whose innocence he's stolen to satisfy his depravity and greed.

Fear and doubt try to creep in, but I shove them down. With care, I return the photo to the file on my desk. Back to work, one step at a time. Gerald's empire will crumble.

It's only a matter of time.

Chapter 24

ALINA

The shrill ring of the phone pierces the silence. I freeze, my pulse quickening. I already know who it is before I even glance at the caller ID.

I steel myself and answer.

"Privet, Alina," Luchenko growls, his gravelly voice dripping with false warmth. "I hope you're finding your new life to your liking."

My stomach twists. He's toying with me.

"What do you want?" I ask sharply. Don't show weakness.

I don't even bother to ask how he got this number. His access to resources is insane.

Luchenko chuckles. "No need for hostility, meelaya."

I shudder at this term of endearment that he insists on using despite my protests.

"I'm simply calling to remind you that I am Yara's father. I have every legal right to see her, as I'm sure you remember. The fact you got her out of the country is... displeasing."

The threat beneath his words makes my blood run cold. He has connections across the globe. If he wanted to take Yara, he could. There wouldn't be anything I could do to stop him. And he knows I know.

I clench the phone tightly, my knuckles white. "You will never lay a hand on her," I spit out through gritted teeth. "I'll die before I let you near her again."

"We shall see," he says softly. "You know you can't hide from me forever, dorogaya."

The line goes dead.

I lower the phone with a shaking hand. Luchenko's call has further shattered the fragile sense of security I've tried to build here... and that was already decimated by Gerald.

Luchenko is right—he has eyes everywhere. Nowhere is safe. Not from him. Not from Gerald, either.

My attempt to put us in a better situation now has us in the firing line of not just one formidable man, but two.

I glance over at Yara, listening to music contentedly on the living room couch. My heart constricts.

I have to protect her from both of them, no matter what it takes.

Chapter 25

ALINA

The cacophony of the crowded mall fades into white noise as I weave between displays of garish luxury, my eyes darting, my body coiled tight.

I'm a fox passing through the henhouse, wary of the pecking order. The other women shoppers eye me with thinly veiled disdain, their judgment searing into my back.

I'm in a designer outfit that Gerald had waiting for me in my wardrobe when I arrived here, but in my mind I'm in a worn cardigan and sensible shoes that scream imposter amidst their designer brands and socialite gossip.

I yearn to melt into the crowd, to camouflage myself among their carefree laughter and trivial concerns. PTA problems. Drama with local charity events.

But I know better. There's no real hiding for me here. I'm simply on borrowed time, my leash extended only so far.

The fact Gerald let me out on a shopping trip without a team of chaperones is a small miracle, but he seems particularly distracted by work lately.

I jumped at the chance to slip away, even if only for an hour or two.

A prickling on my neck turns my blood icy. I'm being watched. Is it one of Gerald's men, sent to monitor my activities? I turn slowly, my muscles tensed to bolt.

"Alina? Alina Petrov?"

My gaze collides with warm brown eyes set in a chiseled face. Caution floods my mind. I resist the urge to glance around for Gerald's goons. Perhaps this man is one, a new hire, sent to follow me around and report back.

The man closes the distance between us, his movements fluid yet non-threatening. He's playing this smart, not spooking the skittish target. Me.

"Got a minute to chat?" His voice is low, meant only for me. "I'm Agent Morello. FBI," he says, discreetly removing an item from his pocket and flashing it to me. It's a badge. And I'm no expert, other than what I've seen in the movies, but it looks legit.

I fight the questions rising in my throat. The middle of a crowded mall is no place for this conversation. But when will I get another chance?

I force myself to nod, despite every self-preservation instinct screaming otherwise.

Morello gestures to a quieter corridor off the main thoroughfare.

I follow on leaden feet, hyperaware of everything around me. The murmur of shoppers fades as we walk, replaced by the rapid buzz of my pulse in my ears.

Morello stops and turns to face me. His eyes are intense but kind, radiating a gentle concern that puts me on edge.

What's his angle here?

"I know you're in a tough spot, Alina," he begins, his voice pitched low. "I want to help get you out of this situation, if you'll let me."

My lips twist. "Help? From a cop?" I utter a harsh laugh. "Where I'm from, your kind don't help people like me. Unless there's something in it for you."

Morello's brow furrows. "I'm not like the police where you grew up, Alina. My only agenda is making sure you're safe."

I shake my head, bitterness welling up to coat my tongue. "Safe? You don't know the meaning. Men like you promise protection with one hand and demand payment with the other." My voice drops to a ragged whisper. "There's always a price."

Morello looks stricken. In another life, I might have felt bad.

But right now, I need to protect myself. From enemies seen and unseen.

No matter how kind the eyes watching me seem to be.

Morello's eyes darken, his mouth pressing into a thin line. For a moment, he looks every inch the imposing figure of authority I've learned to fear.

"I understand your skepticism," he says finally, a hard edge to his voice now. "You've been failed before by people meant to uphold justice. But not everyone is corrupt."

His words pluck a chord deep inside me. I want to believe him, want to grasp at the fragile hope he offers. But I know better.

"Maybe you're different," I reply slowly. "But I can't take that risk. Where I'm from, trust gets you killed."

I expect Morello to argue, to push his point. Instead, he nods, almost sadly.

"You're wise beyond your years, Alina," he says. "Forced to grow up too fast, like so many others are. I'm sorry the world has given you so many reasons to doubt."

His empathy catches me off guard. For a moment, we simply look at each other, separated by a gulf of experience.

In his eyes, I glimpse understanding, not judgment. It stirs an unwelcome feeling—a desire to close the distance between us. To allow someone to truly see me.

The urge terrifies me. I take a step back, steeling myself once more.

"I should go," I mutter. "He'll be looking for me soon."

Morello looks like he wants to object. But he simply nods again, handing me a card.

I briefly glance at it, noting the agency emblem.

"If you change your mind, call anytime. I meant what I said, Alina. I want to help you."

His fingers brush mine as I take the card. A spark shoots through me at the contact.

Wordlessly, I turn and disappear into the crowd, his gaze burning into my back.

I hurry through the crowded mall, Morello's card clutched in my hand.

My heart is racing, my thoughts a turbulent mess.

Part of me wants to trust him. He seems so different from the corrupt officials I've known—sincere, empathetic, willing to help without expecting anything in return.

But I know such men are rare, if they exist at all.

And even if Morello is one of the good ones, he doesn't understand the world I come from. A world where people with power use it only for themselves, where no one helps without wanting something.

I should throw this card away, forget I ever spoke to him.

It's too dangerous to get involved.

Gerald would kill us both if he found out.

Yet even as my head screams caution, my heart whispers hope.

What if Morello really can help me escape? He knew my name, he must know about Gerald and his dealings.

Maybe he has a plan.

I halt, closing my eyes. I see my mother's face, weary and resigned, telling me to keep my head down, not draw attention.

She tried to protect me from harm by remaining invisible.

But I don't want to be invisible anymore. I want my freedom. And Agent Morello represents my first real chance at getting it.

I open my eyes, my resolve hardening. I tuck the card securely into my pocket.

When I get back to the mansion, I'll hide it somewhere safe.

And when the time is right, I'll call.

My heart pounds as I make my way back to the mansion, Agent Morello's business card burning a hole in my pocket. I move swiftly through the expansive rooms, hyperaware of the cameras tracking my movements.

In Yara's suite, I scan for any hidden devices before carefully stashing the card in a slit cut into her mattress. Our only private space.

I sit on the edge of the massive four poster bed, my emotions swirling. Hope and fear tangle within me, but my desire for freedom emerges as the dominant force. I've not been here long, but I've already spent too much time under Gerald's thumb. Initially veiled as caring, his intimidation has shifted into blatant threats.

Running my fingers over the satin comforter, I allow myself to imagine a different life.

A small apartment filled with books and art that Yara and I would choose together.

Friends to share secrets and dreams with.

A guaranteed three meals a day.

No more jumpiness at sudden noises, no more living in terror of displeasing Gerald or Luchenko or any other man.

We don't need all the bells and whistles of a millionaire or billionaire lifestyle.

We just need safety, security and each other.

The image propels me to my feet. I go to the window overlooking the sculpted gardens. Somewhere out there, Morello is waiting to help, asking nothing in return.

I see now that trusting him is worth the risk.

Squaring my shoulders, I make a silent vow.

I will escape this place.

I will take back my life.

A tremulous smile tugs at my lips as I gaze out at the horizon.

With this unexpected new ally, maybe now I have a real chance.

Chapter 26

ALINA

The screen flickers to life, casting an eerie glow in the dark room. My breath catches as Luchenko's face appears, his steely eyes boring into mine.

"It's time to bring Yara home, Alina," his voice rumbles through the speakers, menacing yet calm. "You've had your silly little adventure."

My palms grow clammy, my heart hammering. I want to run but my feet feel rooted in place.

"I've already set legal wheels in motion," Luchenko continues, ice in his tone. "You can't hide from the law, Alina."

I shiver at his confidence—how far does his influence reach?

I'm trapped, caged like an animal.

This fancy room now just another prison.

Can I trust Agent Morello? A spark of hope flickers but then darkens with doubt. The law has never helped me before.

And now I'm going up against two powerful, dangerous men instead of one.

No, I can't risk it. Better to rely on myself, use my wits against Gerald and his guards, and Luchenko and his henchmen.

I will be a lioness protecting my cub.

I don't need outside help that could just make things worse and might end up fucking me over anyway like all men inevitably do.

Especially law enforcement.

I gaze out the window, my jaw set with determination. *No matter what, Yara, I'll keep you safe.*

I just need time to plan.

Luchenko and his goons won't take my daughter—not if I have any say in it.

My mind races as I pace the plush carpet. I'm trapped between two dangerous men—Gerald with his charm and cunning, and Luchenko with his cold ruthlessness. Both present grave threats to me and Yara.

It's hard to know where to start, and how to navigate to avoid either man having their way and destroying our lives even more than they already have.

Gerald's threat feels more immediate, lurking within these mansion walls. I shiver, recalling his subtle touches and veiled threats designed to keep me under his control.

Luchenko's threat has at least come from a distance, through legal channels I don't quite understand. But I know he could wield the law like a weapon, his influence spreading like a dark web.

My thoughts turn again to Agent Morello. He seemed sincere, offering help despite my initial resistance.

I remember the warmth in his brown eyes.

But was it real? Gerald's eyes seemed warm at first, too.

"He's still a cop," I mutter under my breath. I know better than most not to blindly trust law enforcement.

The police back home are easily bought, their laws bent to serve the powerful. Am I naïve enough to believe it's really any different here?

Still, contacting Morello might buy me some time.

Gerald's wrath if he finds out I've gone behind his back terrifies me, but I have to take risks for Yara's sake.

I take a deep breath, steadying my nerves. I'll need to be cunning as a fox circling this den of lions. Perhaps I can exploit the cracks within Gerald's empire, seeking allies among those harboring silent resentments after years of serving his cruel regime.

It's a dangerous game, and I'll need to proceed with utmost caution, using my wits to discern friend from foe. A wrong move could be disastrous. But at this point, I really have no choice.

"Hang on Yara," I whisper. "I'll outsmart them all for you. We'll be free, I promise."

I picture the various servants I encounter day to day. There's Clara, the elderly housekeeper whose weary eyes betray her fatigue at maintaining perfection for Gerald's estate.

And Diego, the groundskeeper who keeps mostly to himself but whose sullen looks reveal his discontent.

They, and others like them, could prove to be valuable allies if I'm able to gain their trust.

But I'll have to be quick, and go up against loyalties that for some go back years, even decades.

I guess I could start small, subtly probing for hints of disloyalty through seemingly innocuous conversations.

Over time, I could then ascertain who might be willing to discretely provide information or other forms of aid.

It's a dangerous game of strategy, requiring patience and perceptiveness.

Patience that perhaps we can't afford.

But for Yara, I'll take the risk.

As I gaze out the window into the night, I feel the weight of trepidation in my heart.

But I'm also reminded of my own fierceness—the fortitude of a mother protecting her child.

"You'll never cage this bird," I whisper defiantly into the darkness.

I will stay cunning, outmaneuvering the lions.

And one day, Yara and I will breathe the air of true freedom.

Chapter 27

ALINA

The marble floors are like ice beneath my bare feet as I hurry down the hallway, clutching Yara's hand tightly in mine.

My heart pounds in my chest, an ominous drumbeat keeping time with each click of my heels.

I can feel Gerald's gaze tracking us, his presence permeating the mansion like a toxic cloud.

Yara's steps drag beside me, her usual exuberance diminished to a timid shuffle.

She keeps her eyes downcast, focused on each footfall, sensing the unease that thickens the air.

I give her hand a reassuring squeeze, wishing I could whisk away the dread that hangs over us.

Rounding the corner, we nearly collide with Gerald's imposing frame, his smile slick like an oil spill.

"Just the ladies I was looking for," he says, blocking our path. "I have a little treat planned for our Yara today."

He reaches out to ruffle Yara's hair but she flinches away, pressing into my side.

My instincts scream danger. This is a trap, I'm sure of it, but I force myself to remain calm.

"Oh, how thoughtful of you, Gerald, but I'm afraid Yara isn't feeling well today." I affect a casual tone despite my pounding pulse. "Maybe another time would be better."

Gerald's eyes flash with irritation before his charming façade clicks back into place. "Of course. Her health comes first."

His smile doesn't reach his eyes.

I nod, nudging Yara forward down the hall, eager to escape.

We've avoided the trap for now, but my relief is short-lived. Gerald's web is woven too tightly around us, and we must break free soon, before his patience runs out.

For now, Yara is safe. I cling to that, whispering a prayer of thanks as we disappear into the cavernous mansion.

My relief at evading Gerald's sinister plans for Yara today is fleeting.

As soon as we're behind closed doors, the enormity of our predicament presses down.

Gerald's web ensnares us more each day, his volatile temper growing ever shorter.

I know we can't delay our escape much longer, but acting rashly could provoke Gerald's wrath and seal our fate.

I mull over how to proceed, wanting desperately to flee, yet cautious of making a fatal misstep.

In a private moment, I pull Yara close, my heart aching at the fear in my daughter's eyes. "No matter what happens, little one, we have each other. Don't ever forget that."

Yara nods, her lip quivering. I smooth back her hair, wishing I could shield her from all of this, but knowing escape is our only hope.

We cling to each other as the light fades, finding strength in our bond. I whisper fierce promises, vowing we will soon be free of Gerald's twisted games. For now, we can only bide our time, trusting our love will see us through.

I notice the subtle and more obvious signs that Gerald's suspicion is growing.

The staff whisper in corners, casting furtive glances my way.

I catch fleeting glimpses of guards stationed just out of sight, confirming my instinct that both Yara and I are being watched more closely than ever.

Gerald's charming façade remains intact most of the time, especially around company, but his eyes follow my every move, calculating and cold. I tread carefully, communicating only in hushed tones when Yara and I are certain we have a moment of privacy.

Our plans for escape must be kept secret, shared through whispers. I hate that Yara must learn this wariness so young, but it's necessary for our survival.

The night we intend to flee arrives. As we sneak through the mansion, our bags packed and pulses racing, my heart sinks. In the shadows near our planned escape route lurk Gerald's men.

I realize with dread that Gerald has us under surveillance far beyond what I realized. Aborting our attempt is painful, but clearly the risks are too great now. Especially when I think back to what happened last time I tried to escape.

Defeated, we return to our opulent cage. I pull a weeping Yara close, making a silent vow. "We will find another way, my little sun. Have faith."

Though freedom slips through our grasp tonight, our determination is undimmed.

We cling to hope through the darkness, two survivors against the odds, unwilling to surrender.

We just might need a hand.

Chapter 28

MORELLO

My phone buzzes in my pocket. I glance at the screen, my brow furrowing. A message from Alina's daughter, Yara.

My gut twists.

This can't be good.

I read her plea for help, anger simmering in my veins.

That bastard Gerald has gone too far this time.

My jaw tightens. I'll get them out of this, no matter what it takes.

But I have to be smart. Gerald is dangerous. One wrong move could make this whole thing blow up.

I type out a reply.

Morello: Thank you for reaching out, Yara. I'm here for you both. We'll figure this out. Delete this message and your other ones as soon as you get this, and sit tight.

Alina

I hum tunelessly as I tidy Yara's room. I scoop up a pile of clothes, revealing Yara's phone underneath, only ever not attached to her when she's taking a shower or asleep. The screen lights up with a new message.

My blood runs cold as I recognize the number from the card handed to me just the other day. A text from Agent Morello? No. It couldn't be. This isn't happening.

"Yara!" I shout, storming into the bathroom where steam swirls around the room. "What the hell is this?"

I brandish the phone, hands shaking with anger. Yara peeks her head around the shower curtain and pales as she sees the object in my hand.

"I can explain—"

"Explain? How could you do this?" My voice breaks.

Fear, disbelief and rage battle within me. I trusted her. We discussed never keeping secrets. And yet, here she is, risking everything by texting with this man we don't even know we can trust.

"I had to!" Yara yells, turning the shower off and grabbing the fluffy towel on the top of the shower casing to wrap around herself. "I won't let you let Gerald hurt us anymore!"

I reel like I've been slapped. *Let* Gerald hurt us? Is that what Yara thinks? That I'm letting this happen?

"Yara, no, I would neve—" I reached for my daughter's hand.

Yara yanks it away. "Don't touch me! I don't know who you are anymore!"

The words pierce my heart. What have I become?

I sink to the couch, head in my hands.

Yara is right. I've failed my daughter. Again.

"I'm so sorry," I whisper. "You're right. I've made awful choices, especially when it comes to men. But no more."

I meet Yara's eyes, fierce determination in my gaze.

"I hear you. We'll let Morello help. No matter what it takes, I'll get us out of this."

Yara stares back, her eyes glistening. Then she rushes into my arms. We hold each other tight, both trembling.

The road ahead is uncertain, but we'll walk it together. And we can deal with the blame and resentment later.

I stroke her hair, my heart breaking. How could I have let things get this bad? Yara is my whole world, yet I've exposed her to danger again and again.

No more. It ends now.

I cup Yara's face, wiping away her tears. "I promise you, I will fix this. Gerald will never lay a hand on you, and neither will Luchenko."

She searches my eyes, looking so young and vulnerable. "How can you stop him? He's too strong. Both of them are. And do you think that Morello is really strong enough to stop either one of them?"

Rage flares in me, white-hot. A twelve-year-old shouldn't have to worry about such things.

Nobody should.

I picture Gerald's smug face and want to smash it in. My hand twitches with the urge to slap, to punish...

No! I catch myself, horrified. What am I thinking?

I take a shaky breath. "Violence won't solve this. But we will find a way, together."

Yara nods, but I see the doubt in her eyes. I don't blame my daughter for losing faith. I've failed her too many times.

But not this time. I'll prove myself worthy of her trust.

Gently, I tilt her chin up. "I know I've made mistakes, my butterfly. All I can do is promise to protect you now. Can you believe in me one more time?"

Yara hesitates. Then, slowly, she leans into her my embrace.

"I'll try, Mama," she whispers.

I kiss the top of her head, a bittersweet ache in my heart. It's a start. This time, I will not fail my little girl.

I hold Yara for a long moment, taking comfort in the familiar scent of my daughter's hair. I know this reprieve is only temporary. We're safe for this very moment in this palatial mansion, locked away in a bedroom. But soon we'll have to face the bleak reality of our situation.

But I push those thoughts away, determined to savor this moment. Right now, it's just the two of us. Mother and daughter. A sacred bond that no one can break.

Finally she pulls back, her expression serious. "What will we do about Mr. Agent Morello? If Gerald finds out..."

I nod grimly. Yara has acted rashly, contacting Morello behind my back. But we're out of options and I can't blame her in the slightest.

She did what I wasn't brave enough to do.

"We'll meet with him. Discreetly," I say. "He has the most chance of being able to help us get away safely."

A spark of hope flickers across Yara's face. Then hesitation. "But what if—"

I squeeze her hand. "No more 'what ifs,' my love," I say. "I'll handle Gerald. You just stay strong for me. Can you do that?"

After a moment, Yara lifts her chin. "I can."

Pride swells in my chest. When did my little girl grow so brave? I pull Yara close again, cherishing the trust between us.

"Then we're going to make it," I whisper. "I promise you, Yara. We're going to be free."

Chapter 29

ALINA

The crystal chandelier glints coldly above the long mahogany table, failing to impart any warmth to the cavernous dining room. I keep my gaze fixed on my plate, hyperaware of Gerald's eyes boring into me from across the table.

"You both seem...distracted lately," he says, shattering the silence. "Anything you'd like to share?"

I force a smile, willing my voice to remain steady. "Just the usual. Nothing out of the ordinary." The lie tastes bitter on my tongue.

My pulse races, knowing his growing suspicion only spells more danger.

"Loyalty is so rare these days," Gerald muses over his steak tartare, feigning a casual tone. "Especially when the future is at stake."

The underlying threat in his words makes my stomach churn. He's fishing for information, suggesting he knows more than he's letting on.

I clutch Yara's hand under the table, squeezing it for reassurance. She's the only thing that matters.

I have to protect her, no matter the cost.

Gerald's gaze bores into me, as sharp and menacing as a dagger. Beneath the table, my legs tremble.

But I refuse to show weakness. He won't see me sweat.

Yara and I are trapped in his web of deception and manipulation. But I swore to myself, we will find a way out.

His charming threats don't own us. And I'll be damned if I let him hurt my daughter.

I nod, pretending to focus on the wilted salad on my plate as my mind races.

Yara and I are under constant surveillance here. Gerald's mansion is less a home than a cage. A pretty cage, but a cage nonetheless.

As soon as dinner ends, I pulled Yara aside, whispering urgently, "He's watching us. Even more closely than before. He knows something is up, so we have to be extra careful."

Her eyes widen in fear. We both know the implications—our every move is being monitored.

The realization of the extent of his surveillance chills me to the core. His net is closing, and before long not even Morello will be able to help us.

The next morning, Gerald corners me alone. His charm barely conceals the steel in his gaze.

"Like we've discussed before, I think it's time you took on more responsibilities around here," he suggests smoothly. "It would be unfortunate if I had to...re-evaluate your role due to lack of cooperation."

The threat beneath his words is crystal clear. Comply, or suffer the consequences.

"And Yara is such a bright girl," he adds. "It would be a shame if her education was disrupted and she had to go into... full-time work. But cooperation ensures her future."

The mention of Yara's name makes my blood run cold.

I confront him, feigning calm despite my racing pulse. "What do you want from us? Clearly you're upset about something. Why this sudden interest in loyalty?"

"It's not sudden, Alina," he replies coolly. "Just more...immediate. I expect your full cooperation. That's all."

His true intentions are laid bare. Submit and obey, or he'll make us suffer. Trapped in his twisted games, I seethe with anger and fear.

But I won't let him hurt Yara. She's all that matters.

My thoughts race as I consider the full extent of the peril we're in. Gerald's charming veneer hides the monster within, a man who will stop at nothing to control us completely.

A man who has proven over and over again to be petty and malicious and vindictive.

Someone who is extremely dangerous not to have on your side.

Fear for Yara's safety wars with anger at my own helplessness. We're well and truly trapped, like prey caught in the jaws of a predator.

But I'm a survivor above all else, and my mama bear instincts are kicking in. I won't surrender without a fight.

Cautiously, I continue preparing for any chance to slip free of Gerald's clutches even with the members of his extensive security detail eyeing us like hawks.

My planning is subtle, my actions discreet, as I attempt to shield the highly perceptive Yara from the harsh reality facing us.

Each small act of defiance fuels my resolve. I'll continue to endure whatever is necessary to keep Yara safe.

Tonight, holding her close, I whisper fierce promises into the darkness.

"He doesn't own us. No matter what threats he makes, we'll find a way out. I'll protect you, always."

It's a vow of both motherly protection and steadfast resistance.

Gerald's manipulations only strengthen my commitment to securing our freedom. It's time to meet with Agent Morello.

Before it's too late.

Chapter 30

ALINA

The stillness of the pond belies the storm brewing between us.

Ducks glide across the glassy surface, oblivious to the gravity of our conversation.

Morello's brown eyes bore into mine, and there's a depth to them I hadn't noticed before. I was too distracted to notice that he's incredibly hot... in an FBI agent kind of way.

"I want you to know that helping you and Yara is my priority. Taking down Gerald comes second."

I fight the urge to roll my eyes. Men and their empty promises.

Yet something in his unwavering gaze gives me pause. Could he be different?

"I look forward to learning more about you, you know. You're a very interesting person," he says, a playful glint softening the intensity of his focus.

I laugh, the sound hollow. "It takes a lot of trauma to become interesting. I'm not sure I'd do it all over again given the chance."

He leans in, his deep voice gentle yet firm. "Nobody asks for the cards they're dealt. It's what you do with them that counts."

"What are you, a motivational speaker?" I scoff. "Because that's corny as fuck."

He chuckles, undeterred. "Hey, it's true. Life is what you make of it."

Something in his lighthearted persistence cracks my skepticism. I glance away, pensive.

"But sometimes life throws stuff at you that you can't come back from."

"Yet here you are," he says softly, turning my chin to meet his gaze again.

I want to pull away, but find myself transfixed. In his eyes I see understanding, respect.

Slowly, I nod. "Yes...here I am."

The space between us crackles with newfound connection. Partnership. Possibility. I feel a glimmer of something I'd long given up on.

Hope.

Morello's eyes hold mine a moment longer before he leans back, exhaling slowly.

The charged atmosphere dissipates as he shifts back into agent mode.

"Alright, time to get down to business. We need to strategize how to get solid evidence against Gerald without exposing you and Yara to unnecessary risk."

I nod, my thoughts refocusing. "Agreed. What do you suggest?"

He steeples his fingers, his brow furrowed in concentration. "I'll keep tracking his movements, look for patterns we can exploit. In the meantime, see if you can get access to his phone or computer—even a few texts or emails could give us leverage."

"Easier said than done," I sigh. "He keeps that phone glued to him and has his men's eyes on me constantly. I could only get away today because I made an excuse about a gynecologist appointment. But I'll try."

"Good. And document anything suspicious he does or says, no matter how small. We need an airtight case."

I chew my lip anxiously. "This could get dangerous fast if he catches on. I need to know Yara will be protected, whatever happens to me."

Morello meets my eyes, resolute. "You have my word—I'll do whatever it takes to keep you both safe."

I search his face and see only fierce determination. Slowly, I exhale, allowing myself to trust.

"Okay then. Let's take this bastard down."

Morello grins. "That's what I like to hear."

We hash out a few more details, then stand to leave. As we walk back through the quiet park, I feel a new sense of purpose.

With Morello by my side, I finally have hope—for justice, and—a strange thought crosses my mind—maybe something more.

We reach the park entrance and pause, the weight of our task lingering between us. Morello turns to me, his eyes full of warmth and understanding.

"It won't be easy, but we've got this, Alina. Together. One step at a time."

I manage a small smile, comforted by his reassurance. "One step at a time."

He squeezes my shoulder gently.

The simple touch sends a spark through me.

I meet his gaze, seeing my own tentative longing reflected back.

Slowly, reluctantly, we step apart.

But as I walk to my car, I feel Morello's eyes on me.

I turn back. He lifts his hand in a silent wave, his lips quirked in a half-smile.

My heart flutters.

With everything at stake, I hardly dare acknowledge the attraction growing between us.

But in that lingering glance, I see a future where we might explore this connection without fear. A future that, with Morello's help, I finally dare believe could be possible.

I drive away with hope for freedom, for justice, and maybe even for love.

The road ahead is uncertain, but now there is renewed hope. And that makes all the difference.

Chapter 31

ALINA

I glance around the dimly-lit corridor, my pulse drumming in my ears. As far as Gerald's concerned, we're on a school trip, an overnight stay at the children's museum.

I even drove us to the school in case his goons were following us, lugging in sleeping bags and other items on the list the teachers had prepared.

But, under the guise of darkness, we made our excuses with the school, feigning Yara's fear at having to spend the night away from her precious creature comforts.

Now, we're far away in a covert location with the one man who could possibly save us.

The shadows seem to creep and curl around us as we huddle together, their smothering darkness both shielding us and heightening the tension coiled in my muscles.

Yara's voice trembles slightly as she asks, "Will it really be like the movies, Mr. Agent Morello?"

He smiles, the gesture warm and reassuring on his usually serious face. "Better. Because we're writing our own ending, kiddo."

I can't help the swell of affection as I watch Morello's interaction with my daughter. He's so gentle, so patient with her questions. It's a side I never expected to see from the intense agent.

"We've got one shot at this." Morello's voice hardens, expression somber once more. "Everything's got to go just right."

His finger traces an invisible path on his phone's screen, mapping out the route we must take to escape Gerald's far-reaching grasp. Adrenaline surges through me, equal parts fear and anticipation. We're in this together now, bonded by our shared mission.

I meet Morello's gaze, reading the promise there. He'll keep us safe or die trying.

Something powerful passes between us in that loaded moment, speaking of possibilities beyond this dark night.

Morello's hand brushes against mine as he points out the last checkpoint, a jolt of electricity sparking at the contact.

"We'll get through this," he says softly, holding my gaze. I nod, my throat tightening with hope tinged with an unexpected attraction.

He leans back, the hint of a playful smile teasing his lips as he launches into an animated retelling of a past escapade. Yara's eyes widen, a delighted laugh escaping her as Morello regales us with the daring tale.

The sound of my daughter's laughter in this dim, tense space is like a ray of light piercing the darkness. I can't help but join in, the genuineness of my smile startling after so long spent locked in fear.

For a fleeting moment, we are simply three friends sharing a story, the danger ahead forgotten.

As we sober, the weight of our task settles once more. But we stand together now, bonded.

Morello's eyes burn with quiet ferocity as he swears, "I will protect you both, no matter what comes. You have my word.

His vow resonates through me. While Yara is preoccupied with a game on her phone, I find a private moment, needing him to know what this means.

"Thank you," I whisper, "for giving me hope again. For giving me the strength to fight back."

We stand so close. It would be so easy to close the distance... but Yara's approach startles us apart, the spell broken.

Disappointment wars with relief inside me at the interruption.

But this isn't the time or place to explore the pull between us. Escape comes first.

The night envelops us like a cloak as we make our final preparations, concealed from watchful eyes.

We speak in hushed tones, reviewing the plan, synchronizing each minute.

No detail is too small—our window to slip these chains will be narrow.

Yara checks her backpack one last time, nerves and excitement playing across her face. She glances at me, doubt flickering in her eyes. "Will we really make it, Mama?"

I squeeze her hand, pushing down my own uncertainties. "We will. I promise."

Morello finishes loading the truck, every movement precise and purposeful. He turns to us, resolve etched on his features. "It's time."

As we walk to the truck, Morello and I share a loaded look. One that speaks of trust, of possibility. Of a future neither of us dared hope for until now.

My heart is heavy with the perilous road ahead, but lighter knowing I won't walk it alone.

I watch Morello drive away, Yara sleeping soundly beside me.

I gently wake her and we head back to the mansion while it's still dark outside, navigating by the school to gather our sleepover items and making apologies for our early departure the previous evening.

Dawn will fully break soon, and with it, our bid for freedom. I close my eyes, allowing myself to imagine the life that could be waiting on the other side of this darkness. A life unbound by fear, filled with light—and maybe even love.

Chapter 32

ALINA

The diamond chandelier glints coldly as Gerald strides through the cavernous foyer, his polished Oxfords clicking sharply on the marble floor. I freeze as his icy gaze fixes on me. Oh god, what have I done now to enrage the beast?

"Care to explain this?" His voice is lethally soft as he holds up the business card between two fingers.

My heart stutters. Morello's card. How could I have been so careless?

"Oh, that?"

I force an airy laugh as my mind scrambles to come up with a plausible, acceptable reason I would have this in my possession.

"Yara probably picked it up at the immigration office. You know how kids are, collecting little souvenirs everywhere they go."

Gerald's eyes narrow, but his smile remains, like a snake baring its fangs. He steps closer, backing me against the paneled wall. The scent of his spicy cologne overwhelms me.

"Don't take me for a fool, Alina," he murmurs, his breath hot on my cheek. "You've been making some very interesting...connections."

I meet his gaze evenly, refusing to show weakness. "I don't know what you mean."

His hand shoots out, gripping my jaw. "It would be a shame if you lost your place here."

I wrench away, heart hammering. He wants to control me, but I won't break.

Gerald's smile widened. "Changes are coming, Alina. I expect your full cooperation. Yara's livelihood is counting on it."

There is no warmth in those once-kind eyes. Only threats and dark promises.

Alone in our room, I gather Yara in my arms, holding her tight as fear and determination war within me.

"We won't let him win," I whisper, stroking her hair.

I will keep her safe, whatever it takes.

Yara clings to me, her body trembling. My brave girl. Gerald has no idea of the strength in this small heart.

"I'm scared, Mama." Her voice is muffled against my shoulder.

"I know, my love. But we're together."

I kiss the top of her head.

"Remember what Agent Morello said? There are good people who want to help us."

At the mention of Morello, Yara looks up, her eyes shining with fragile hope.

My own hopes rest on him now too. His card, though it raised Gerald's suspicions, reminds me we aren't alone.

As the mansion settled into uneasy sleep, I lay awake plotting our escape.

The risks are greater than ever, but so is my determination. I will outmaneuver Gerald.

Moonlight filters through the curtains as I gaze at Yara's sleeping form. My brave, beautiful girl. I will set her free. For real this time.

"Whatever it takes," I whisper. As long as we're together, there is hope.

Yara's breath slows to the steady rhythm of sleep. I gently brush a stray curl from her face, my heart swelling with love and fear. She looks so small and vulnerable in the massive four-poster bed.

I have to be strong for her. Strong enough to defy Gerald and escape this gilded prison.

Quietly, I creep to the window and peer out at the moonlit grounds below. The mansion is eerily still, the only movement the swaying of trees in the night breeze.

Somewhere out there, Morello waits. I cling to the belief that he can help us get away safely.

But I can't rely solely on him. When the opening comes, I have to be ready.

My mind races, calculating risks, plotting diversions. Gerald's men are everywhere, vigilant. Slipping away unnoticed will take luck and nerve.

I glance back at Yara, looking so tiny amid the brocade pillows. My heart constricts. No risk is too great to protect my child.

"Sleep well, little one," I murmur. "This will all be over soon."

I will not let Gerald extinguish the light in those bright eyes. The love swelling in my heart hardens into steely resolve. We will be free.

Chapter 33

ALINA

The night air is cool against my skin as I step outside, the moonlight casting an eerie glow across the mansion grounds. I shiver, though not from the chill.

My heart pounds as I make my way toward the shadows of the garden, nerves and anticipation churning inside me.

This clandestine meeting with Morello feels dangerous, forbidden. And it is.

But I can't resist the magnetic pull I feel toward him, this man who has shown me both tenderness and strength when I needed it most.

I both long for and fear what might pass between us in the secrecy of the night.

"Alina," his voice comes, low and smooth as velvet. I turn to find him emerging from the darkness, his tall frame backlit by the moon.

My breath catches at the intensity in his eyes.

He moves toward me, tilting my chin up with a gentle finger until our gazes locked.

"You don't need to be afraid of me," he murmurs. "I told you, we're in this together now."

My lips part, but no words come out.

His face is so close to mine, his earthy, masculine scent enveloping my senses.

I want to melt against him, to trust in the sincerity of his words. But the specters of my past hold me back, whispering warnings of betrayal.

Sensing my hesitation, Morello trails his fingers down my neck in a feather-light caress.

"Let me prove it to you," he whispers before his mouth claims mine in a searing kiss.

My reservations burn away in the heat of his passion, my body coming alive under his touch.

For this one perfect moment, the darkness doesn't seem so threatening after all.

When we finally break apart, I'm breathless.

Morello's eyes search mine, his strong hands still cradling my face.

"Alina..." he begins, but I silence him with a shake of my head.

"We shouldn't have done that," I say, my voice unsteady.

As much as my body sings from his kiss, my mind is awhirl with doubt.

We have far more pressing concerns than exploring this dangerous attraction.

Morello nods, his jaw tightening. "You're right. This isn't the time. I'm sorry."

He releases me and stepped back, his face becoming an unreadable mask.

I immediately miss his warmth, but try to ignore the pang in my chest. There are more lives at stake here than just ours.

We turn our focus back to finalizing the escape plans, speaking in hushed tones as we check our supplies and go over the route again.

Morello is all business once more, but I can't stop replaying the kiss in my mind. I've kissed my fair share of men, but I've never felt anything like that before.

But is it real, or just another manipulation from a man claiming to want to help me?

"We need to move," Morello says abruptly, snapping me from my thoughts.

His eyes dart around warily before coming to rest on mine. In them I see understanding and regret.

This is not the time to analyze what passed between us.

All that matters now is getting through this night.

I take a deep breath and give him a single, sharp nod.

We've made our leap of faith. Now it's time to see where we land.

The night is still around us as we stood poised to make our escape.

A heavy fog has rolled in, muffling any sounds and making the darkened mansion look eerie and unfamiliar.

Taking advantage of a well-timed shift change, I slip back inside and take Yara by the hand, her small form bundled in every layer possible.

I put a finger to my lips, reminding her to be quiet, and we find Morello waiting in place.

Morello's hand finds mine in the darkness, his warm, calloused fingers intertwining with my own. I glance at him in surprise.

"For luck," he murmurs.

Despite my doubts, I don't pull away. We stay that way, hands clasped, as we slip through the side door and out into the murky night.

The fog swirls around us as we hurry across the grounds, making our way toward the hidden section of fencing Morello had scouted out days before. My heart pounded, my senses hyper-alert. Each shadow looks like a lurking threat.

I stumble on an uneven patch of ground and Morello's grip tightens, keeping me on my feet. We're in this together now, our fates interlinked, for better or worse.

Somehow, we make it to the fence undetected. Morello gives me a boost over the top and I land lightly on the other side, my breath loud in my ears. He hoists Yara over soon after, and I carefully lower her to the uneven ground.

A moment later, he's beside us again.

We pause, glancing back at the dark silhouette of the mansion one last time. Then Morello takes my hand again, his eyes meeting mine.

"Let's go," he says. And together, we melt into the fog and the night beyond.

For a moment, I inhale the sweet scent of freedom.

But, true to form, this feeling is very short-lived.

The gunshots pierce the silence like thunder. My heart leaps into my throat as Yara's hand slips from mine.

"Get down!" Morello tackles us to the ground, shielding our bodies with his.

My breath comes in panicked gasps. We were so close to freedom just seconds ago.

More shots ring out, bullets spraying the dirt around us.

Yara whimpers, her small frame trembling against me, and the sound just about destroys me.

"Stay with me, baby," I whisper.

Morello's eyes scan the tree line, his jaw set. "We need to move, now!"

He hauls me to my feet, keeping low as he drags us toward the brush.

Adrenaline pulses through me.

I grab onto Yara, holding her hand tight, for a split second wishing she was younger and smaller so I could just scoop her up and carry her.

Just a little further. We can make it if we just keep moving.

Suddenly Yara cries out. I glance down to see blood blooming on her shirt.

"No!" My scream is raw and primal. I stumble, nearly dropping her.

Morello whirls back and notices the scarlet hue, stark against the bright yellow of her shirt. His face drains of color.

"Go!" he shouts. "Get her out of here!"

I clutch Yara close as more shots explode around us.

We dive behind a boulder.

She's still breathing, but her eyelids flutter.

"Stay with me, baby," I beg, applying pressure to the wound. "Mommy's here."

Footsteps crunch on the gravel.

I look up to see Morello standing over us, gun drawn. He fires at unseen assailants.

"I'll take her and you run!"

He hauls me to my feet.

"I'll cover you!"

I blink back tears as I hand Yara to him. Our eyes meet, saying everything words cannot.

Then I'm running alone into the shadows, my baby's fading cries echoing after me.

It's agony, counterintuitive to a mother's love.

But I plan on being a distraction.

I crash through the underbrush, thorns tearing at my clothes and skin.

My breath saws in and out of my lungs. Behind me, gunshots still crack through the night air.

I have to keep going. I can lead them away, buy Morello and Yara time to escape.

Suddenly, a dark shape lunges from the bushes.

Hands grab my arms, yanking me to an abrupt stop.

I struggle wildly, but another man appears and helps subdue me.

"We got her!" one of them shouts.

Floodlights switch on, blinding me.

I hear a car door open, followed by steady footsteps on the gravel.

Blinking, I make out a tall, slender figure approaching. Moonlight glints off his sleek hair.

Gerald.

He smiles coldly. "Did you really think you could escape me, Alina?"

I thrash against my captors' grip. "Let me go, you bastard!"

Gerald's expression hardens. He backhands me across the face.

Pain explodes through my cheek.

"Such language," he tuts. "I expected better from you."

He leans in close. The subtle notes of his cologne make my stomach turn.

"Now, why don't you tell me where you've hidden Yara?" he rasps, a drop of his saliva landing on my cheek. "Be reasonable, and no one else has to get hurt."

I spit in his face.

He jerks back, his eyes flashing.

"Go to hell!" I yell hoarsely.

Gerald straightens his tie and shrugs. "Okay, have it your way."

He nods to the men restraining me.

One of them backhands me, just as I hear a familiar voice scream, "Leave me alone!"

My stomach drops further and my blood runs cold.

I hear footsteps stomping through the brush, and moments later Yara is dragged into the open.

There's no sign of Morello.

Gerald opens the car door. "Take her," he says, gesturing toward Yara.

"No!" I cry. "I'm coming too!"

"Nope, that's where you're wrong," says Gerald. "You've been nothing but a thorn in my side, and now I get to have a little fun. You see, it's clear to me that your daughter is your kryptonite. So I'm going to take her away from you. And you truly will have nothing."

Blood runs cold in my veins as I watch Yara be bundled into the car.

"I'm so sorry," I cry out as the door is slammed and the vehicle begins to move away.

One of Gerald's remaining goons approaches me and jabs a needle into my neck.

The world spins. Darkness creeps into my vision. As I sink into unconsciousness, my only thought is of Yara.

I'm so sorry, baby girl. Mommy failed you.

Chapter 34

ALINA

Before

I shield Yara behind me, my body trembling as Luchenko's men surround us in the alley.

His cold eyes bore into mine while he approaches and strokes Yara's hair.

She whimpers, shrinking away from his touch.

"Finally kotyonok." He reaches back out and takes hold of her chin, tipping it upward so he can see into her eyes. "Ah yes, we have the same eyes, you and me."

But he's only partially right. Their eyes may both be the same mesmerizing blue, so vibrant it's almost disarming, but while his are cold and ruthless, hers are wide with fear.

"Don't call her that," I hiss through clenched teeth.

My stomach churns, fury and fear twisting inside me. He has no right to speak to my daughter with such familiarity.

He does many things that bother me—murder, human trafficking, drug and arms smuggling—but his overfamiliar use of terms of endearment for my daughter are what makes me insane.

Luchenko's lip curls. "She's only alive because of me. Her talents are wasted with you."

I know he's trying to rile me up, and as much as I try to calm myself, it's working. Judging from the look on his face, he's going to keep going until I snap.

He continues. "In fact, I'm surprised she lived this long... you can barely keep yourself alive, let another human being. If I wasn't here to collect her, I'm sure it would only be a matter of time until child protective services came to pick her up."

Yara's eyes flicker between us, showing a combination of confusion and hurt.

"Don't listen to him, baby!" I cry. "He's only trying to upset us both."

He cocks a brow. "Your mother is an idiot."

"You don't know what you're talking about. You are just a DNA supplier. You will never be her father."

"Well, you are a whore." He pauses, locking eyes with my daughter. "Yara, she told me she wished you'd died in the womb."

I spit in his face.

His hand cracks across my cheek in a blaze of pain before I can react.

My head whips sideways, my hair flying. The slap echoes down the alley.

I bite my tongue to choke back a cry, refusing to show weakness.

Luchenko grabs my chin, his manicured fingernails digging in. "You both belong to me, whore. Never forget that."

I jerk my head away. "I don't belong to anyone, especially not you. And neither does she."

But my stinging cheek betrays me, my hand pressed over it.

Luchenko chuckles. "Still living in fantasy land? You're mine. Always have been."

His hungry gaze rakes over me, and then turns to Yara.

"And I've come to collect what's due. Whether you decide to be stubborn or not, it's your choice. I can leave you here. But the girl is coming with me."

I glare at him. My defiance is only emboldening him further. I know he enjoys it when I fight. So I need to change tacks. "What about your wife?"

"Marie?" He shrugs. "She serves her purpose. It's a transactional arrangement at this point. She lives her life and I live mine. You know this, Alina. Why is it so hard for your little pea brain to comprehend?"

Despite his condescending tone, his eyes undress me as if my visible discomfort only excites him more.

I flush, my stomach knotting with unwanted heat.

I hate that he knows my body so intimately. That I'd even enjoyed his touch once.

His eyes feel like extensions of other parts of his body as they trail over me, and I shiver.

How could I ever let somebody so evil, so depraved, touch me? He's old enough to be my grandfather. I never wanted this life.

But Luchenko and my father had an "arrangement."

And then there was Yara.

And by then I was trapped, destined for a life intertwined with this madman's.

I failed her then. But not today.

Today we escape him for good.

I steel myself, meeting Luchenko's icy gaze. "You took my innocence. Robbed me of a future. But Yara is my redemption."

Luchenko sneers. "Still clinging to hope, little dove? There's no escaping your fate. And, in case you didn't realize it, it takes two to tango. Fathers have rights too, you know. Especially with lawyers like mine, and a system designed to protect the patriarchy. You're screwed if you think you're going to pull the 'poor single mother, woe is me' card. The moment I snap my fingers, I'll have full custody."

He moves closer, backing me against the brick wall. I press back in an attempt to shrink into myself, willing myself not to tremble as my blood simultaneously boils. His breath grazes my ear, and I shudder, the little hairs on my neck standing to attention.

"We could be a family, Alina. Doesn't our daughter deserve that?" He smirks, knowing his words will infuriate me.

Revulsion rises in my throat. "Yara deserves better than you."

Luchenko's eyes flash. His fist slams into the wall beside my head. I flinch despite myself.

"Watch yourself," he growls. "You're forgetting who you're dealing with."

My heart hammers, but I lift my chin, defiant. "No. For the first time, I see you extremely clearly."

His mouth twists in a cruel smile. "Brave words, Alina. But they won't save you."

He grabs my wrist, bruisingly tight. I struggle in vain as he drags me down the alley toward a waiting car.

I won't let it end like this.

Yara is my chance for redemption.

And I won't fail her again.

Chapter 35

MORELLO

The pre-dawn air is thick with tension as I peer through night vision goggles, surveying the shadowy perimeter of the airfield. My heart pounds with adrenaline and determination. This is it—the moment we've planned for. Failure is not an option.

I glance over at Kane, his jaw set with focus, his eyes scanning for any sign of movement. Beyond him is Cole, her face obscured by tactical gear, exuding coiled power like a panther waiting to strike.

My team is ready.

Lives depend on our success.

And not just any lives.

I spot headlights cutting through the darkness—the SUV carrying Yara.

My chest tightens, imagining her fear. I have to reach her first. It's been three long days, and this is our one shot to get her out safely before she's whisked overseas to goodness knows where.

Kane tenses, anticipating my signal.

The SUV rolls to a stop, surrounded by armed silhouettes.

I steady my breathing, pushing down the rage I feel for the monsters who have chosen to terrify a child and steal her from her loving mother. Not yet. Wait for it...

"Now!" I hiss.

Kane explodes into motion, sprinting towards the SUV. Gunfire erupts, shattering the night's calm.

Adrenaline floods my veins as I charge forward, focused only on my goal. Bullets whizz past, but none will stop me. I have a job to do.

I reach the SUV and wrench open the door. Yara stares at me wide-eyed, shaking with fear and relief.

"I've got you, you're safe," I say gently.

Her small hand grips mine like a lifeline as I scoop her into my arms.

Kane lies down covering fire as we sprint for safety, the promise of a new sunrise guiding our escape.

I cradle Yara close as we race towards the tree line, the sounds of gunfire and shouts fading behind us.

Her small body trembles against mine, her breath coming in panicked gasps.

"Shhh, just keep your eyes on me," I murmur. "We're almost there."

I can see the clearing up ahead where our extraction team waits.

Kane and Cole flank us on either side, their weapons raised, ready to eliminate any threat.

We break through the tree cover and I nearly collapse in relief at the sight of the idling chopper. The pilot spots us and begins spinning up the rotors.

I hurry Yara into the helicopter's cabin, shielding her body with mine until we're safely inside.

Kane and Cole pile in after us and we lift off just as our pursuers emerge from the trees, firing futilely at the rising aircraft.

Yara buries her face in my shoulder, finally releasing the tears she's bravely held back until now.

I stroke her hair, my heart swelling with gratitude and purpose.

"Let it out, little one. You're safe. You'll be back with your mama soon."

She's endured a nightmare, but we've snatched her back from the brink. I vow then that no matter what comes next, I will keep her—and Alina —far from harm's reach. This is only the beginning.

Alina

I pace the safehouse floor, weariness and worry etched in every line of my body. I've been waiting for hours since Morello left on his dangerous mission to intercept Yara's transport. Endless scenarios of everything that could go wrong plague my thoughts.

Finally, I hear the distant drone of helicopter blades. I rush outside just as the black speck grows larger, its shape becoming distinct as it approaches.

Relief floods my veins at the sight, followed quickly by a wave of apprehension. Just because someone is approaching doesn't mean it's Yara.

And even if she is in there, she could be injured, or... I can't bear to think the worst...

The chopper touches down and the doors slide open.

Part of me wants to cover my eyes and have someone provide a recap when it's all over, but my motherly instincts overwhelm me.

Instead, I put my selfish fears aside and run toward the aircraft.

Morello emerges first, Yara bundled protectively in his muscular arms.

My breath catches at the sight of her, disheveled but unharmed.

I surge forward as Morello sets Yara down, sweeping her into a fierce embrace.

"You're safe, you're here. My sweet Yara," I murmur, tears spilling down my cheeks.

Yara clings to me, her thin body wracked with sobs. Thank god her wound was superficial, patched up by Gerald's men and then checked on by the FBI medic in the rescue chopper.

After long moments, I lift my head to meet Morello's gaze.

My gratitude wars with lingering mistrust, causing my mouth to tremble as my eyes fill with tears.

It's hard to find the right words in this situation. "You saved her," I say simply.

Morello nods, his expression serious. "I made you a promise."

His actions prove his words were true, yet doubt still nags at me.

I can't afford to let my guard down, no matter what grand gestures he made. He was just doing his job, after all, and even though it felt incredibly personal to me, perhaps for him it was just another day at the office.

Yara tugs at my hand, pulling me from my thoughts.

There will be time later to unravel Morello's motives. For now, I push aside my questions and focus on the precious girl before me. She's tired, but doesn't seem to have any physical injuries. Although I'm sure this whole ordeal has left just another layer of psychological scarring that will take many years to unravel.

Back at the safehouse, we retreat to Yara's room and I lay with her, holding her in my arms.

Before long, she snores softly, the weight of the day's events lifting from her as she lays securely ensconced in the comforting cocoon of a dream about more pleasant things.

Later, while Yara sleeps, I join Morello in the safehouse kitchen. He motions for me not to make a noise, and I listen intently as he debriefs the operation, clinical and precise in his details.

He trusts me enough to listen, and overhearing the conversation allows me to fill in some of the gaps. Gerald is an even worse man than I thought, with a complete disregard for human life.

And Morello clearly went out on a limb to save Yara the way he did.

When he finishes, I shake my head in wonder. "I don't know how to repay you for what you've done."

Morello's eyes glint with purpose. "It's not over yet. But I swear to you, I'll do everything in my power to keep you both from harm."

His words spark the tiniest flicker of hope in my heart. But only time will tell if he's worthy of my full trust.

I'm well and truly done with rushing things when it comes to men.

For now, I take comfort in Yara's safety and the promise of tomorrow.

I study Morello's face, searching for any hint of deception. But his eyes hold only sincerity and determination.

"We're not out of the woods yet," he says gravely. "Both Luchenko and Gerald's reaches are long. Neither of them will give up so easily."

He gazes at me, his eyes kind.

"But I think you know that."

I suppress a shudder at the mention of the two men's names.

Even half a world away, the shadow of Luchenko's menace hangs over us.

And Gerald, of course, is much, much closer.

"What happens now?" I ask quietly.

Morello's jaw tightens. "Now we stay vigilant. My team will continue monitoring for threats. I'll keep you updated on any developments."

He hesitates, then reaches out to squeeze my hand. "But you have my word, I won't let anything happen to you or Yara. No matter what comes next, I'll protect you both."

His rough palm against mine kindles a warmth deep inside. But fear keeps me from embracing the feeling.

"I wish I could believe that," I whisper.

Morello tilts my chin up to meet his gaze. "Have faith in me, Alina. I know it won't be easy, but I mean what I say."

Looking into his eyes, I feel the first cracks form in the walls around my heart. I want to trust this man, consequences be damned. But the shadows of the past lurk close, and, after all, it was only recently I placed trust in a man that led to this very situation.

With a shaky breath, I manage a small nod. I know he wants more, but it's all I can offer for now.

Perhaps, in time, that will change, and I'll have more of myself to give.

Morello

I feel like a hypocrite. Moments after promising Alina that I'll keep her and her daughter safe, I'm forced to renege on my promise and put them both back directly in harm's way.

I feel ill at the thought of breaking the news. But the alternative, in Alina's eyes, would be much worse.

"We tried to get a warrant to storm his place, but the higher-ups aren't signing off on it. We're going to have to do things differently."

"So you're going to go against your superiors? Won't that get you in trouble?"

"I mean, theoretically. I could face disciplinary action for an intentional protocol breach. But I'm not going to just let you sit there in danger for however long, and I know you are terrified of being deported back to Luchenko. All of that aside, my main priority is taking the action necessary to eliminate Gerald as a threat from your and Yara's lives, and that means taking decisive action. So here we are."

"So what do you have in mind?"

"We need to poke the bear. To raise the stakes."

"That sounds dangerous."

"Well, yes. It is. But unfortunately, it's the only way I think we're going to get him at his most vulnerable. With the limited resources available to me, to us, we can't storm the mansion as we ordinarily would. He has a large team, a solid infrastructure with more weapons than he could ever need. That would be too dangerous."

"So the plan is..?"

"We're going to use you as bait. Unfortunately, we may need to include Yara as well. But one thing is for sure—Gerald, in all his twisted ways—seems to have some type of sick obsession with you. In the timeframe we have available, having you lure him out into the open where we can actually get at him seems like the only option."

Her face twists into a frown, her eyes a window into her mind that mulls over the risks involved.

I feel sick for even asking her, but I know there's no other option.

"What if he... becomes violent? What if he tries to hurt Yara?"

"I'll have some men who I trust with me. We're under-resourced but I won't be completely without backup. We'll have arrangements in place to ensure the appropriate action can be taken if anything gets out of hand."

Her eyes grow large. "You mean—"

I put up a hand to silence her. "The less you know, the better. I've told you too much already."

She takes a deep breath. "Well, this sounds like our only option. And I'm sick of being out of choices. So I'm going to choose to do this. I'm trusting what you're saying—that doesn't mean I trust *you*—and it does seem to be the only way to escape Gerald without going back home, which I'm not prepared to do."

"Are you sure?" I ask, quirking a brow. "You're going to have to be braver and stronger than you've ever been, to get through this. And I think you can do it, but you need to believe it as well."

Alina's gaze meets mine and she nods, determination burning fiercely in her emerald eyes.

She throws her shoulders back as if steeling herself for war. "I'm ready to go. Anything for my daughter."

Chapter 36

MORELLO

The sun dips below the horizon, shadows pooling around the dilapidated warehouse like blood.

I crouch behind a rusted shipping container, my heartbeat thundering in my ears. Not from fear—I don't feel fear in situations like this anymore.

No, this is anticipation.

The hunt.

Through a gap in the metal, I glimpse Gerald standing over Alina and Yara, a smug grin twisting his lips as he toys with them with a gun in his hand.

Bile rises in my throat.

The moment Alina lured him out to the meeting spot, of course Gerald flew into a jealous rage.

"Where have you been?", "How dare you stay away from me?", "You stupid bitch! I'll kill you and your daughter if you ever leave my sight again" were all heard over the radio.

It was almost unbearable, listening to his harsh words and the fear in their voices.

The situation continued to escalate, Gerald's fury only intensifying, when he forced them to move to another location at gunpoint to, in his words, 'teach them a lesson'.

I hate that we had to put them in harm's way once again, into the clutches of an unhinged man with nearly unlimited resources. A man who truly believes they both belong to him. Because in his world of trafficking and misogyny, women are merely possessions that can be traded and discarded on a whim. A profitable enterprise with an unlimited supply and an even more unlimited demand.

I remind myself that while they are currently very much in danger, it's not for long. And it's an unavoidable means to an end.

I check my weapon one last time and burst through the warehouse door.

"Let them go, Gerald," I growl. "This ends now."

Gerald's head snaps up, his eyes narrowing.

But he doesn't move, and he doesn't release his captives. The bastard is actually enjoying this.

"Well, well. If it isn't the gallant Agent Morello."

His smirk widens, showing his too-white teeth.

"Thank you for leaving your business card at my house. I've done a lot of research on you. Here to play hero? Trying to make up for all your past fuck-ups? There's quite an extensive list."

I keep my gun trained on the center of Gerald's forehead, ignoring the trembling in my arm.

If I need to shoot, I can't miss.

Won't miss.

"There's no playing here. It's over."

A mocking laugh. "You think so?"

Gerald grabs Yara's arm, yanking her in front of him as a shield.

"Is that what you said when you let little Debbie Frost die because your aim missed and struck her instead of her kidnapper?"

He glances down at Yara, as if unperturbed by the firearm I have trained on him.

"It would be a shame to repeat that mistake again, in front of Alina, wouldn't it?"

Panic surges through me, a million thoughts crashing through my mind.

He's right. I can't shoot, not with Yara so close, but if I don't—

I'm paralyzed by indecision as every piece of firearms and combat training I've ever received flies through my head. *Advance, retreat, de-escalate, eliminate the threat, protect human life, get approval, follow your instincts.* All of it makes sense, and none of it makes sense.

A sharp cry cuts through my spiraling thoughts.

I snap my gaze to Alina just in time to see her slam her elbow into Gerald's gut.

Gerald's breath whooshes out in a pained gasp and his grip slackens.

Yara wrenches free, scrambling away to Alina's side.

In that fraction of a second, I squeeze the trigger.

The shot echoes through the warehouse, impossibly loud.

Gerald crumples.

I find myself moving before I even realize it, crossing the space between them in three long strides.

I kick the gun from Gerald's limp hand and drop to my knees, feeling for a pulse.

Nothing.

Gerald is gone.

And the two women he's been terrorizing—the two women I had vowed to protect, no matter the cost—are finally, finally safe.

From him, at least.

I look up to meet Alina's gaze, and see my own bone-deep relief and something else reflected in her eyes. Something like gratitude, and maybe, just maybe, a spark of something more.

A smile tugs at my lips as the wail of sirens in the distance grew louder.

We've made it. All of us. Together.

The smile slips from my lips as a fiery bolt of pain lances through my side.

I glance down to see a growing crimson stain seeping across my shirt.

In the chaos, I hadn't even felt the impact of the bullet. Now it's making its presence known, and the icy fingers of shock are starting to creep in.

"You're hit!" Alina gasps.

She's at my side in an instant, her hands fluttering over the wound.

"Oh God, there's so much blood."

The panic in her voice snaps me out of my daze.

"It's okay," I say, fighting to keep my own voice steady. "The vest caught it."

I fumble for the Velcro straps of my Kevlar, peeling it back to reveal a deep wound along my ribcage, skirting the side of the vest.

"Not life-threatening, but it's going to need stitches. Probably a lot of them."

The words are an attempt to soothe myself as much as them, because there's more blood pumping out of me than any stitches could fix.

Judging from the expressions on both of their faces, they're not buying my words any more than I am.

Alina makes a small, distressed sound, and Yara whimpers beside her. Their terror is almost enough to make me wish the bullet had pierced something vital.

Almost.

I can't stand to be adding to their pain.

I reach out to squeeze Alina's hand, dredging up a reassuring smile even as my body grows cold and I find myself shaking uncontrollably.

"Like I said, I'm not going anywhere."

The wail of sirens grows louder, and then the warehouse is filled with chaos as the SWAT team swarms in.

Medics descend upon us, ushering me onto a gurney.

Through it all, Alina refuses to leave my side.

Her hand is a steady, comforting weight in mine until they load me into the ambulance.

As the doors slam shut, cutting off my view of her, a strange sensation blooms in my chest.

Not pain, for once, but something warm and almost pleasant.

Hope.

Moments later, the air vibrates with the sound of approaching helicopters and vehicles—the full FBI SWAT team descends upon the scene with overwhelming force.

They're safe for now at least.

And then everything fades to black.

Alina

Gradually, the chaos fades into relief, as the realization sinks in that the terror is finally over. We're finally safe. From Gerald, at least.

I hold Yara tight, tears of relief and residual fear mingling as I whisper, "We're safe, solnyshko. We're safe."

Yara nods against my shoulder, still trembling.

There's a spark of hope in my eyes as I gaze at Gerald's prone form being loaded into a body bag and wheeled away.

The monster who haunted our American nightmares is gone. We're battered and scarred, but we survived.

But then my heart leaps to my throat at the sight of Morello, a choked cry escaping me. Not him. Please, not him.

I watch helplessly as he's loaded onto a gurney and then into the nearby ambulance, blood seeping from the bullet wound in his abdomen.

After all he's done to save us, I can't lose him now. We can't lose him now.

I rush to his side as the SWAT medics descend upon us, their shouts fading into the background. His eyes flutter open, meeting mine for a brief moment.

The warmth I've come to cherish behind those serious eyes makes my breath catch.

Then his eyes close again and the medics take over, working swiftly to stabilize him.

I try to get closer, but they usher me away and ask me to give them space while they work.

"You have to save him!" I urge, grabbing one of the medics by the arm. I can't stem the panic in my voice. "Please, he can't die!"

The medic gives me a grim look, then focuses on the task at hand. "Ma'am, please. We can't have you hovering right here."

I frown and step back, helpless, as they prepare to move him.

Yara comes up beside me, slipping her hand into mine and squeezing tight.

I cling to her, and it's my turn now to draw strength from her presence.

"Can we ride with him?" I ask, addressing the lead medic. "Please, we have to be there when he wakes up."

After a brief hesitation, he nods. We climb in after the stretcher, the doors slamming behind us

The ambulance lurches into motion, sirens blaring, as we speed through the gathering dusk.

I grasp Morello's hand, cold and limp in mine, blinking back tears.

"You have to make it," I whisper, as much to myself as to him. "You have to."

The uncertainty of his fate hangs over us, a dark cloud marring the relief of our escape.

All I can do is pray, as the ambulance races on through the deepening night.

Chapter 37

ALINA

The fluorescent lights flicker above me, a buzzing drone that echoes down the sterile hallway.

Each step feels heavy as I clutch Yara's small hand, her presence the only thing keeping the panic at bay.

The harsh beeps of monitors grow louder the closer we get to his room, my heart pounding in time with their incessant rhythm.

I peer through the window, my breath catching at the sight of Morello lying motionless amidst the web of tubes and wires.

Bandages wrap his broad torso, a stark white contrast to his deeply tanned skin.

Even now, under the harsh hospital lights, he radiates a rugged strength that makes my pulse quicken.

"He'll be okay, won't he Mama?" Yara's soft voice pulls me from my daze.

I squeeze her hand, willing my voice to remain steady. "Of course sweetie. He's a fighter."

Morello stirs as we enter the room, his eyelids fluttering. I perch on the edge of his bed, the warmth of his hand sending tingles up my arm.

"Hey tough guy," I whisper. "You really scared me back there."

His eyes meet mine, creased with pain but still intensely focused. With a gentle squeeze he conveys what words cannot, calming the storm inside me.

Yara hops up beside him, worry creasing her young face. "You'll get the bad guys, won't you Mr. Agent Morello? The ones that are still left?"

The corner of his mouth twitches in a hint of a smile.

"Don't you worry kiddo. I'm not going anywhere."

His voice comes out gravelly but resolute.

Relief washes over me as I study his rugged features, taking in every detail.

However vulnerable he may seem in this moment, I know his strength and determination will pull him through.

And I'll be right here, ready to explore what lies between us when he's back on his feet.

For now, just feeling his warmth and gazing into those soulful eyes is enough.

I take a deep breath, trying to steady my nerves as we sit in silence, the steady beep of the heart monitor punctuating the stillness.

Morello's eyes are closed now, his breathing slow and labored.

Yara fidgets next to me, too young to grasp the gravity of it all.

I brush her hair back gently. "Why don't you go get a snack from the vending machine down the hall? Get something for Mr. Agent Morello too for when he wakes up." I can't resist using her adorable name for him. It makes me smile every time I hear her say it, a hint of normalcy and levity amongst the dark storm.

She nods and skips out of the room, comforted by having a task.

Alone now, I scoot closer to Morello, keeping hold of his hand. With my free hand I trace the line of his jaw, rough with stubble, and then smooth back his dark hair from his forehead.

"You have to pull through this," I whisper. "We've been through too much for it to end here."

I think back on our journey, how standoffish I was when he first approached me, and then subsequently when he protected us and masterminded our escape from Gerald.

Slowly, his gruff exterior gave way to playful banter, then meaningful conversations late into the night after Yara fell asleep.

Somewhere along the way, his role transformed from information-seeker to bodyguard to confidant to something more. Something neither of us has dared speak aloud, but which simmers unspoken between us.

I lean in, brushing my lips lightly against his. They're dry and chapped, but the spark is undeniable.

"I'm not ready to say goodbye," I breathe.

His eyes flutter open to meet mine once more.

This time, his squeeze of my hand feels purposeful rather than reflexive.

He's not giving up this fight.

Or on us.

I exhale in relief as Morello's eyes focus on me, conveying a reassuring alertness despite his weakened state.

His lips part slightly, rasping out a barely audible "Alina..."

My name on his lips sends a shiver through me. I smooth his hair back again, needing the contact. "Shh...don't try to talk. Just rest."

His brows furrow in that familiar look of determination as he struggles to speak again.

"Are...are you okay? Is Yara okay?"

His concerns are not for his own condition, but checking on my wellbeing and my daughter's.

So like him.

I nod, blinking back tears. "I'm fine, thanks to you. That was too close of a call."

His eyes cloud with pain and regret. "I'm sorry...I should have..." His voice trails off in a fit of coughing.

I squeeze his hand firmly.

"No. You have nothing to apologize for. You've done so much for us already."

I lean in, speaking earnestly.

"Let me take care of you for once."

The corner of his mouth quirks up slightly. "Yes ma'am."

Relief floods through me at that glimpse of his humor returning. I study his face, this man who has come to mean so much to me, wanting to etch every detail into my memory.

"Get some rest," I say gently. "We'll talk more when you're stronger."

I smooth his hair back one last time as his eyes drift closed.

But our hands remain clasped together, speaking the words we cannot yet say.

I sit back in the chair beside Morello's hospital bed, watching the steady rise and fall of his chest as he rests.

My mind races with the events of the last 24 hours—the shootout, the terror of not knowing if he would survive, and the heart-stopping moment when he regained consciousness.

Under the harsh fluorescent lights, I study his face, taking in every cut and bruise. Evidence of his strength, and his sacrifice.

My heart aches, knowing how close I came to losing him before we even had a chance.

Guilt wells up inside me.

He took those bullets meant for me and Yara. Were it not for his protective instincts, his sense of duty, he wouldn't be lying here.

I know I have no right to ask more of him, to want more than his role as the agent assigned to gather information, to help us escape, and then to guard us.

But I can't deny what my heart knows to be true.

Somewhere along the way, my feelings for Morello have grown into something deeper. Something terrifying in its intensity.

In this quiet moment, I can no longer avoid the truth—I care for him in a way I haven't allowed myself to care for someone in a very long time.

Forget what I thought I felt for Gerald.

This is the real thing.

Maybe it's foolish, hoping for a future neither of us dared envision before.

But, brushing my fingers over his, feeling the warmth of his skin, I make a silent promise. I will stay by his side as long as it takes for him to recover.

And when he's well again, we'll have a chance to explore what lies between us. At our own pace.

Without the shadows of dangerous men breathing down our necks.

It won't be easy—the obstacles are many.

For one, Luchenko is still very much alive and obsessed with Yara. That's not just going to randomly change—he's her biological father, after all, and me hating that fact doesn't change it.

But I have hope. Here and now, with Morello, I feel a sense of home that has eluded me for so long.

And for the first time in years, I allow myself to believe that, even with all we've endured, somehow real, pure love can still find a way.

Chapter 38

MORELLO

The crackling fire fills the cozy cabin with warmth and light.

Shadows dance on the walls as I lay on the sofa, my torso wrapped in bandages. The pain is still there, but it's dulled to a persistent ache thanks to Alina's attentive care.

I watch her now as she heats a pot of stew, humming softly to herself. Her dark hair is pulled back in a messy bun, loose strands falling across her forehead.

She moves with easy grace, her full lips curved in a hint of a smile.

My heart stirs, an unfamiliar yearning rising within me. No one has shown me such care and compassion since...since my nonna when I was a boy.

Alina glances over, meeting my gaze. Her gorgeous emerald eyes soften. "How are you feeling?"

"Better," I say. "Thanks to you."

A blush blooms on her cheeks as she brings over a bowl of stew.

I struggle to sit up, wincing.

"Here, let me help." She sets the food aside and slides her arm around my back.

My breath catches at her touch.

Gently, she eases me up and arranges the pillows behind me.

Our faces are inches apart.

Her lips part slightly, and her gaze drops to my mouth.

Desire courses through me. I nearly give in to the magnetic pull between us.

But no, it's too soon. I don't want to take advantage of her kindness. And the last thing I want to do is scare her off which is apt to happen after all she and Yara have been through.

This is the time to take things slowly, and to let her take the lead. She'll come to me, if she wants to, when she's well and truly ready.

And I'm absolutely willing to wait.

Clearing my throat, I reach for the stew. "This smells amazing. You didn't have to go to so much trouble."

"It's no trouble." She tucks a lock of hair behind her ear. "I like taking care of you."

A lump forms in my throat. When was the last time someone had said that to me?

I take her hand, running my thumb over her knuckles.

"Thank you, Alina. For everything."

She smiles, giving my hand a squeeze. "We're in this together."

Together.

The word settles around me like a warm blanket.

With Alina by my side, I could face anything.

I savor the stew, the rich broth warming me from the inside out.

Alina watches me eat with a satisfied smile.

"This is incredible," I say between bites. "Where did you learn to cook like this?"

"My mother taught me."

Her expression turns wistful.

"Cooking was one of the only ways we got to spend time together. She worked so much..."

I set down the bowl, sensing there's more to the story. "You must miss her."

Alina nods, her eyes glistening. "Every day. I wish..."

She stops herself, shaking her head slightly.

"What is it?" I ask gently.

She hesitates before responding. "I wish she could have had an easier life. And not had to worry about me for so many years. And I wish that she could be here with us now. I feel so guilty leaving her."

My heart aches for Alina, and for the mother she had to leave behind.

I take her hand again, tracing circles on her skin with my thumb.

"It's not too late, you know. After all this, after we take down Luchenko and his men, you could try to bring her here. In the circumstances, you might even be able to get her application expedited through some refugee program."

Hope flickers in her eyes. "Do you really think so?"

"I do."

I bring her hand to my lips, brushing a soft kiss over her knuckles.

"You deserve to be happy, Alina. And your mother deserves to be safe with you and Yara."

She inhales sharply at the contact, her cheeks flushing. The air between us seems to crackle.

Slowly, she leans in, her eyes searching mine.

I meet her halfway, unable to resist any longer.

When our lips touch, sparks ignite within me. The kiss deepens, filled with longing and promise.

In this moment, the past and future fade away.

There is only Alina, her body pressed against mine, her fingers tangled in my hair.

We break apart, breathless.

She rests her forehead against mine, a smile playing on her lips.

No words are needed. The kiss said everything our hearts long to express.

Alina's eyes flutter open, still hazy with desire. I brush a strand of hair from her face, tucking it behind her ear.

"I've never felt this way before," she whispers. "Like I can finally breathe again."

Her candor emboldens me. "Me neither. Being here with you, it's like the world makes sense again."

She nuzzles against my chest, listening to the steady beat of my heart.

I hold her close, overcome with protectiveness. My wounds are healing nicely, and her weight against my chest no longer hurts. Breathing no longer hurts. I've even been able to get in a couple of jogs in the nearby woods as well as some weight training. There's nothing like a severe injury to make you appreciate how good it feels to be healthy and well.

After a moment, she peers up at me, a mischievous glint in her eyes. "Well, Agent Morello, now that you're feeling much better, I believe we have some training to do."

I chuckle, the mood shifting. "That we do."

Reluctantly, we untangle ourselves and head outside to begin our session.

The late afternoon sun filters through the trees as I show Alina basic self-defense techniques. She's a quick study, focused and determined.

We spar playfully, our bodies moving as one. With each grapple and block, our chemistry intensifies. I'm impressed by her skill but even more so by her spirit.

Underneath her poise is an indomitable will, a refusal to be anyone's victim ever again.

As the sun dips below the horizon, we halt our training, both flushed and panting.

Alina's tank top clings alluringly to her curves. I try not to stare but fail.

Noticing my distraction, she saunters over with a knowing look.

"Like what you see, Agent?" she asks, peering up at me through thick eyelashes.

I growl low in my throat, pulling her to me. "I'll show you what I like."

Our lips crash together once more as we lose ourselves in each other.

The rest of the world fades away, and all that matters is the passion that burns between us in this kiss.

I take a deep breath to steady myself as Alina pulls away, her cheeks adorably flushed. There's an unspoken understanding between us now. The chemistry we've tried to resist can no longer be denied.

There's a loud bang and the cabin door bursts open and Yara comes bounding out, oblivious to the charged moment she's interrupted.

"Morello, look!" She holds up a drawing proudly. "It's us escaping the bad guys!"

I smile as I take in the colorful scene—two figures that fairly accurately resemble Alina and I, holding Yara's hand as we flee an ominous shadowy shape.

I take the drawing from her to look at it more closely. This isn't just a child's drawing, this is the work of a budding artist. Impressive. "That's fantastic, Yara. You really captured the action. I had no idea you were such a talented artist."

Her face lights up at my praise. Despite our harrowing circumstances, Yara's resilience and optimism never cease to amaze me. She and others like her are the reason we fight so hard in my line of work—to protect the innocent and give them a chance at a better future.

As Yara chatters excitedly about her artwork, I notice Alina watching us, a tender expression on her face.

She reaches out and squeezes my shoulder, a silent message of understanding passing between us.

I cover her hand with mine, hoping she senses how much her support means to me.

With Alina by my side, I feel for the first time that we might actually succeed in taking down the remainder of Gerald's corrupt empire, as well as threats from further afield like Luchenko.

The touching moment is interrupted by the rumble of Yara's stomach.

We all laugh.

"I think that's our cue for dinner," Alina says warmly. "Who's up for spaghetti?"

Yara cheers and races up to her room to finish her homework and get ready for dinner, the aroma of simmering tomato sauce soon wafting from the kitchen.

Alina throws me a playful wink as she stirs the large pot on the stove.

I take a deep breath, inhaling the tangy scent of the woods mingled with homey smells of a meal being prepared.

It's all so normal, so right.

Hard to believe that just beyond these walls, a dangerous threat still lurks.

But I won't let that darken this moment. For now, we're safe, we're together...and that's enough.

Over dinner, we keep the conversation light, sharing funny stories and laughing more than we have in weeks.

Yara regales us with tales of her adventures in the forest, including befriending a family of rabbits and spotting a deer through the trees.

"Can we keep him, please?" she begs, her eyes round with hope.

Alina and I exchange amused looks. "I don't think your new friend would like living in the house," I say gently. "He needs to be free in the woods."

Alina smirks and looks at me. "Just don't turn your back for too long, or she'll have an entire animal sanctuary up in this safehouse."

Yara pouts briefly before perking up again. "Okay, but I'm gonna visit him every day!"

After we finish eating, Alina brings out the chocolate chip cookies she helped Yara bake earlier. The gooey sweetness is the perfect end to our meal.

"You can cook too?!" I exclaim, and Yara beams.

As we sit relaxing with our dessert, I feel a sense of peace and belonging that's eluded me for so long.

But the reprieve can't last forever. As much as I want to pretend otherwise, we still have difficult decisions to make.

Clearing my throat, I meet Alina's eyes, knowing she understands what has to come next.

"Yara, do you mind giving Alina and me a few minutes to talk?" I asked. "We need to discuss some...grown-up stuff."

Yara skips off happily to read in her room, and silence descends, broken only by the crackling fire.

Alina reaches for my hand, her gaze steady and resolute. "It's time, isn't it?"

I nod. "We can't stay hidden here much longer. If we're going to stop Luchenko for good, we need to make our move. You can't spend the rest of your life in hiding, on the run. That's no way to live."

Her fingers tighten around mine. "Just tell me the plan. I'm with you, whatever it takes."

I outline my strategy, aware of the risks it entails. But with Alina by my side, I know we can face the danger ahead...together.

I spread the maps and case files out on the table, the web of evidence Luchenko has woven over years of corruption and violence. Alina studies them intently, her brow furrowed in concentration as I walk her through the details.

"His American businesses are just a front," I explain, tapping one of the documents. "Covers for importing firearms and other illicit materials. Including women and young children. If we can get concrete proof of the illegal operations behind it, we can bring the whole American wing of his empire down."

It's sad to think Alina has been trapped now by two men who run sophisticated human trafficking operations. But, from experience, I know the industry is much more prevalent than people realize or prefer to think about.

Unending demand, unending supply.

She nods, her eyes blazing with purpose. "So we need to get inside his operations. Past his security, his men. It won't be easy."

"No, it won't," I agree. "But I have an informant on the inside, someone who can get us the evidence we need. He's taking a huge risk, and we'll need to move fast once he makes contact again."

I see the concern in her eyes, the unspoken fear that this unknown ally could betray us.

Gently, I squeeze her hand in reassurance. "We can trust him. He wants him stopped as much as we do."

Silence falls between us, the weight of what we face sinking in.

But as we sit together in the quiet cabin, I feel a sense of conviction I haven't known in years.

With her by my side, it's possible to believe we just might succeed.

Alina takes a deep breath, then meets my gaze unflinchingly. "When do we start?"

I smile. No matter what's coming, we'll face it together.

Side by side, two allies bound by trust and so much more.

Just like Gerald, Luchenko's days are numbered.

Justice will be served.

Chapter 39

MORELLO

The first rays of sun slice through the blinds, stirring me from sleep.

I blink, squinting against the intrusion of light.

The safe house is quiet, almost peaceful, a far cry from the chaos that drove us here.

I creep down the hall, following the aroma of freshly brewed coffee.

Alina stands at the stove, humming softly as she flips pancakes.

Yara sets the table with mismatched plates and utensils, beaming with pride at her contribution.

"Morning," I say. Alina's smile lights up the room. "Coffee?"

I nod, taking the warm mug she offers. The bitter liquid jolts me awake.

Yara bounds over and takes a seat beside me.

"Mr. Agent Morello, look!" She holds up the potted plant I gave her yesterday. A tiny green sprout pokes through the soil.

"It grew!" she squeals with excitement.

I nod. "It sure did. And with care and patience, it will grow strong," I say.

Her eyes shine with wonder.

I hope one day she'll see herself that way too—capable of flourishing even through adversity.

Alina watches us, an unreadable expression on her face. I meet her gaze. Something passes between us in that moment, an awareness I don't dare put words to.

Not yet.

Alina

I watch Morello and Yara huddled over the little plant, their heads bent together.

He's so gentle with her, patiently explaining how to help the fragile sprout grow.

His presence has brought light back into her eyes, as well as a sense of security I thought we'd both lost forever.

I retreat to the living room, emotions swirling within me. It's more than gratitude I feel for this man who saved us, who risked his own life and very nearly lost it to protect us.

He's restoring our faith that goodness still exists in this dark world.

That people like us, who life had battered and bruised, can still bloom again.

My heart aches at the thought of losing him, this unexpected source of hope and...something far deeper.

Footsteps sound behind me.

I turn to see Morello, concern creasing his brow.

"Everything okay?" he asks.

I nod, not trusting my voice.

He's so close I can see flecks of amber in his warm brown eyes.

I feel exposed under his gaze, as if he can read my unspoken thoughts.

"She's quite the little sprout herself," he says, glancing back toward the kitchen where Yara still tends to her plant.

"Thanks to you," I whisper.

He looks at me then, really looks.

And in that moment I know—he feels it too. This bond between us, new tendrils twining, seeking the light.

I reach for his hand, no longer content to leave things unspoken.

His fingers curl around mine, large, rough and tender all at once.

"Whatever comes next, we'll face it together," he says, both a vow and a promise.

I cling to his hand, my heart overflowing.

For the first time in forever, I believe it just might be true.

And it's only taken saving both of our lives, killing another man, and almost being killed himself to prove it.

I open my mouth to respond, but before I can form the words, Yara's excited shout rings out from the other room.

"Come quick, it's sprouting more now!"

Morello and I exchange a look, both reluctant to break the intimacy of the moment but eager to nurture Yara's joy.

Hand in hand, we make our way to the kitchen.

Yara stands on her tiptoes, peering intently into the potted plant.

"See, right there!" She pointed to a second tiny green shoot emerging from the dark soil.

"Well would you look at that," Morello says, bending down to inspect it. "That little guy really is determined to make his way into the light. Two new shoots in one day!"

I squeeze Morello's hand, understanding his metaphor. After so much darkness, here is solid proof that goodness can still grow.

Yara's delighted smile is like the sun breaking through clouds.

Later, as Yara waters her new sprouts, sure that they've both grown even more in the last hour or so, Morello pulls me aside. No words are needed. The look we exchange speaks volumes—of shared pain and second chances. Of a bond forged in fire, deeper than either of us could have expected.

Come what may, we'll face it together. We're now a team.

I nod, overcome with emotion and unable to conjure up just the right words. But then again, words aren't always needed.

There is still so much uncertainty ahead, but in this moment, I feel a sense of peace.

As the day goes on, our unlikely little family falls into an easy rhythm.

Yara chatters away as she tends to her plant.

Morello regales us with funny stories from his childhood.

I cook up a simple but hearty lunch, savoring the feeling of normalcy.

Laughter fills the cozy kitchen. For the first time in a long while, my smile comes easily and reaches my eyes.

Watching Yara and Morello together fills me with gratitude and contentment.

I know now that I'm falling for him—this brave, caring man who has brought light back into our lives.

When Yara finally heads up to her room to read and talk to her friends online, Morello and I retreat to the porch with mugs of hot tea.

We sit in comfortable silence as the sun dips low on the horizon, setting the sky ablaze in dazzling hues of orange and pink.

"It's beautiful," I whisper.

Morello reaches for my hand. "So are you," he says. "Extremely beautiful."

He tucks a lock of hair behind my hair with his other hand as he gazes down at me.

"And this is a beautiful new beginning," he adds softly.

I lace my fingers through his, a promise written in that simple touch.

As the sun slips below the trees, I rest my head on his shoulder.

The future is uncertain, but we'll face it hand in hand.

Chapter 40

ALINA

I ache for him, my every nerve ending on fire as I stare at the outline of Morello's hard length straining against his pants. I have to have him, need to taste him, to soothe the ache in my core that only he can fill.

In one swift motion, I drop to my knees before him, my hands shaking as I undo his belt buckle.

His cock springs free, thick and throbbing, his head already leaking in anticipation.

"Oh, fuck," Morello groans, his hands fisting in my hair as I take him into my mouth.

I moan around him, an overwhelming sense of power surging through me as I feel him shudder under my touch.

My tongue swirls around the head, savoring his salty, musky flavor.

Slowly, I slide him deeper into my mouth, my throat constricting around his girth.

I know I'm playing with fire, but the high stakes only turn me on more.

"Alina, baby," he groans, his voice a mix of pleasure and restraint. "Fuck, you're killing me."

He pauses.

"And I'm more than okay with dying this way. Holy fuck, you're good at that."

I look up at him through hooded lids, my mouth full of his cock, a naughty grin on my face.

This very real man, the formidable FBI agent Morello, reduced to moans and curses by my touch.

It's empowering and freeing, like nothing I've ever experienced before.

I bob my head faster, taking as much of him as I can, my tongue swirling around his shaft and teasing the sensitive spot just underneath the head.

"Oh my god, the throat. Yes," he rasps.

I love the way his fingers dig into the couch, as if he's battling for control.

I know deep down that he'd never hurt me, but the primal part of me thrills at the idea of him losing himself to my touch.

"Ah, fuck, Alina," he moans, his voice gritty with restraint. "You're gonna make me..."

That's all the encouragement I need, knowing his pleasure is completely within my control, and mine alone.

I suck harder, my moans vibrating around his length as I use my hands to massage his balls.

His cock twitches in my mouth, and with a roar he comes, spilling his release into my waiting mouth.

As I swallow, my core throbs with envy. I want him inside me, deep, to feel that power, that connection.

I stand up and straddle him, my wet core inches from his face. "Your turn, Agent Morello," I purr, running my nails down his chiseled abs.

Morello

My hands grip the couch as Alina straddles me, her wetness dripping onto my face.

Her scent fills my nostrils, intoxicating me as my cock still twitches from what has to be one of the most epic blowjobs I've ever received in my life.

I can't get enough of her.

As I lap at her pussy, her moans spur me on, pushing me to give her the release she so desperately needs.

Her nails dig into the leather of the couch, her body trembling above me.

"Oh fuck, Morello," she moans, her hips grinding against my face. "Don't stop. Right there."

I can feel her tensing, and I know she's close.

I redouble my efforts, my tongue plunging deeper inside her, and swirling around her clit.

"Yes! Oh God, yes!" she screams.

I chuckle, the vibrations shooting straight to her core. "Call me Vincent, . I want to hear you scream my name."

My tongue continues to dance over her sensitive spots, my fingers sliding inside her, teasing her, stretching her, preparing her for what's to come.

Alina's moans fill the air, mingling with the sounds of the city outside.

"Vincent," she moans, her voice shaking with need. "I'm close, I'm so close."

"That's it, Alina," I growl, my voice thick with arousal. "Let go for me."

Alina comes, her juices coating my face as she shudders above me.

I drink her in, every drop, relishing in her pleasure.

I love the way her body clenches around my tongue, the way her nails dig into my shoulders.

I'm lost in her, consumed by her.

I don't care that we're in danger, with the world crumbling around us.

All that matters is her.

As her moans subside, I look up at her, my face drenched in her essence.

Alina's chest heaves, her eyes hazy with lust.

"Damn," she breathes out, collapsing on the bed beside me.

I stand up, naked, my cock rock hard once again, and lead her to the bedroom.

"There's more," I growl.

With a groan of desire, I push her onto the bed and flip her onto her stomach, her hands pressed into the cool headboard.

She gasps, her ass in the air, her pussy glistening with desire.

Unable to resist, I once again bury my face between her legs, this time from behind.

She gasps as I slip my tongue into her entrance, almost sending her leaping off the bed.

She moans, loud and wanton, as I lick and tease her swollen bud from behind.

I lap up her juices, her taste addicting me like nothing else.

"Morello," she gasps, her nails digging into the sheets. "Vincent fucking Morello!"

With one last, hard flick of my tongue and a deep, steady thrust of my finger, Alina shatters, my name on her lips a keening cry of release.

Her entire body trembles as wave after wave of pleasure washes over her.

As her orgasm begins to subside, I reach forward and entangle my hand in her's hair, and she gasps as I pull her head back, exposing her delicate throat.

"You don't know the things I've thought about doing to you, bella," I growl.

My tone is rough with lust and need, and I notice her shiver involuntarily.

"Show me," she breathes.

I can tell that she's finally starting to trust me, even though she worries she shouldn't.

My body aches for her.

I want to protect her and fuck her brains out all at the same time.

My cock throbs for her.

Slowly, I insert one finger inside her, then another, stretching her as she moans.

"Morello," she groans, arching her back. "I need you."

I tease her entrance with my hard length, denying her the relief she so desperately craves.

She shivers at the sensation of my warm breath against her ear. "I've wanted you like this from the moment I saw you, Alina."

"And I've wanted you, Vincent," she pants as her breath recovers.

I almost lose myself at the sound of my name on her lips.

"You've got me, baby," I growl, lining up my cock with her wet entrance. "Tell me to fuck you."

"Fuck me, Vincent," she moans, her voice hoarse with need.

And I do.

I plunge into her from behind, deep and relentless, our bodies slapping together in rhythm.

I can feel her walls clench around me, her nails digging into the bed.

Alina, without knowing it, has become my lifeline, my salvation in this dark world.

Thoughts of our dangerous lives, of the FBI, the mafia, all of it melts away as I sink into her pussy, our bodies molding together like they were made for each other.

"Oh, God! I'm close again," she screams, her back arching.

My pace quickens, pounding into her, unwilling to let her go. "But I want to be on top. Now!"

She twists her head to look at me behind her, her emerald eyes filled with hunger.

"Alina, are you sure?"

"Never been surer," she breathes as I turn and lie on my back.

She lowers herself onto my thickness.

I fill her perfectly, stretching her as she clenches around me in ways I haven't felt in years, or maybe ever.

My hands grip her hips as I guide her movements, our bodies meeting in a symphony of moans and gasps.

Our union is fierce, hungry, as if each thrust stakes a claim, a promise.

It's as if we're soulmates, fated to collide despite the odds.

Alina, the woman with ties to two very dangerous, powerful men, and me, the FBI agent sworn to take both of them down.

In some ways, we should have been enemies, but our love is a force of nature, unstoppable, unyielding.

Alina

I can't believe this is happening.

Morello, of all people, the hottest FBI agent I've ever laid eyes on. The hottest *man* I've ever laid eyes on.

Our bodies are intertwined, moving in a rhythm that's equal parts desperate and electric.

His strong hands grip my hips, guiding me up and down as I ride him, my soaked pussy clenching around his thick shaft.

With each thrust, fireworks explode behind my closed eyes, and a deep moan escapes my lips.

"Yes, baby, take it all. You're so fucking wet," Morello groans, his voice a deep, commanding rumble that sent shivers down my spine.

His eyes, usually so guarded, are now full of raw lust and desire as they bore into mine.

The intensity of his gaze alone is just about enough to send me over the edge.

I lean forward, my breasts brushing against his muscular chest, and whisper in his ear, "I've dreamed about this for so long."

My breath is hot against his earlobe. It's the truth. As much as I tried to avoid it, to stay far away as possible because of his occupation, I spent countless nights fantasizing about this very moment, but I never thought it would actually happen.

Morello's hands slide up my thighs, his calloused fingers teasing my sensitive nipples, causing me to moan louder. "Oh, fuck, I can't get enough of you," he growls, his hips bucking upwards, meeting my thrusts with an urgency that matches my own.

Our bodies move together in a primal dance, our hips slapping together as we fuck against each other, our moans and gasps filling the dimly lit room.

This feels surreal. After being pursued relentlessly by powerful men with ulterior motives, I'm now here, in bed with someone I initially identified as the enemy.

But in this moment, none of that matters.

All that exists is the two of us, lost in a sea of lust and desire.

As the tension builds within me, my nails dig into Morello's biceps, my orgasm barreling towards me like a freight train. "I'm...I'm..." I pant, struggling to form words.

"That's it, baby, let go," Morello growls, his grip on my hips tightening as he hammers into me one final time. "God, Alina, you feel so fucking good. I can tell you're getting close. Now, I want you come apart for me. Come all over my cock, baby."

With those words, my world explodes into a shattered kaleidoscope of colors.

Cries of pleasure spill from my lips, my body shuddering around him as I come apart in his arms.

Morello isn't far behind, his own climax shaking his entire body as he growls out my name like a prayer on his lips.

As our breathing slows, we collapse onto the bed, tangled up in the sheets, our hearts pounding in unison.

I can feel the weight of Morello's muscular form pressing me down into the mattress, but I don't care.

In this precious, stolen moment, only we exist.

"I...I should go," I whisper, the reality of our situation seeping back in.

Without hesitation, Morello wraps his arms around my waist, pulling my body closer to his. "Stay, just till sunrise," he mutters, his voice gruff with emotion. "Don't go now, please."

And, for once in my life, I don't argue or run. I close my eyes, inhaling the scent of him as sleep slowly starts to claim me.

Tomorrow, the world could well come crashing down around us, but for now, we have this.

We lie tangled in each other's arms, our bodies spent, our hearts pounding. I nestle into his strong embrace, my fingers running idle patterns on his chiseled chest.

"What now?" I whisper, dreading the answer.

His grip tightens around me, as if he could keep the world at bay forever.

"I don't know," he admits, his voice gruff with emotion. "I just know I can't imagine my life without you in it anymore."

As my breathing slows, Morello pulls me back into his embrace, spooning my naked body against his.

"Shh," he soothes, running his fingers through my damp hair.

"It's just us now, Alina. Forget the world outside."

Chapter 41

ALINA

The stillness of the forest is shattered by the crack of gunfire. I jolt upright, adrenaline flooding my veins even before my brain registers the danger. Morello is already in motion, his hand on his holster, his eyes scanning for the threat.

"To the cellar, now!" His voice is tight, urgent.

I don't hesitate, grabbing Yara's hand and pulling her from the table. My only thought is getting her to safety.

We race for the cellar door as another shot splits the quiet morning air, closer this time.

Yara, startled, lets out a small cry, her fingers digging into mine.

"It's okay, I've got you," I say, my voice amazingly steady despite the jackhammering of my heart.

We reach the cellar and I usher Yara inside.

I take her face in my hands, looking into her wide, frightened eyes. "Stay here, no matter what you hear. I'll come back for you, I promise."

I secure the door, shutting out the light.

In the distance, I hear Morello's shouted commands mingling with the rap of gunfire.

I say a silent prayer he'll be okay and make my way upstairs, gripping the heavy iron fireplace poker.

If Morello needs me, I'll be there.

I'll do anything to protect my daughter, and the man who's kept us safe and freed us from Gerald.

I creep up the cellar stairs, the poker clenched in my sweaty palm.

My ears strain for any indication of how the confrontation outside is unfolding.

More shots ring out, closer and more rapid now. I freeze, willing my pounding heart to steady.

Was that a cry of pain? Morello's? Luchenko or one of his men? I can't tell.

Cautiously, I crack open the cellar door.

Morning light streams in, dust dancing incongruously in the sunbeams.

I slide through the opening, poker at the ready.

As I enter the kitchen, a figure suddenly fills the window, barreling toward the back door.

Morello.

He crashes through, slamming the door behind him. His shirt is torn, and his face smudged with dirt and blood. But his eyes are alert, flickering to me and then scanning the room for threats.

"We've got to move," he says tersely. "Luchenko's men flanked me. He'll be coming."

On cue, the front door splinters open.

Luchenko strides through, ruthless and scarred face set in a mask of cold rage.

He levels his gun at Morello.

"You just had to make this difficult," he hisses. "I tried to end it cleanly."

Morello raises his hands, shifting to place his body between me and the gun.

"It doesn't have to go down like this," he says evenly. "We can talk."

Luchenko lets out a sharp laugh. "The time for talking is done." His finger tightens on the trigger.

I react on pure instinct, adrenaline surging through me.

With a guttural cry, I charge forward, swinging the poker with all my strength.

It connects with Luchenko's wrist with a sickening crack.

His shot goes wild, the gun falling from his grasp.

Before he can recover, I swing again, striking the side of his head.

He collapses heavily.

Morello blinks at me in shock. "Remind me not to make you angry," he says, giving me a wry, relieved grin.

Morello moves quickly, securing Luchenko's hands behind his back with a zip tie.

Luchenko lets out a low groan, starting to stir back to consciousness.

I stand over him, the poker still gripped tightly in my hands. The adrenaline is fading, leaving me shaky and lightheaded.

Morello puts a steadying hand on my shoulder. "It's okay. You can let go now."

I release a long breath, setting the poker down.

My hands tremble.

I acted on pure instinct to protect Morello.

But seeing Luchenko lying there, knowing I'm capable of that violence, leaves me deeply unsettled.

Morello seems to sense my distress.

"You did what you had to do," he says gently. "It's not in your nature to hurt without reason. Don't doubt yourself."

I nod, though his words only partially reassure me.

I know he's right—I'd had no choice.

But it doesn't change the fact that I nearly killed a man today.

The biological father of my child.

"I should check on Yara," I say, needing to see my daughter safe. Needing that reminder of why I had fought so hard.

Morello inclines his head in understanding. "I'll keep watch on our friend here until back-up arrives."

As I descend into the cellar, Yara flies into my arms. "Mama! Are you okay?"

I hold her tight, stroking her hair. "I'm okay, baby. Everything is going to be okay now."

And saying those words to her, feeling the warmth and weight of her in my arms, I start to believe them.

What matters isn't how close I'd come to the edge today.

It's that my daughter is safe. We are free.

I nod slowly as I try to process everything that had just happened.

The violence, the fear, the desperation—it all feels surreal now in the dim quiet of the cellar.

Yara looks up at me, her eyes wide. "Is the bad man gone? Mr. Luchenko?"

"He's not going to hurt us anymore," I say, smoothing back her hair.

I don't want to frighten her with the details.

"The police are coming to take him away."

"Good," she says fiercely, and I have to smile at her courage. "That's where the bad guys belong. In the slammer!"

My brave girl.

I take a deep breath, steadying myself before I speak again. "Yara, I need you to stay here a little longer while I go help Morello. Can you do that for me?"

She bites her lip but nods.

"That's my girl." I press a kiss to her forehead. "I'll come get you soon. Everything will be okay now."

Leaving her there, even knowing she's safe, tears at my heart.

But Morello needs me.

I climb the cellar steps slowly, emerging into the morning light.

Morello has bound Luchenko's hands and feet.

The man lies motionless, blood matting his elegant hair.

I look away quickly.

"Backup's on the way," Morello says.

His voice is steady, but I can see the tension in his shoulders, the bruise darkening on his temple.

"Are you alright?" I ask softly.

He nods. "I've had worse."

But his eyes tell a different story, haunted and weary.

On impulse, I reach out and take his hand in mine.

Offering a small measure of comfort, connection.

His fingers curl around mine. We stand in silence then, two souls marked by the day's violence but bound now by so much more.

Together, we wait for the sound of sirens in the distance.

The wail of sirens grows louder as several police cars pull up the long driveway, their lights flashing brightly.

Morello gives my hand a gentle squeeze before letting go to confer with the officers now spilling out of the vehicles.

I hang back, suddenly feeling unsure and exposed.

My eyes fall on Luchenko again, taking in the rise and fall of his chest as he lies unconscious.

Just looking at him makes my stomach turn, memories of our shared past and his torment flooding my mind.

But seeing him defeated also stirs a sense of grim satisfaction.

I've finally fought back.

Morello guides the officers as they haul Luchenko to his feet and lead him to one of the waiting cars.

He casts his eyes over his shoulder, meeting my gaze with a look of pure venom that makes me flinch.

But then he's gone, disappearing into the back of the police car.

I let out a breath I didn't know I'd been holding.

It's over.

My knees nearly buckle in relief.

Morello is suddenly at my side, his hand hovering just over the small of my back.

"Let's go get Yara," he says gently.

I retrieve my daughter from the cellar, holding her close as we walk outside.

My heart swells as I watch the police cars disappear down the driveway, carrying Luchenko away for good.

He may have been able to avoid justice up until now, but with an ironclad international case against him, this is going to be a near-impossible situation for him to squirm out of.

Morello wraps his arm around both of us. "It's a new beginning," he murmurs.

I lean into him, feeling Yara do the same on my other side. A new beginning for the three of us. Together.

Chapter 42

ALINA

The quiet crackle of the fire is the only sound in the dim living room.

I sit, near-motionless, Yara's head resting in my lap as I gently stroke my daughter's hair.

The past few weeks have been a blur of fear and uncertainty, but now a fragile sense of peace settles over us.

Morello stands silhouetted against the window, his phone pressed to his ear.

His shoulders tense as he listens intently to the voice on the other end.

When he finally turns around, the firelight dances across his face, highlighting the hint of a smile tugging at his lips.

"Good news?" I ask hopefully.

Morello nods his smile growing. "That was the lead agent on Luchenko's case. They formally charged him this morning."

Yara sits up, suddenly alert. "They did?!"

"Yes, and the case is definitely moving forward," Morello confirms. "Interpol coordinated with FBI and local police. Luchenko's locked up and awaiting extradition. It's over."

I let out a shuddering breath, the fear and tension that has gripped me for so long finally releasing.

I sink back into the couch, my hands trembling.

Yara throws her arms around my neck. "We are home here now, right Mama? With Mr. Agent Morello in America? We don't need to go back?"

"Home," I repeat in a whisper.

I look up at Morello with glistening eyes.

"I didn't think we'd see the day."

Morello kneels beside me, his strong hand grasping mine.

"You and Yara never have to look over your shoulders again. It's a new start."

I cling to his hand like a lifeline, overwhelmed by the promise of freedom.

For the first time in forever, hope blooms in my heart.

I sit there for a moment, letting the reality sink in.

After years of fear and running, it's finally over.

Luchenko and Gerald are gone, one dead and the other locked away where they can never hurt me or Yara again.

I took a deep, steadying breath as the tension that has coiled inside me for so long begins to unwind.

Yara, sensing the shift, curls up in the nook of my arm. "What happens now?" she asks softly.

I stroke her hair. "Now we start again. We find a new home, a new life here."

I look over at Morello who is watching us with a gentle smile.

"Maybe somewhere near the ocean this time."

Yara's face lights up. "I can learn to surf!"

I laugh, the sound light and airy, as I picture Yara catching waves.

It's so long since I've heard myself laugh with joy that I almost don't recognize the sound.

"We'll see about that." My smile fades into a more serious expression as I meet Morello's gaze again.

"Thank you," I say, my voice thick with emotion, tears threatening to spring forth. "For everything. For keeping us safe, giving us hope..."

My words trail off as I struggle to find the right ones.

Morello moves closer, his hand coming up to cradle my cheek.

"You never have to thank me," he says softly. "I made a promise to protect you both, no matter what. And I always follow through on my promises."

I shiver at the similarity between his words and Gerald's as his eyes bore into mine, layered with meaning.

But as I see the kindness radiating from within, my heart quickens.

In this moment, I know for sure that he's nothing like Gerald, or Luchenko, and know that his commitment to both me and Yara runs far deeper than duty.

Here, in this quiet moment, the future feels limitless.

I smile up at Morello, allowing myself to get lost in his warm brown eyes for a moment.

An unspoken understanding passes between us, a new layer to our relationship born from shared trauma and triumph.

Clearing my throat, I stand up, shifting the mood. "Well, I don't know about you two, but I'm starving. How does pizza sound to celebrate?"

Yara jumps up eagerly. "Yes! With extra cheese? And pineapple? "

I laugh. "Of course, sweetie."

Morello quirks a brow and pulls a face. "Oh, you like pineapple on your pizza? I heard that's immediate grounds for deportation."

For a second, Yara looks worried.

"Too soon," I scold Morello.

"Just joking, just joking!" He puts up his hands in mock defense, and Yara and I both laugh.

As I go to grab the takeout menu, I feel lighter than I have in years. Lighter than I can remember ever feeling since I was a young child, in fact.

The evening passes in a blur of easy laughter and hope, the three of us chatting about plans for the future over steaming slices of pizza, pineapple and not.

Yara's eyes shine as she talks about going back to school, making new friends, and learning to surf.

Morello and I share relieved smiles, Yara's tenacity and resilience almost unbelievable, and the worst behind us at last.

Later, after Yara is tucked into bed, I join Morello on the back porch overlooking the moonlit yard.

Cicadas hum in the darkness, creating a soothing chorus.

"It's really over, isn't it?" I murmur.

Morello slides an arm around me, radiating strength and comfort. "It's over. You're free."

I nestle against him, wondering how I could ever repay the man who saved us from the shadows. And not just from one incredibly dangerous man with global reach, but two.

As if reading my mind, Morello tilts my chin up to look at him.

"This is about more than duty for me now," he says, his voice a low rumble. "You know that, right?"

Heart pounding, I nod. "I know."

Under the stars, we seal a silent promise for the future with a lingering kiss.

My lips tingle as we part, my pulse racing.

Morello's hand comes up to cradle my cheek, his touch impossibly gentle for a man of his formidable presence.

"I didn't know if this could be real," I admit in a hushed voice. "If we could have this."

Morello presses his forehead to mine. "It's real. I'm here, for as long as you'll have me."

Emotion swells in my chest. Just days ago, my world had consisted of nothing but fear and uncertainty.

Now here I sit, in the arms of this incredible man who had vowed to keep me and Yara safe.

I think of his tireless dedication, the way he'd shielded us without hesitation or complaint. The way he breached protocol and risked his own life multiple times in order to save ours.

He could have walked away after neutralizing the threat, could have moved on to the next case.

But he'd chosen to stay, to see us through to the other side.

And I realize then that he isn't just our protector anymore.

Somewhere along the way, he has become our family.

"Stay with us," I whisper. "Not just for now, but always."

Morello's eyes darken, relief and desire mingling. "Always," he echoes.

He draws me close once more beneath the boundless sky.

And though challenges still lie ahead on the road to our new life, in this perfect moment, there is only joy.

I gaze up at Morello, hardly believing this is real.

After everything we've endured, it still seems far too good to be true that I can feel this safe, this cared for.

Morello brushes his thumb over my cheek, his eyes searching mine. "What are you thinking?" he murmurs.

I lean into his touch. "That I don't want this moment to end," I admit.

His expression softens. "It's only the beginning for us," he promises.

Slowly, giving me time to pull away, he lowers his mouth to mine.

The kiss is gentle at first, both tentative and reveling in this new-found connection.

Then it deepens, days of longing and fear giving way to relief, desire, a tacit promise of devotion.

I slide my arms around Morello's neck, pressing closer as his strong arms envelop me.

I can feel the heat of his body even through our clothes, solid and real.

When we finally break for air, I lay my head on his chest, listening to the steady beat of his heart.

"I never thought I could feel this way again," I whisper. "After everything..."

Morello presses a kiss to my hair. "I know," he says simply.

And he does know—he's been there through all of it, and has seen me at my most broken.

He could have run, but he chose not to. And he's choosing to be here now.

Silently, we stay wrapped in each other, the past fading into memory as we turn our gazes to the future.

There will still be challenges ahead, healing and adjusting to build a new life.

But the three of us will face it all together.

Chapter 43

ALINA

The morning sun warms my face as I stand on the front step, squinting against the bright rays.

Yara's hand clutches mine tightly, her fingers trembling ever so slightly.

"This is it, Yara. Our new beginning," I say, my voice catching with emotion. I glance down at my daughter, her wide eyes fixed on the little yellow house in front of us.

Yara doesn't respond. She continues staring, her lips pressed together in a tense line. I give her hand a gentle squeeze.

"I know it looks different than our old place, but this can be home too," I say softly. "We'll make lots of happy memories here."

Yara finally looks up at me, her brows furrowed tight with uncertainty. "Are you sure the bad men won't find us again?" she whispers.

My heart aches at the fear in her voice. I glance down at her and brush a loose strand of hair from her face.

"I promise you, we're safe now. No one will ever hurt you again. Both Luchenko and Gerald are gone and can never touch us again. And I won't be putting us in the way of any more dangerous men."

I pull her into a hug, feeling her small frame relax slightly in my arms.

We stay like that for a moment, the hopeful rays of sunlight bathing us in their glow.

When I pull back, Yara gives me a timid smile. "Okay Mama. I trust you."

I stand and take her hand again, giving it an encouraging squeeze.

Together, we step over the threshold into our new home and our new life.

Yara clutches her backpack straps tightly as we approach the front doors of her new school. She stays close to my side, her usual bubbly energy replaced by hesitant steps.

I give her shoulder a gentle, reassuring rub. "You've got this, Yara. It's always scary starting somewhere new, but you're going to do great."

She looks up at me, eyes wide. "What if the other kids don't like me?"

"They'll love you," I reply without hesitation. "Just be yourself and I know you'll make friends in no time."

Yara takes a deep breath and gives a determined nod. As we reach the entrance, she pauses and glances back at me one more time.

"You can do this," I encourage. After a moment, her lips curve into a small, brave smile. Then she turns and walks through the doors, her head held high.

I watch her go, heart swelling with pride. My little girl, so resilient. This is just the first step in her new life here, and she's already facing it with courage.

The other school, the one Gerald enrolled her in, might have better credentials, but the kids were mean and she deserves to go somewhere a little lighter and more carefree.

Education is important, but so is happiness, and safety, and security, and a sense of belonging.

Over the next few days, Yara gradually begins to open up about her school experiences. Each afternoon when I pick her up, she bubbles over with stories about her day.

"...And then Lily shared her cookies with me at lunch!" she exclaims one evening. "She's really nice. I think we're going to be best friends."

Hearing Yara sound so happy and carefree again brings me immense joy. She's adapting quickly, making connections. Thriving.

This is a far cry from her experience at the other school, and a testament to her resilience.

One day, she bursts out of the front doors, grinning from ear to ear. "Mama, I made a new friend today!" she shouts.

As we walk to the car, she chatters on animatedly about a girl named Leah. "She likes horses too, and she has the coolest unicorn backpack! Oh, and we're going to work on a project together in class... and our teacher is really nice, and she taught everyone about my name and a bit about where we're from. And everyone thought it was really cool, and..."

I can't stop smiling as I listen to her tales, each new friendship and positive tale about an experience in class a balm to my soul.

My brave, resilient girl. She has so much joy and light within her, and now she's free to share it with the world.

As I watch Yara blossom in her new environment, I find my thoughts drifting more and more to Morello.

During quiet moments, memories of our time together come flooding back. His steadfast courage in the face of danger. The warmth and kindness in his eyes when he looked at me. The way he made me feel truly safe for the first time in years.

I can't deny that I miss him. That I think about reaching out. But a pang of guilt always follows. I should be focusing all my energy on Yara, on making sure she has the stable, loving home she deserves. And I should leave him to focus on his career.

One night after tucking Yara into bed with a story and a kiss on her forehead, I go to the living room and sink down onto the couch. Sipping chamomile tea, I stare into the darkness outside the window.

My emotions churn within me, a stormy sea of joy, longing, and doubt.

I'm ecstatic to see Yara so happy here. Her bright spirit fills me with hope.

But my heart aches too. Late at night, when she's asleep, the loneliness sets in. I yearn for companionship. For Morello's steadying presence.

Should I really be thinking about him so much? Wanting him here?

No, Yara has to be my priority. Her needs come first. But...maybe my needs matter too.

The thought surprises me, and I let it sink in. It's not selfish to want happiness for myself as well. To want love again.

With a sigh, I set down my empty teacup. My feelings remain complicated, but realization dawns that embracing my own joy doesn't diminish Yara's. Her resilience amazes me daily.

Perhaps it's time I find some of my own.

I reach for my phone, scrolling to my mom's number. She answers on the second ring.

"Hi sweetie, everything okay?" Her warm, familiar voice instantly puts me at ease.

"Yeah, we're good. Just..." I hesitate. "I've been thinking about Morello a lot. I feel guilty wanting something for myself when I should be focused on Yara."

"Oh honey," she says gently. "Of course you want love again. Needing companionship doesn't make you selfish. It makes you human."

"But I am selfish, trying to find a man and dragging Yara all the way across the world."

"Alina, imagine if you had never left the home country. You would be in an even worse situation with Luchenko. Surely you must know that. You must forgive yourself for trying to find a better life for you and your daughter."

"You warned me, though. You said that Gerald seemed too good to be true, Mama."

"Yes, but I'm not always right. And at some point, you need to make your own decisions. Just because he turned out to be another evil man doesn't mean you didn't make the best decision out of a bad bunch."

"Why do you never judge me, mama? I feel like any other woman would be so critical of a daughter like me."

"You're my greatest pride and joy, Alina. You and Yara together. You burn so brightly and I have every confidence you'll get through this."

"What if he just turns out to be like Luchenko and Gerald, though? They started out nice as well."

"Look in your heart for the answer, my love. You know him better than me, but I think you realize he could never be like them. His soul is that of a good man."

I let her reassurance wash over me. She's right.

"It's okay to want happiness for yourself too. You being fulfilled is part of being the best mom for Yara."

I nod even though she can't see me. My eyes prickle with tears. After everything, I'm still learning to validate my own needs.

"Thanks, Mom," I whisper. "I think I needed to hear that."

We chat a few more minutes before saying goodnight. I set the phone down, feeling lighter. My guilt begins to lift, replaced by clarity. I deserve joy, too.

The next evening, I'm making dinner while Yara works on art at the table.

She's drawing a picture of the three of us—her, me, and Morello.

Each drawing she does gets more and more realistic, a budding talent that I'm finally able to encourage with pencils and nice, thick paper and other art supplies.

"I want you to be happy, Mama," she says, not looking up from her sketch. "You always take care of me, but who takes care of you?"

Her simple wisdom strikes deep. My eyes well up as I look at her, heart overflowing with love. Even after everything, her compassion astounds me.

I sweep her into a hug. "You're so right, sweetie. I should find someone who takes care of me too."

She grins up at me. "Morello makes you happy. You should call him!"

I laugh, kissing her forehead. My remarkable girl. With her support, I feel ready to reach for joy again. For both of us.

I take a deep breath as I dial Morello's number, my heart pounding. What will he say after all this time? Will he even want to talk to me?

I pushed him away so far after things settled down, I could totally understand if he didn't want to hear from me ever again.

My fingers hesitate over the call button. Doubt creeps in, making me question this impulse. But I think of Yara's drawing, her wish for my happiness.

I press call.

After two rings, he answers. "Alina?" His warm, familiar voice washes over me. "I can't believe it's you."

"Hi Morello." I try to steady my voice. "I'm sorry I haven't called. I just...needed some time."

"Of course. I understand." There's no judgement, only kindness. Just like I remember. "I'm so glad you called. I've thought about you every day."

My breath catches at his words.

We talk tentatively at first, the conversation halting. But slowly we rediscover our rhythm, laughter and memories filling the gaps.

"I missed this," Morello says after a funny story about his work. "Missed you. No one makes me laugh like you do."

My cheeks flush, warmth spreading through me. "I missed this, and missed you too," I pause, then continue softly. "I was scared to want this again. But I'm ready now."

"I'll be here, Alina. Whenever you're ready." His voice is earnest. "We have something special. I still feel it, do you?"

"I do." Joy wells up inside me. We talk late into the night, the connection between us still strong.

With Morello, anything seems possible.

A new beginning, together. For real this time.

I take a deep breath as I end the call with Morello, feeling lighter than I have in weeks.

A smile tugs at my lips as I think about our conversation, the possibilities blooming.

I'm filled with clarity in this moment, watching my daughter work on her art as I reflect on how I felt while talking to Morello.

My quest for happiness doesn't take away from hers—it adds to it.

By embracing my own joy, I become a better mother.

"You're so right with what you said before, Yara. We both deserve to be happy."

I squeeze her hand, my voice thick with emotion.

"And if Morello makes me happy, and seeing you like him so much, then I think we should see where this new beginning takes us."

Yara lets out a cheer, throwing her arms around me. "Finally," she says, rolling her eyes with wisdom far beyond her ears.

I laugh, hugging her back.

As I look forward to what lies ahead with Morello, a sense of peace settles over me.

My joy is just as essential in creating a fulfilling life for us both.

Chapter 44

MORELLO

My gaze sweeps over Alina's face, memorizing every curve, every freckle, as if I could burn her into my memory.

I reach out a hand, caressing her cheek, our fingers entwining.

"I don't want to ever let you go again, Alina."

My voice is hoarse with emotion, and my eyes are shining.

My heart swells and a lump forms in my throat as I watch her blink back tears.

"Neither do I. But it's not just about us. We have Yara to think about."

"I know." I furrow my brow, my warm, calloused hand stroking her cheek. "And I meant what I said. I want to be there for both of you. I want to be a father figure for her. The one she's never had."

A fat tear slides down Alina's cheek, but she wipes it away. "You do know this won't be easy, right? Yara's been through so much. She's skittish around men, and who can blame her?"

"I'm patient," I reassure her, rubbing her back. "I'll take it as slow as she needs. I'll be there for her when she's ready, and for you too."

My gaze heats, deepening with desire.

"I still can't believe you're here, that I can hold you like this again."

I lower my head, capturing her mouth in a hungry kiss.

Alina moans into the kiss, the fire we'd both missed so much igniting within us.

The tension between us is palpable, as if our time apart has only stoked the flames.

"Mmmm, Morello," she purrs, tangling her fingers in my hair, "I've missed you so much."

I growl in response, deepening the kiss, my hands roaming every inch of her body, reacquainting myself with her delicious curves.

Alina arches into me, as if reveling in the familiarity of my touch.

Breaking apart, both breathless, I study her.

"I want this, Alina. I want you, and Yara. I want us to be a family, if you'll have me."

"I've never wanted anything more," she whispers, clinging to me. "But it won't be easy. There'll be... complications."

"I know," I say, chuckling softly, "But I'm an FBI agent, I thrive on complications."

I sweep her up in my arms, carrying her to the bedroom.

"Now, let's pick up where we left off."

Our clothes fall to the floor in a frenzy, revealing the bodies that have ached for one another for so long.

We move together as if no time has passed, as if we've never been apart.

"Vincent," Alina gasps, arching her back, her sharp nails digging into my shoulders.

"I've got you, Alina," I growl, my voice strained with desire. "I've got you, and I'm never letting go."

Climaxing together, our bodies intertwined, I know this was what we've both been missing.

It's as if she's finally allowing herself to fall into the depths of the ocean that is our love, submitting to the waves of pleasure crashing over her.

As my words sink in, Alina's eyes fill with unshed tears.

"I love you," she gasps, clinging to me as if I'm her lifeline, which I'm always happy to be for her. "I'll always love you."

I smile against her neck, a single-handed wave of relief washing over me. "I love you too, Alina. More than you'll ever know."

Breathless, Alina collapses against my chest, our heartbeats pounding in unison. My strong arms encircle her, as if I fear she might slip away at any moment.

"Morello," she sighs, nuzzling into my neck, "I don't know if I can do this again. Lose you... I-I don't think I'm strong enough."

I tighten my hold. "I know, baby girl, me neither. But one thing is for certain. I could spend my whole life searching, but I know it'd be futile. I'll never meet someone remotely like you ever again. You're it for me, Alina. You're my universe. Nothing matters without your smile, your laugh, your touch. I thought I had it all, but you've made me realize my life was nothing without you."

Alina blinks back more tears as she gazes me, running her finger down one side of my jaw. "You do yourself a disservice speaking that way."

"No, I honor you by speaking this way. And I promise to treat you exactly the way you deserve—like the queen that you are—for the rest of your days. And beyond, if I have my way. The same goes for Yara.

She's the princess in this castle, and I would lay my life on the line for her many times over."

The mention of her daughter brings tears to Alina's eyes. I know from what she's shared that so many men have said similar words, but they'd been empty, used as pawns to play with her emotions.

But my words are real. I am here for them.

And it just feels so perfect, I don't know if any of us can handle it.

Alina

"Please don't fuck this up, Alina. Just this one thing. Let us finally have this one nice thing," I think to myself, gazing up at Morello and thinking about how perfect everything feels in this moment.

As the words form in my mind, my heart pounds out a frantic beat.

The weight of the promise and the knowledge that this is real, that Morello truly means it, is heavy on my chest.

Yet, as I look into his intense, unwavering gaze, I find the strength to give him the only answer my heart can bear.

"I..." My voice catches in my throat as he reaches up to brush away the single tear that escaped my eye, "I..."

The anticipation hangs thick in the air as Morello's breath stills, waiting for me to finish.

"I..." I swallow hard, my heart pounding out of my chest, "I'll... I'll try not to fuck it up too."

A slow, tender smile stretches across his lips, "That's all I can ask for." He leans in, closing the distance between us, and presses a soft, reverent kiss to my trembling lips. This kiss is different, sealing a promise, promising a future.

Through the blur of my tears, I see stars exploding behind my eyelids, and I know I've finally found my home.

My heart pounds in my chest as I press my body against Morello's, our heated breaths mingling in the dimly lit room.

His eyes, usually so stoic and guarded, blaze with a fire that make my knees weak.

After everything that's happened, the tension between us is too much to bear any longer.

I trace my fingers along his jaw, my fingertips dancing over his stubble, and he shivers, goosebumps breaking out on his arms.

"I've been wanting to touch you again so badly," I whisper, my voice husky with desire. "Now it's all I want to do."

Morello's temporary restraint breaks like a dam, and he growls, "Me too," before his lips crash against mine.

The kiss is anything but gentle, our tongues clashing in a wild dance as we devour each other. I moan into his mouth, the sound spurring him on as one of his hands finds its way to my hip, pulling me even closer.

The other dips lower, sliding under my shirt to caress my soft, bare skin.

"I need more," he rasps, his voice raw with need.

I don't hesitate; I unbutton his pants and free his hard length from its confines.

"Me too," I say, running my fingers along his shaft.

"Fuck, Alina," he groans, his brows furrowing in pleasure. "I can't take it anymore."

Heat pools between my thighs as he roughly kisses me once more, backing me up against the wall, his grip on my throat both thrilling and terrifying.

"Neither can I," I moan, arching my hips against him as his hands frenziedly explore my body.

I wrap a leg around his waist, my core aching for him.

With a growl of desire, Morello sweeps me off my feet and carries me to the nearby bed, our clothes flying off, our kisses ravenous and desperate.

Our union is explosive, our bodies intertwining in a desperate dance of lust, love, and longing.

"I want you," Morello growls, his voice guttural as he tastes my neck, one hand sliding down to cup me between my legs.

"Yes," I moan, arching my hips into his touch.

Slowly, Morello lowers his head to my core, his tongue flicking at my clit, sending me reeling over the edge.

I cry out, my nails digging into his back as the orgasm hits me like a freight train.

As my breathing returns to normal, I look into his eyes, the darkness in them both terrifying and arousing.

But he doesn't stop there.

Morello's skilled hands leave no inch of my aching body untouched, eliciting moan after moan.

He knows just how to touch me, as if he can read my mind.

His mouth and hands travel all over my body, from my earlobes to my hardened nipples, to my soaked pussy.

"Morello, I need you inside me again," I pant, my hips gyrating against his rock-hard arousal.

"You've got me," he growls, entering her with a single, powerful thrust.

We move as one, our bodies slick with sweat and desperation.

Our hips collide in a frenzied rhythm, our moans muffled by each other's lips.

It's primal, this dance of lust and lust alone.

"I'm close again," I whimper, my nails digging into his back as I clench around him.

"Me too," he grunts, "Feel it, Alina, feel how much I want you."

"Fuck, Alina," Morello groans, his grip on my hips tightening as I clench around him. "You feel so damn good." His eyes bore into mine as he pushes deeper and harder, claiming me in a way no one else ever has.

I arch my back, his words sending a shiver down my spine. "God, Morello, I... I can't..."

"Let go, Alina," he growls, his voice thick with desire. "I've got you."

That's all it takes. With his low, guttural words in my ear, a climax tears through me once again, setting me ablaze from the inside out. Tears of relief and ecstasy spill down my cheeks as I convulse around him.

Morello's strokes grow even wilder, his own release approaching. "Me too, baby, I'm coming too." With one final, deep thrust, he stiffens inside me, his body shuddering with pleasure as he collapses on top of me.

As our breathing slowly returns to normal, we lie tangled together, naked and sweat-soaked, our hearts still racing in time with one an-other's.

Sunlight filters through the blinds, casting a soft glow on our flushed faces.

My head is resting on Morello's chest as we catch our breaths, our legs entwined.

We know that tomorrow could bring more challenges, more danger, but for now, we've stolen one perfect moment.

The aftermath of our lovemaking leaves me feeling more exposed than I care to admit.

Not just physically, but emotionally too.

My heart is bare, and my walls have dissolved like sugar in a warm tea.

Morello's words still echo in my head, and I wish I could bottle up this feeling and savor it forever.

"I love you," I whisper, my voice barely audible against his chest.

Morello's arms tighten around me in response. And for once, words aren't needed.

Morello

I stroke Alina's hair, unable to believe she's here, in my arms, after all we've been through.

I never thought I'd have her this close again, let alone hear her whisper words I thought I'd never deserve.

Pulling Alina closer, I hold her tightly against me, her front pressed against my chest, and I inhale her sweet scent.

I need her to believe me, to know that I'm in this for the long haul.

"I'll do everything in my power to give you and Yara the best life possible. I swear it."

As we lie together, entangled in each other's arms, the room around us fades away, and all that matters is the two of us and the love we've found in the unlikeliest of places.

The neighborhood lights twinkle outside the window, a reminder of the world I've always fought to protect, but for now, we have this sanctuary.

A place where we can pretend to be normal, where we are simply a man and a woman in love.

Alina

Morning sunlight streams through the window as birds chirp outside

I wake up first, careful not to disturb Morello's sleep. He looks peaceful in his slumber, and I hate to wake him. But we have a mission to complete.

Gently, I slip out of bed, donning the oversized t-shirt he lent me the night before and tying my hair up in a messy bun.

Morello

I stir awake, feeling the absence of Alina's warmth beside me.

My eyes travel around the unfamiliar room, orienting myself.

I hear the quiet hum of the coffee machine downstairs, my senses heightened from years on the job.

I smile, realizing it's our first proper morning together in this new place.

In this new life.

Throwing on gray sweats, I pad barefoot to the kitchen, where I find her, clad in my shirt—the sight of which makes me instantly hard—her back to me as she brews coffee.

I wrap my arms around her waist, nuzzling her neck. "Good morning, beautiful."

Alina jumps, nearly spilling the scorching liquid.

Whirling around, she sighs with relief upon seeing it was only me.

"Y-you scared me!" she admonishes, a blush creeping up her cheeks.

"Sorry, I didn't mean to startle you," I say my hands sliding from her waist to the counter as I pour my own cup of coffee. "So, what's the plan today, partner?"

"Well," she says, a funny smile on her face, "This is going to sound random, but I'm guessing you have a passport... and I've been looking at some travel websites..."

Chapter 45

ALINA

The photo album weighs heavy on my lap, each page a window to our past. Yara leans in beside me, her wide eyes searching the faded polaroids and scraps of a life I barely recognize.

"Is this you, Mama?" she asks, pointing to a young girl with haunted eyes. I nod, swallowing against the lump in my throat.

Yara traces her finger over the cracked plastic protecting the photos. "You look scared," she says softly.

I take a shaky breath, blinking back tears. My little girl who had known too much fear herself, so perceptive and wise. I wrap an arm around her, pulling her close.

"Did you ever think we'd be happy like this?" Her question, asked with such innocence, clenches my heart.

I press a kiss into her hair. "Never," I admit. "But we made it, little one." I'm not going to be able to call her that much longer. Even now, it's a stretch—she's almost as tall as me.

She snuggles against me, filling my soul with light.

The past lingers, its ghosts never far, but with Yara in my arms and Morello at my side, I have all I need.

I close the album, the memories still vivid though dulled by time.

"Let's take a walk," I say. "There are some places I want to show you."

Yara skips beside me, her hand tucked in mine as we make our way down the cracked sidewalks of my old neighborhood.

I point out the tiny corner store that sells candy by the piece, the graffitied basketball court where I had my first kiss.

With each familiar sight, I share a piece of our history, the good and the bad.

Yara listens, wide-eyed, as if I'm describing a foreign land instead of the streets I once called home.

I pause outside the old apartment building, gazing up at the sagging fire escape.

"This is where I first learned to fight for us," I told her. Where I swore nothing would break me, not poverty, not violence, not fear.

Yara squeezes my hand, our silent language of love and understanding.

The neighborhood holds ghosts, but it forged me too.

Every challenge made me stronger, more determined, until I was finally able to take control of our destiny.

I pull Yara close again, filled with overwhelming gratitude for the little girl who gave me purpose.

My choices took us away from here, but her love has led me home, even if briefly.

I nodded slowly as we walk, lost in memories.

The cracked sidewalks and faded graffiti stir up complicated feelings—nostalgia, grief, pride.

This place represents where we come from, the good and bad.

I lead Yara to a small park, the same one where I met with Dominika right before we left for America, the grass now overgrown but still a rare oasis of green in the concrete jungle.

We sit on a bench and I take a deep breath, knowing it's time to share parts of my past I'd kept hidden even from her.

"I made a lot of hard choices, back then," I begin.

Yara watches me closely, her eyes intent.

"Choices I thought would protect us, but that put you in danger too."

My voice catches and I look away, ashamed.

But Yara reaches for my hand, her fingers curling around mine.

"That's all over now, Mama," she says gently. "We're okay because of you."

I turn back, tears blurring my vision. Her simple faith in me is humbling.

She's right—the past is done.

All that remains is our future, one I vow to fill with joy and safety.

I pull Yara into a fierce hug, letting go of the final shadows.

My mistakes haven't defeated us; they have made us stronger.

Together we have survived, and now we will thrive.

Later that evening, after Yara is tucked into bed, Morello and I sit out on the back porch with glasses of wine.

The night air is cool and still.

I tell him about my day—the walk down memory lane, running into old friends, the talk with Yara.

He listens without interrupting, his steady presence soothing me.

"I was afraid my choices back then made everything worse," I confess. "But Yara reminded me our struggles made us who we are."

Morello reaches over and took my hand.

"She's right," he says. "Your past didn't break you, Alina. It built you into the strong woman you are today."

I exhale, feeling the last of the guilt lift from my shoulders.

We sit in comfortable silence for a few moments.

"What do you see for us in the future?" I ask eventually.

Morello's eyes light up. "Peace. Watching Yara grow into an amazing young woman. And..." he hesitates, a shy smile teasing his lips.

"And what?" I prod.

"Maybe a brother or sister for her someday?" His voice is tentative but full of hope.

My own heart swells at the thought. "I'd like that," I whisper.

We talk late into the night about plans and dreams—all the possibilities our future holds.

The contrast with our hushed, worried conversations of the past is stark.

But the darkness is behind us now.

Ahead lies only joy.

Two weeks later

The morning dawns bright and clear. Yara is already up, brimming with energy.

"What should we do today?" she asks, bouncing on her toes.

Morello and I exchange a glance. "Actually, we were thinking we could plant a tree," I say. "To celebrate our new start together."

Yara's eyes grow wide. "Our own tree? That's perfect!"

We head out to the backyard with shovels and a young sapling Morello had picked out. The three of us begin digging, the soil cool and crumbling beneath our feet.

With each shovelful, I feel us putting down roots. This tree will grow just like Yara—strong and resilient.

She chatters away the whole time, voicing plans for the treehouse she wants to build, and the picnics we'll have in its shade. Her enthusiasm is contagious.

Finally we stand back, admiring our work. The little tree stands straight and proud. The late sun casts a warm glow over our home.

"We made it," I whisper, almost disbelieving the peace we've found. Pride and gratitude swell in my heart.

Yara throws her arms around me. "Together we can do anything," she says. "You've taught me that."

I hug her tight.

With Morello's arm around us both, I know she's right.

The future holds nothing we can't face—not as long as we have each other.

Later that evening, after Yara goes to bed, Morello and I find a quiet moment alone together.

"I meant what I said. I promise I'll always protect our family," he says, his voice low and serious. "I'll make this the life you and Yara deserve."

His unwavering commitment makes my heart swell. No words could fully express what it means to me.

Instead, I draw him close and kiss him deeply, sealing our unspoken promise to one another.

A promise of love, security, and hope for the future.

Afterward, I stand gazing out the window at the velvety night sky. The stars glitter like diamonds.

Yara's soft snores drift from her room down the hall. Morello's strong presence beside me is a comfort.

My reflection shifts from our difficult past to the promising future ahead. The lessons we've learned have shaped us all.

Fear has turned to confidence in facing each new day.

I smile serenely, my heart and soul bursting with gratitude. The road here has been long and arduous, but together we've made it through.

As I stare into the vast night sky, I know there's nothing our little family can't handle.

Not anymore.

The future holds endless, shining possibilities.

And I can't wait to start the next chapter.

Epilogue

ALINA

The early morning sun spills through the curtains, bathing our bedroom in a warm, honeyed glow.

Beside me, Morello stirs, his muscular arm draped loosely over my waist.

I smile, drinking in this quiet moment of intimacy.

It's hard to believe there was a time I dreaded the sunrise, when darkness felt safer.

But with Morello's steady strength beside me, the light no longer holds shadows of fear.

Morello's stomach rumbles, and I chuckle. "Someone's ready for breakfast."

His eyes blink open, his gaze tender. "I could eat."

His gaze trails down my body and I playfully smack his arm.

"There'll be plenty of time for that later," I grin.

We dress leisurely, our fingers trailing, our lips brushing together casually as we stand side by side. The simple joy of having this—someone to share lazy mornings with—still feels new, a gift I'll never take for granted.

As we descend the stairs, the scent of sizzling bacon and fresh coffee envelops us.

I give Morello a sideways glance.

We're the two who usually cook around here.

Yara stands at the stove, humming tunelessly as she flips pancakes.

"Morning, munchkin," I say, kissing the top of her head. Her smile lights up the room.

"I made breakfast all by myself!"

"I see that!" I laugh, looking at the flour that coats one side of the kitchen counter.

"It smells amazing." Morello grabs plates and mugs. "Look at you, junior chef extraordinaire."

Yara giggles. "I wanted to surprise you."

As we gather around the table, sunlight streams through the window, bathing our little makeshift family in its glow.

Morello squeezes my hand, his eyes crinkling.

"Can you believe this is our life now?" I ask softly.

"It feels like a dream," he says.

"A happy dream." Yara bites into a strip of bacon with relish. "We're like superheroes now. Breakfast superheroes!"

Her quip startles a laugh from me. Morello grins, leaning back in his chair.

"That we are, kiddo."

Yara's joy is contagious. The laughter bubbles up inside me, sweet and light.

My heart is overflowing.

The laughter lingers as we finish up breakfast. A new energy buzzes through me—today is the day. I've been waiting for this moment for years.

"Your mom's flight gets in soon, right?" Morello asks.

I nod, butterflies swirling in my stomach. "Her plane should be landing within the hour."

It's been over two years since I last saw my mother in person, except for the brief visit back home—and that was extremely traumatic, because it felt like I was ripping my heart out by leaving her again.

We've talked on the phone when possible, but today's reunion will be emotional.

I can't wait to embrace her and show her the life I'm building here. And to make her part of it.

After the dishes are cleared, we pile into Morello's truck and head for the airport.

Yara bounces around in the back seat, just as excited.

"I can't wait to see Grandma!" she exclaims.

Her words make my heart buzz.

The bond between my two favorite women has always been so strong.

Despite the anticipation, nerves creep in as we wait at the arrival gate.

Morello gives my hand a reassuring squeeze.

I cling to it like a lifeline.

Then I see her. My breath catches.

She's older, her dark hair now streaked with grey, but her eyes—my eyes—are the same.

I'm frozen in place as she rushes forward.

Her arms wrap around me and the years collapse.

I'm a little girl again, safe in my mother's embrace.

Tears flow down both our cheeks.

"Oh, my Alina," she whispers. "My sweet girl. Being here with you, it makes everything complete."

I can only nod, overcome with emotion. The pain of our separation melts away in this moment.

Morello stands back with Yara, giving us space for our reunion.

When we finally separate, my mother pulls them both into fierce hugs.

"Welcome home," I tell her, meaning it with my whole heart.

I take a deep breath as I look around at the crowd gathered in our backyard. Neighbors, friends old and new—so many people here to welcome my mother into our little community.

She fits right in, already chatting and laughing with our next-door neighbor, Delia. Despite the slight language barrier, I can tell they'll be fast friends.

Morello slips an arm around my waist. "You okay?" he asks, noticing my misty eyes.

I smile up at him. "Better than okay," I reply. "This is more than I ever dreamed was possible."

He kisses my temple. "You deserve it all, Alina."

From the corner of my eye, I see Yara showing my mom her latest art project. My heart swells at how quickly they've re-bonded.

My mother may have been kept away for a couple of pivotal years of Yara's life, but she dotes on her now like she's trying to make up for all that lost time.

Later, we sit in the garden—my refuge, the place I've poured my energy into cultivating beauty.

The fading light casts a golden glow over my mother's face as she tells us her plans to offer cooking classes, sharing the food of our homeland with others.

"Maybe Yara can help me decorate," she says with a wink.

Yara lights up. "I can make signs for your class! And menus!"

We continue chatting as the sun sinks lower, making plans.

It's strange; after so many years just focused on survival, now I have the space to dream again.

I smile as Yara chatters enthusiastically about helping my mother with her cooking classes. It's been so wonderful having my mom here with us, like the missing piece of our family has finally fallen into place.

As the sun dips below the horizon, we fall into a comfortable silence and I take in the scene before me—my mother and daughter side by side, Morello with his arm wrapped around my shoulders.

My heart feels so full.

After everything we endured, all the fear and heartbreak, somehow we made it here. To this moment of peace. Together.

I catch Morello's eye. "Can you believe this is real life?" I whisper. "That we get to just...be happy?"

He presses a kiss to my hair. "You and Yara deserve every bit of this joy. I'm the lucky one."

Yara overhears him saying her name and immediately pipes up. "We're all lucky!"

I laugh. "You're absolutely right, butterfly."

I open my arm and she comes over and snuggles into me.

Morello envelops us both in his strong embrace.

Over Yara's shoulder, I meet my mother's glistening gaze.

"I love you," I mouth silently.

She presses a hand to her heart.

We stay huddled together as the first stars appear, filling the sky with their brilliance.

The trials of our past brought us to this moment, this new beginning.

And our future has never looked brighter.

After we finally peel ourselves apart and head inside, I find myself lingering as the others get ready for bed.

I'm not quite ready for this magical evening to end.

I step out onto the back patio, breathing in the night air.

The moon casts a soft glow across the yard and I'm struck again by the beauty and peace of this place.

Our sanctuary.

Closing my eyes, I allow my mind to drift back through our journey.

The fear that gripped me, the pain that felt endless.

The strength it took just to survive.

I remember the first time I let myself trust Morello, let myself believe I deserved care and affection.

The terrifying vulnerability of opening my heart again.

And Yara. My fierce, resilient girl.

She gave me purpose when I thought all was lost.

Her smiles heal my soul a little more each day.

We endured the unendurable. And came out the other side. Together.

I open my eyes, a few tears slipping down my cheeks.

But they are tears of gratitude.

Of awe at how far we've come.

The past will always be with us. But it doesn't define us. Not anymore.

With my family surrounding me, and a wide-open future ahead, I have everything I need.

Everything I never dreamed I could have again.

There is no more waiting for the other shoe to drop.

Instead, joy, love, hope—they live inside us now. And all those things will light our way, wherever we go from here.

I'm ready and open for whatever comes next.

Can't wait to see what comes next? Enjoy this exclusive bonus scene.

Also By

Blood and Sand (Dark Reverse Harem Mafia Romance)

- Sea of Snakes(Book 1)

- Sea of Sinners(Book 2)

- Sea of Rage (Book 3)

- Sea of Pain(Book 4)

- Sinners, Rage & Pain: The Brixton Trilogy(Books 2, 3 and 4)

- Sea of Demons(Book 5)

- Sea of Redemption(Book 6)

Standalones

- Rucked (sports romance – rugby why choose)

- Pretty Lovely Lies (FBI/mafia romance, single parent, international)

- Ruthless Choices(romantic horror)

Palm Falls Series (mafia romance – interconnected standalones)
- F*CKBOYS(dark revenge romance, second chance, enemies to lovers)

- Bronson & Wren's story (title TBC) – preorder. Releases July 2024

Billionaire's Takeover Collection

- Irreversible Decision

- Compelling Proposal

- Love Merger

- The Billionaire's Takeover Collection (all 3 of the above!)

Novellas

- Love in a Seedy Motel Room

Sign up for my newsletter herefor the latest on new releases, promos, giveaways and events!

Join me on social media:

Facebook: @heidistarkauthor

Instagram: @heiditstarkauthor

TikTok: @heidistark_author

Twitter: @heidistarkauthr

Websitehttps://heidistarkauthor.com

Acknowledgements

Thank you to everyone who continues to support me through my writing journey.

To my incredible beta and ARC teams and street team, my editing team, Isa and the rest of the squad, all of the incredible book groups that keep me up to date with what you're interested in reading – Booktok Baddies, $mut $luts, The Smuthood and B.A.N.G. Book Club to name a few.

And to Fang. I'll take you across the world, wherever I go xo